Tempting Vivi

TEMPTING **VIVI**
HEROES OF HENDERSON: BOOK 3.5

A DuVal Cousins Novel

Published by Kelly Girl Productions
©Copyright 2015 Liz Kelly
Cover design by Tammy Kearly

ISBN: 978-0-9860864-0-3

For more information on the author and her works, please see
www.LizKellyBooks.com

To

Nance
World's Greatest Teacher. Period.

and

The Fideles of Wake Forest University
"Raise Hell"

CHAPTER ONE

May

"You're breaking up with me?" Vivi DuVal's eyes shot wide as her mouth gaped open. "Now?" she sputtered.

"Well, yeah."

She watched as Kevin sort of grimaced. Definitely looked sheepish. She considered his lean build and pretty, pretty face. And, oh God, that hair. It was always so well groomed. She liked that. She liked groomed.

What she didn't like was being dumped just as she finally had a moment to breathe.

"You're breaking up with me now, right after I've finished my last exam? With one week to go until graduation?" she said, her voice escalating. "Right before Beach Week?"

"Vivi, Vivi, Vivi," he sighed, motioning them both over to a bench in the center of campus. "There's just something you need to know. About me. About us."

"Is this about me throwing myself at you after Wine and Roses?"

He cleared his throat. "A little bit."

"But that was such a great night. You can't blame a girl for wanting a little more, after we danced the way we danced all night long."

"I understand. I do. That's why we need to talk."

"I thought we were so compatible. We've been to all of your fraternity dances. Had a great time at all my Fidele social events."

She stopped and sucked in a breath, her arms splayed out to stop everything. "Wait. Is this because I'm bossy?"

"No, Sugar Belle, you're not that bossy. You're a natural-born teacher. You're gonna be great leading a classroom."

"But I've neglected you, right? Graduating in three years hasn't been easy with the double major and all. I know I've neglected my social life, but I really thought you and I were good."

"We are good. I'm still crazy about you. And Sugar Belle, trust me. You're perfect just the way you are. You're just not perfectly perfect for me."

"You've found someone else?"

"Not exactly."

"What does that mean?"

Kevin sighed. "It means that you're still a little young and naive and have yet to figure out what most of my close friends suspect."

"You're saving yourself for marriage?" she whispered.

He smiled at her. A patient, sorry smile. And then the words dropped out of his mouth. "I'm gay."

Blank stare.

"I like guys," he offered.

"I know what gay means, Kevin. I'm not *that* young or naive. I just don't…" she hesitated, shaking her head, trying to clear it, "…understand. How are you gay? Why…why would you keep asking me out if you were gay?"

"Because I'm social, and I like to dance, and I like you, and I like your friends and I wanted to be a part of everything without making waves. I wanted to have fun and enjoy myself during college."

"We made out. You felt me up on every damn date," she insisted. "What the hell?"

"I like your breasts," he said. "I like kissing. I'm just more attracted to guys."

"So you used me?"

"I didn't use you, Sugar. I like you. You know I like you. A lot. No one's more fun on the dance floor. But after the incident in the car the night of Wine and Roses, I figured I'd better let you know about me. Still, Sugar, it shouldn't really change that much between us. You're one of my best friends. "

That statement made Vivi gasp.

That best friend statement was the arrow that shot through her shock and triggered the avalanche of pain...and heartache...and self-doubt...and insecurity.

Oh, wow, the insecurity.

Vivi was fortunate. She had a lot of close friends. She had girl friends and guy friends, and now she could add Kevin to that list, she supposed. But the wound his words opened was dark and it was deep. Because she didn't want another friend. She'd thought she was someone's love interest. She'd thought he was interested in her romantically. She'd thought she was dating this guy for real, not for show.

"I showed you a good time."

She heard his words as if she were underwater, and although she looked toward Wait Chapel, which stood at the end of the beautiful lawn, she couldn't see it. Yeah, he had shown her a good time. She couldn't deny it. Such a good time she did not see this coming.

"You used me, Kevin. You wanted me on your arm so you could have fun and not...make waves."

"I didn't use you. We went out on dates and enjoyed ourselves. We had fun together. Just because I wasn't hell-bent on getting you into bed at the end of those dates doesn't change the good times we've had."

She looked at him then. Really looked at him. Kevin's neat appearance was not unusual on Wake Forest's campus. His pretty looks didn't scream gay. Maybe his hair was a little too...styled all the time. He never had a hair out of place. Oh, man. She had really appreciated all that about him. And she'd had no idea he wasn't physically attracted to her. No idea he played for the other team. *Not that there was anything wrong with that.* That thought made her laugh out loud right before she burst into tears.

"Well, maybe I would have liked to have been with somebody who was hell-bent on getting me into bed at the end of the night.

Lord, am I an idiot? I had…" she sputtered, "…I literally had no idea."

"Sugar Belle—"

"How could I not have known?"

"Well, hell. How would you know unless I told you?"

"I don't know. I think a girl should be able to sense these things. But you—you were handsy. You kissed my neck all the darn time." Her temper subsided into anguish. "You were sweet and so much fun, and I just thought I was lucky to have a gentleman like you interested in me. Giving me space to do my work and showing up for me on the big nights." She breathed a long, steady intake, hiccuped, and then let her breath out.

"I never intended to hurt you, Sugar Belle. I'm crazy about you and I enjoyed being invited to your events. Maybe from your point of view it looks like I used you, but that wasn't my intention. I like being with you. You know that. We always had a great time together. I guess I figured what's the harm?"

"The harm is that I thought you were romantically interested in me for a long-term relationship. The harm is that I planned on us spending more time as a couple now that we're graduating. The harm is that I'll never be able to trust my instincts about men or anything else ever again!" She shouted that last bit and stood up, pointing a finger at her…her…buddy.

Oh, God. I'm losing it.

Vivi reined herself in right there in the middle of campus on a beautiful late spring day. She didn't want to cause a scene. She didn't want to say something she'd later regret. She needed to go process this news by herself. Give herself time to mourn what she thought she had.

"I'm gonna go," she told Kevin. "I'll…I'll go to the beach with the girls, and maybe if I've wrapped my head around this by the time I get back, we'll be able to have a civil conversation. But right now, I'm really pissed off at you."

Kevin grabbed her finger. "If I had told you I was gay when we first met, would you have hung out with me?"

"What?"

"If you knew, when we met? Would you have treated me differently?"

"I wouldn't have asked you out, and I certainly wouldn't have made out with you, or put my hand down your pants, or let you touch me," she said, feeling herself blush with mortification.

Oh, God.

"Really Kevin. This is all so unfair. I'm...I'm...I gotta go. I'll talk to you at graduation."

CHAPTER TWO

"You see those girls over there?"

Lane Kettering followed his cousin's thumb as it pointed over Trevor's shoulder. Yeah, he'd seen those girls. There wasn't a group of guys on this beach a mile north or a mile south who hadn't seen *those* girls.

"Your mission, should you choose to accept it—and let me just clarify that any of my beer you plan to drink this weekend hinges on your ability to accept it and git 'r done—is to go over there and get them to join our party."

"Our party?"

"Yeah. Our party. Our, you know," he circled his hands indicating their surroundings, "party."

"We're sitting here on the beach."

"Exactly. And they're sitting on the beach. But chances are it'd become a party if we were all sitting on the beach together."

"But they just got all set up over there, with their girly umbrella, and chairs, and coolers, and shit."

"Dude. You play football. How hard is it going to be for you to help move all that shit over here?"

"What if they don't want to move over here?"

"I'm sending you in to convince them they do indeed want to move over here. And I'm motivating you with beer. You need to earn your keep this weekend, and you're gonna start by doing this." Trevor started poking him in his chest. "Use all of that bulging-bicep charm of yours and woo them over here."

"Woo them?" he said with a raised eyebrow.

"Woo them," Trevor replied.

"Come on. This is a bachelor party," Lane protested. "I thought it was supposed to be a long weekend with the guys. Beach, beer, and golf. My brother's getting married in a month. We don't need girls."

"Oh, we need girls. That's what a bachelor party is all about. The girls. I mean, yeah, your brother is all hooked up tight—and I'm happy for him and everything—but the rest of us, we need girls."

"Lindsey is not going to like this."

"Which is why Lindsey and her bridesmaids are having their bachelorette party in New York City instead of Myrtle Beach. They're going to have their own good time while we have ours. And whatever happens here, stays here. No one is the wiser. Got me?"

"Got you. Still, mind if I ask Tray if he's down with this?"

Trevor moved in and started poking Lane in the chest again. "He's fine with this. Trust me. I'm running the show. Just go over there and give it your best shot."

"Hey, Tray," Lane yelled, his eyes not leaving Trevor's. "Mind if Trevor and I ask those girls over there to join us?"

There was a moment of silence. Lane guessed his brother was checking out the girls. "Not if y'all can keep your mouth shut the next time you see Lindsey. She's freaking out enough that I'm spending the next four days with you yahoos."

"I hear ya," he said loudly, watching Trevor's mouth form into a broad, I-told-you-so smile. Lane lowered his voice. "Look, Trev. I'm happy to be here, I really am. But I am not interested in watching my brother be set up to cheat on his fiancée."

"Hey," Trevor said, holding up his hands. "One lap dance. That's all we're allowing the poor boy. I like Lindsey, too," he said, smacking Lane on his bicep. "Best thing that ever happened to him. But like I said, the rest of us are footloose and fancy free. You included."

Lane wanted to roll his eyes. Yeah, he was footloose and fancy free. Of course he was. But he'd been invited to this shindig solely because he was related. To the groom. And it was becoming clear that all the other graduating law students, like his brother, along with his two cousins were planning to treat Lane as their lackey. Which he was actually okay with. If nothing else, he figured they were bound to make his birthday entertaining.

⌒⌒⌒⌒

"Caroline, will you please stop ogling those guys. They're starting to stare back at us like we're stalkers or something."

"I'm not ogling unnecessarily. I'm trying to read their T-shirts. One says Gamecocks, but I think a couple others say Carolina Law. I'd love to go over and find out if they're law students. See if they have any advice for when I start in September."

"We are here to relax after four long years of college. Please don't bring up grad school," Heather said.

"Or jobs," Hayden moaned. "I'm sort of freaking out about not having a job."

"Or final exams, since I'm not sure I've passed them all." Jody's voice escalated, "What if I didn't pass them all?"

"No freaking." Kate said. "There will be no freaking on the beach. We've already had enough freaking out on the long car ride down here."

All eyes shifted toward Vivi.

"As if I don't have a reason to freak," she started. "Kevin is gaaaaay." Once she saw them all roll their eyes, she held up her hand and said, "Fine. I get it. You've heard enough." She got out of her beach chair and flung her towel out away from the rest of them. "I'll just lie over here in the sand quietly and contemplate how much money I spent on my first Brazilian bikini wax for a guy who isn't interested in me below the waist."

"Shhh, one of the T-shirts is coming this way," Liz said, hushing her up. "Caroline, here's your chance."

Vivi just groaned into the sand. "He's probably gay," she muttered as she turned her head away from her girlfriends who were tired of hearing her woes. Away from any approaching Carolina Law students.

She was cranky, crazy tired, and unfit for company. She knew it and didn't blame the girls for shutting her up. She'd like to shut herself up, too. Shut her mind off from reviewing every date she'd had with Kevin over the last couple of years. They amounted to about ten, which was actually enlightening now that she added them up. Ten dates. Not really the long-term relationship she'd conjured up in her brain. She and Kevin were never a couple. They escorted each other to various social events. They had fun. They'd made out, which now just seemed weird, and she'd mistaken all of it. Especially mistaken him.

Wow.

The smart girl in the class sure looked dumb now. She shuddered, imagining delivering her speech at graduation while the rumor floated among the graduates and their parents that the valedictorian might be book smart, but just plain naive when it came to personal relationships. That she'd spent too much time trying to be an A student, graduate early, double major, and impress her favorite professors, all while maintaining a fingerhold on a social life.

Well, that had sure backfired.

She felt her body give in a little bit to its fatigue. Felt the sun coaxing her into a nap. Felt her brain zoning out to the quiet timbre of a male voice.

"Hey, y'all go to Wake Forest?" she heard him say. "Y'all've got a great baseball season going right now, don'tcha?" She liked the voice. It wasn't loud or brash; it was pleasantly lulling her into a relaxed state. Soothing her tired, frantic brain. "Smart girls…come on over…law students…" the voice went on, lulling her into a much needed rest. "… Yeah, Carolina…good party…I'll help…" the voice went on until she eased out of her conscious mind and drifted off to sleep.

❦

"Where's Vivi?" the one nicknamed Southie asked after all the introductions had been made and the girls' chairs strategically placed to be straight on with the sun. Lane was still working on their umbrella. Not ever having been a beach bum, he was finding it trickier than it looked. Jody, the one in the teeny-weeny bikini, jumped up to show him how it was done.

"Thanks," he said, looking up and noticing one chair had been left behind. "I'll, ah, just go and get that," he said, pointing.

"Bring Vivi over too," he heard as he headed off and waved in acknowledgement. He didn't see any Vivi. He planned to grab the chair and then go for a run on the beach, letting the party get started without him. He wasn't interested in answering a lot of those introductory questions. Then he'd hit the ocean and the kick-ass surf that seemed to be gathering momentum, eventually easing back into the group as unnoticed as possible.

Pretty girls, he thought. Seemed nice too. Friendly. He put his hand on the back of the last chair before he noticed the adorable little bare ass all dressed up in an aqua blue thong-styled bikini bottom with a big bow at the top. He smiled, considering this an early birthday present from the Universe.

Vivi?

Lane stole a quick glance over the rest of her, making sure she wasn't actually witnessing him salivating over her perfectly round, slightly tanned derriere. 'Cause it was pretty, and that bow made it downright cute—and man, now he was starting to feel it in his shorts.

She faced away from him, thank God, and from what he could tell, she was sound asleep. Probably had a big night last night. The skin of her back was left bare to his eyes too. For a second he thought she was topless, and his eyes bugged open. You could get arrested for a lot less on this public beach, he thought before he noticed that she wasn't topless, just had untied her straps.

Interesting.

He looked over his shoulder back at the party going on just down the beach. Coolers were being opened and beers and whatnot were being dumped into Tervis tumblers. Yep, the party was starting all right. He looked back at Sleeping Beauty and decided she needed her rest. So he took off his sunglasses and shirt, laid them on the empty chair, and went for his run down the beach.

Too bad he didn't take his brain with him.

His mind couldn't shake thoughts of those perfect, plump, silky-smooth mounds of flesh, separated by a strip of blue. Frankly, it was the most ridiculous bathing suit he'd ever seen. A big ol' bow right at the small of her back, like her sweet little ass was a gift waiting to be unwrapped. Damn he'd volunteer for that. He started looking around at what other girls were wearing. The beach was starting to fill with all sorts of college students ready to let off steam after final exams. Lots of tiny little bikinis, not so many thongs, and definitely none as pretty and fine as his Sleeping Beauty.

His.

That made him laugh and turn on the power boosters. He needed to get a grip.

About forty-five minutes later, he slowed to a jog, and then a walk, noticing his brother's group way up the beach, but letting his eyes surf back across the sand for Beauty. He couldn't find her at first, now that the sun was high and the beach was full. Maybe she'd woken up and joined the party. Nope. There she was, in the same position he'd left her. All curves, not a hard angle to be found. Her hair was dark, he noticed for the first time as he approached. And it was probably long, though it was hard to tell how long. It was all twirled up on the back of her head and held in place with a clip or something. He stopped in front of the beach chair where he'd left his shirt and sunglasses, toed off his running shoes, and pulled off his socks, all the while glancing over, and over, and over again at her perfect backside.

Man, I hope she put sunscreen on that thing, he thought as he turned and headed into the ocean. *Otherwise she's gonna have a hard time sitting,* he laughed to himself.

His brother Tray joined him in the water, swimming over and dunking him, or at least trying to dunk him. Lane had a good three inches and fifty pounds of muscle over his big brother. Of course, he was slightly shorter than his brother in the smarts department, so there was that.

"Great waves," Lane said.

"Yeah. Unusual." Tray said. "You go for a run?"

"Gotta stay in shape."

"That you do."

"How's it going with those pretty Demon Deacons?"

Tray laughed. "Fine. Good. They're funny. Makes me miss Lindsey."

Lane smiled. "I'm glad to hear that."

"Yeah. I'm hooked. Been crazy about her since day one at Carolina. I'm not sure why we're even doing this."

"Because Uncle Chuck has a sweet condo on the beach and offered it up for your bachelor party. And what better way to celebrate my birthday?" Lane laughed as his brother tossed him a sneer. "Come on. We'll have a good time, get our tans on, and before you know it, you'll be stuck with Lindsey for-ev-a and only wishin' for time with your old law school buddies. Enjoy this. It's the only bachelor party you're gonna get."

"I am. I will," Tray amended. "And I really appreciate you being here. And, you know…"

"Being the manservant to all you Doctors of Law?"

Tray laughed. "Yeah, and that."

"I don't mind, bro. Whatever you need. I really don't mind. I'm here to serve."

They bodysurfed for a while, and when a couple of Tray's buddies hit the water further up the beach, Tray swam over to be with them. Lane told him he wanted to grab his shirt and shoes. He didn't bother to mention that he wanted to get another look at Sleeping Beauty. He shook himself off like a dog as he walked up the beach, took his shirt and wiped it over his face and hair, using it as a towel. He was starting to wonder if Beauty was passed out, or even breathing. Shit. Maybe she'd OD'd on something horrible and had been left by him and her friends to die alone in the hot sun.

"Hey," he said.

Nothing.

"Hey," he said a little louder. He was actually starting to feel a little panicky. There was not a lot of evidence that she was alive. Maybe he was detecting a slight rise and fall in her back, but it was really hard to tell. He looked over his shoulder up the beach to where all her friends were now sitting. He wanted to call out, but they were quite a distance away with a good five groups of beachgoers set up between them and him now. And really, he didn't want to look like a dick, raising an alarm when there wasn't one. Still, he thought, looking back at Beauty, he needed to be sure.

Maybe if he just…

CHAPTER THREE

Vivi could feel her consciousness being drawn from somewhere deep, back up to the surface. She became more and more aware of the surf, and mildly aware of some shuffling going on around her. Maybe somebody said something? She wasn't sure. Felt too good lying there, resting in the sun to care. She kept her eyes closed but turned her head in the other direction, smiling.

Bump.

Hmm?

Bump, bump.

What the hell?

Bump—bump, rock, rock, rock.

Her eyes sprung open and she saw an ankle. An ankle attached to one well-sculpted, light-haired calf. An ankle attached to a masculine, sand-covered foot standing close to her. One foot. The other was out of her view. The other, she surmised, was bumping her ass.

"What the hell are you doing?" she asked, holding a hand on her bikini top and looking back over her shoulder as best she could without getting up. The sun shone directly in her eyes, backlighting the culprit.

"Ah, sorry. I was…um, nudging you."

"With your foot? On my rear end?"

"With a toe," he corrected. "I, ah, was tempted to use my hand, but I thought you might have a problem with that."

"But you didn't think I'd have a problem with your toe? Poking my ass?"

She heard him laugh. A short, semi-embarrassed-but-not-really kind of a laugh. "I was worried you'd OD'd or something. You've been still the better part of an hour."

"I was napping," she said, exasperated, as she laid her head back down on the towel. "I was tired, and I was sleeping, and it was wonderful," she whined, "and now you woke me up." Her head sprung back up, and she looked in his direction. "Do I look like a drug addict to you?"

He snickered as he plopped down into the beach chair next to her. *Her* beach chair. "Well, I've never actually seen a female drug addict lying nude on the beach before, so how was I to know?"

She watched as he put on his sunglasses, stretched his legs out, and laid his head back like he intended on sunbathing. In *her* chair. She tried not to notice his handsome profile.

"I'm not nude."

"Closest thing I've seen to it on a public beach," he commented with his eyes closed. Then he turned his head and lifted his sunglasses, giving her a look at his startling green eyes. "Might want to rub some suntan lotion on that ass of yours. It's getting a little red."

"Ah!" Vivi scrambled to hook her bikini top in the back and tie it up around her neck. "Why the hell are you looking at my ass?" she shouted.

"Why the hell are you leaving it on display?"

"Oh my God," she grumbled, scrambling to stand up fast. "I'm wearing a bathing suit," she said, letting her hand motion to her bikini top and her bikini bottom. She felt her hair start to fall down so reached up to grab the clip, and that's when everything went a little wavy. No, no, that's dark, that's....

"Oh shit," she heard him say. Maybe he sprang up out of the chair, but she couldn't see anything except for black. She felt her brain go blurry, felt arms catch her as she stumbled to the side, and felt her whole body lean heavily against a cool wet surface—ah, that felt good—as she shifted all the way to the ground.

The next thing she knew, she was being pulled awake, as if snatched from a dream. She didn't know where she was, but she felt comfortable as a cool hand stroked her brow.

"Beauty? Wake up, S.B. Come on. Wake up." She heard the words from a distance as she felt a gentle tap on her cheek.

She moved her mouth toward the tap and bit the first thing she could reach.

"Ouch," he shouted. Then he laughed. "Sleeping Beauty has a dark side," he said as she opened her eyes.

She found herself with her head in his lap. Weak. "Sorry," she mumbled, limply bringing up a hand to run it over her face. "Did I…"

"You fainted," he said. He had a really nice voice. Just loud enough, with a seductive quality. It made her want to close her eyes and go back to where she'd just been. "Too much partying last night?"

She turned on her side and snuggled in closer, her hands coming up under her head.

"Oh…hey…ah," he stuttered as he shifted her head around, disturbing her descent back into oblivion.

What the?

Her eyes popped open. She started to scramble again, to sit up and get her head out of this poor guy's crotch, but he held her still, telling her to relax, that it was okay, and that she didn't want to stand up too fast again or the same thing would happen. She felt his hand on the top of her head, stroking, soothing, and it felt nice, and safe, and…

Embarrassing.

"I am so sorry," she muttered, starting to shift slowly and remove herself from his lap. His hands took hold of her shoulders and helped her sit. She leaned one hand on the towel and stopped moving, trying to get her bearings.

"You okay?" he asked while rubbing the center of her back. He sat taller than she did. She had only to look over her shoulder to scan the breadth of his chest situated directly in her line of vision. She barely glanced up at his face before she had to right herself.

"I feel weird." She took a deep breath in and out. "I've gotten dizzy from standing up too fast before, but I've never fainted. Ever."

"Probably the sun. And you jumped up pretty quick. You might be dehydrated if you had a lot to drink last night."

She crossed her legs in front of her and put her elbows on her knees before laying her head in her hands. She didn't feel good. Really wanted to lie back down. So she twisted and folded herself into the fetal position, laying her head at the opposite end of the towel.

"No-no," she heard. "S.B. You've got to wake up, or I'm really going to start to worry." She felt a hand skim over her hip, felt the sun being blocked, his body producing shade. "If we can get you down to the water, cool you off a little, I think that might help."

Vivi opened her eyes and rolled onto her back, blinking up at the shaggy wet hair falling forward as the toe poker had her caged beneath him. His green eyes had a look of alarm. Her instinct was to soothe him. So she reached up and gently touched her open palm to his cheek.

"I'm okay, I think," she said, trying to reassure him. "I just— Ouch!" she cried when he turned his head and bit her fingers.

"Tit for tat. Come on," he said with a smile, pulling back and grabbing both her hands in his. He stood, trying to get her to stand with him.

"I don't want tooooo," she moaned. "I'm tired, and I'm sad, and my life hurts."

He stopped tugging on her, but kept a good grasp on her wrists. "Your life hurts?"

"Yes, my life hurts," she insisted. She looked at him then. Really looked at him, and his perfectly unkempt, wet, sandy-blond hair, his strong chin, and those smirking lips. He was handsome. Ruggedly handsome. Which had never been her thing. "Oh God," she groaned out loud, reminding herself of how un-rugged Kevin was.

"Come on, Sleeping Beauty. You need to get in the ocean. Let it revive you. Then we'll find you some water.

"I've got a bottle of water somewhere," she said, wanting to burst into tears. She needed to get a grip. This poor stranger, this ruggedly handsome stranger, was having to deal with her in a state of complete physical and emotional lethargy. "You go," she suggested. "I'll be fine."

"Ha," he barked out. "Come on. You can barely stand. Seriously, how drunk did you get last night?" His tone sounded disgusted.

"I didn't drink last night," she claimed as vehemently as she had the strength to. "I packed. We got up real early this morning and drove five hours to the beach. I just haven't slept well in a while. Exams. Gay men. That sort of thing."

"Gay men?"

She waved the words away. "Never mind. Just…hand me my water bottle."

Toe Poker looked around and came up empty-handed. "Come on. Let's get you cooled down," he said, gently taking her hand. When it was taking her too long to stand, he just grabbed her around her waist with one arm, swung her legs up into his other arm, and trotted them off toward the water.

"Wow," she said. "That was…that was kinda cool." She swung one arm around his neck to steady herself. "You're…strong."

"You're light," he countered, his eyes trained on the waves in front of them.

"I weigh well over a hundred pounds."

"I bench press well over that."

"So you're not gonna drop me?"

"Not by accident," he said, slanting a crooked smile at her. Their eyes met for the first time.

Wow. She felt herself blush. Felt her chest tighten and felt her inner self shrink down into shy mode. *Shy? I'm not shy. I'm…I'm confident. What the hell?* She found herself struggling to get out of his grasp. "Put me down."

"No," was all he said, as he kept walking.

Oh—okay, her shy self thought, with a timid little smile and the nagging desire to tighten her arms around his big, broad, shoulders.

Oh, please.

Confused and exhausted, Vivi didn't trust herself to speak, and as Toe Poker had made it onto the wet sand, she figured he'd be putting her down soon enough. But he kept walking. When the water was up to his knees, she said, "Okay. This is good."

But Toe Poker kept on wading into the surf, turning his back when they reached the breaking waves, letting them slam into him, protecting her as best he could. He turned back around and moved a little quicker, taking the two of them out deeper.

"Can you swim?" he asked.

She just nodded her head, thinking about how good the water felt, how it soothed her. Then she started to notice how lovely it was to be held in his arms and how romantic this would be if she actually knew this guy. If they were actually a couple.

The water was covering most of her when he stopped. He carefully dipped to the side and placed her feet on the sand before pulling his arm out from under her legs. He kept a tight grip around her waist even as she pulled her arm from around his neck.

"How do you feel? Is this helping?"

She nodded her head, feeling better enough to be embarrassed but not good enough to stop leaning against him as she was buffeted by the incoming waves. "Thank you," she managed. Then she bent her knees and let the water soothe her all the way to her neck. "This feels good. Definitely helping."

"Maybe you had heat stroke," he said, watching her with his hands on his hips.

She shook her head in the negative. "I haven't had anything to eat in a while. I'm sure jumping up from a sound sleep in the hot sun did it. Like you said, I'm probably dehydrated. How come you know so much about all this? Are you a med student or something?"

Toe Poker snorted out a laugh as he looked down the beach. "Not nearly. I don't have the head for Latin or the stomach for the blood."

She smiled then. Right at him. Like she was flirting. "Then it's a good thing I only fainted. You wouldn't do me any good if I'd been attacked by a shark."

His eyes scanned the horizon as if he were seriously looking for sea predators. Then his gaze landed on her with what felt like a thud. Hard. Pointed. Serious. "I won't let anything happen to you."

That sort of took her breath away.

It definitely made her feel shy again. And made it hard for her to drag her gaze from his. She took another look at his broad shoulders, gorgeous chest, and what she could see further down whenever the water ebbed. He wasn't like, muscle bound or anything. He was just in really good shape. Cute too, in a disheveled—didn't shave yesterday or today—sort of way.

Not really her type, but then her type was gay, so maybe disheveled and unshaven was a step in the right direction.

Unsure how to respond, she gave him a quick smile before letting herself float on her back, spreading her arms out to keep from being rocked too much by the roll of the tide. The water felt good on her head, soaking her hair. She reached up and dragged the clip out from where it was hanging and held it in her hand as she floated. She felt her toe being pinched, and she was dragged slowly through the water.

"Don't want you floating away," he said quietly in response. "My name's Lane by the way."

Vivi tucked her knees and stood, the water now up to her chin and his chest.

"Shane?"

"No. Lane."

"Lane? I've never heard that name before."

"Family name. You know, as in, Lois Lane? My mother's maiden name is Lane."

"Hmm." She smiled. Couldn't help herself. "You're a Superman fan."

"No. Yes. Well, I just use that as an example because everybody's heard of Lois Lane. It's easy."

"Your mother's name isn't Lois, is it?"

"No. Bizzy."

"Busy Lane?" Vivi said, wide eyed.

He shook his head and eyed her from the side. "You making fun of my momma now?"

"No," she said, laughing. "No. I'm not. It is funny though."

"Well, she's Bizzy Kettering now, anyway."

"So you're Lane Kettering," Vivi said, liking the sound of his name. "I'm Vivi DuVal. I'm with," she looked up the beach and pointed, "my sorority sisters."

"From Wake Forest," he confirmed.

"Go Deacs," she said. "I wasn't being very pleasant so I don't blame them for ditching me. I definitely needed a nap." She floated backward keeping her head upright, but bringing her toes to the surface, using her hands to tread water. "Definitely needed an attitude adjustment."

"They didn't really ditch you. They sent me back to get you, but you were asleep."

"Ah, so you're with the Carolina Law students?"

"Ah, yeah, so to speak. My brother and his buddies are graduating next week. Beach Week and his bachelor party all rolled into one."

"That'll be fun."

"Should be."

"You sound a little skeptical."

"I'm not...you know, one of them. I'm just here because Tray's my brother. I'm the best man, so..."

"They had to invite you."

"You got it."

She felt herself smiling. "So are you graduating undergrad?"

"No. No, I...um...I'm not graduating this year."

"Next year?" she quizzed.

"I'll be a senior next year."

"Oh. Well, I'm graduating a year early because I thought that was going to make me look smart. I think that's my fatal flaw, always trying to look smart. Because it turns out that working hard enough to graduate early was a really dumb move," she said, startling herself with the truth. She tried to find footing in the sand beneath her. "Whoa."

Lane pulled her against him, the surf up to his chin. "I think we floated out a bit. Come on, I'll drag you back in." When she found her footing, he released her.

"How old are you?" he asked. "Because you look a lot younger than your friends. Maybe it's because you're wet, but..."

Vivi laughed. "I am younger. A lot younger in some cases. But my birthday is tomorrow," she said, brightening. "I'm finally turning twenty-one."

Lane choked. "You're twenty?"

"Today I'm twenty. Tomorrow, I'll be twenty-one."

"Tomorrow?"

"Yes. Tomorrow. Tomorrow it's good-bye fake I.D. and hello tequila."

"Oh, Lord. I can just imagine Miss Thong after a couple shots of tequila. You faint in the damn sun. How are you going to handle tequila?"

"I can handle tequila. And what's wrong with a thong?"

"Have you ever had tequila? Nothing's wrong with your thong."

"No, I've never had tequila. I've been…busy. Like your mom," she snickered. "And I like my thong."

"My mom's name is spelled B-I-Z-Z-Y. Not busy like a damn bee. And I like your thong too. It's just a little…"

"A little what?" she snapped.

"Distracting. Unconventional. Eye-catching. With that big bow just sitting there screaming 'Here's your present.'"

Her mouth dropped open.

"Look," Lane said, floating her to him again. "It's a great suit. Really great. And if anyone should be wearing it, it's you, 'cause there isn't a girl out here on this beach with a finer ass than yours. But with that cute little bow and your…"—he seemed at a loss for words—"…ass,"—he shook his head—"you're going to be attracting a lot of attention."

"Maybe that was the idea," she said, irritated.

"Well, then it's working. Working really well."

Lane's green eyes held her silent. She couldn't look away. Didn't know what she was angry about. The moment stretched out. Finally he broke eye contact, looked up the beach toward his crowd.

Her crowd.

Their crowd.

"I meant that as a compliment," he said, bringing his face back around to hers. "I'm not sure it came off like that."

She felt herself sink inward, dipped down into the water to her chin, trying to figure out how she felt. Self-conscious for sure. Embarrassed? Maybe. Happy a man liked looking at her ass? Yes, she admitted.

Oh, God. She felt so uncertain of everything right now.

"Lane?"

"Yeah?"

"When we get out of the water, can I borrow your T-shirt?"

CHAPTER FOUR

Lane kept checking his watch. The Demon Deacon hot-babe contingent should have arrived over an hour ago. They'd agreed. All of them. On the beach this afternoon. While Vivi sat there all covered up in his T-shirt, which hung down to her knees. And the ball cap she stole from him too. They'd all agreed to meet at the Hot Fish Club after dinner for drinks and to listen to the band. Have a good time. But so far, they'd been a no-show, and his cousin Trevor was talking up the idea of moving their group to a strip club.

Shit.

He'd been nursing a beer, sitting on a bar stool, eyeing the door, waiting for Vivi to make an appearance. Not because he thought he had a chance in hell with her, but because he'd heard a rumor and he wasn't happy about the impending consequences.

Seems while he'd been staring at Sleeping Beauty's ass, her friends were feeding his brother's buddies a story. A gossipy story. A very interesting, very gossipy, very telling story. Something about Vivi's boyfriend of the last two years turning out to be gay. He was short on the details, but once they were all back in his uncle's condo, he had heard plenty of suggestive comments about how Vivi was probably lookin' for a very physical heterosexual experience—phrased not so delicately—as the guys laughed at her expense. He tried to keep his head down and bite his tongue. Tried not to be bothered by their suggestive comments. Tried to tell himself that Vivi DuVal wasn't as vulnerable as she appeared earlier in the day and could probably handle herself. Until he remembered her tequila comments and how she had felt in his arms.

Soft. Soft-soft-soft. And little. And young. And fresh and pretty and self-deprecating about being too smart. She was vulnerable physically because of her weight and height, not to mention the lack of sleep and nourishment. And maybe she was vulnerable emotionally because of her recent breakup. Listening to those horny sons of bitches carrying on about Sleeping Beauty brought back the fear he'd felt as he stood over her body on the beach worried that she'd OD'd. He couldn't just stand by and listen any longer. So he cleared his throat and spoke up.

"She's only twenty. Leave her alone."

All heads turned and stared. Trevor started to make some wisecrack, but Tray stopped him by grabbing his arm and asking Lane, "You like her?"

He shrugged. "She said her life hurt. Fainted in the goddamn sun. She doesn't need…this," he said, indicating their ribald conversation.

"You're right," his brother said. "We'll stop talkin' about it and stand down."

"Good," was all Lane had to say. And he appreciated the nod Tray gave him.

Somehow, Lane Kettering had appointed himself Vivi DuVal's protector. And beyond that, he just wanted to see her again. Talk to her. Make sure she was all right. But he hadn't gotten her phone number, and she and the other girls appeared to be no-shows. So he was feeling a good bit of disappointment as he followed his brother's crowd toward the door of the bar.

Since he'd never been to a strip club before, you'd think he might be feeling a little more excited. It was likely he'd never see Vivi DuVal again, so he needed to get a grip and stop pining for a girl he barely knew. Even if they did share the same birthday—something he never got a chance to tell her.

But glancing up, hope engulfed him as one of Vivi's friends came through the door just as Trevor was moving out. The two of them stopped and chatted, a couple more of the girls joining the conversation as they entered, both of their groups now clogging up the doorway as they reunited.

Vivi was not there. Lane kept his eyes glued to the door as the rest of the girls kept coming. But Sleeping Beauty with her dark hair and soft little body had yet to make an appearance. Lane rolled his eyes as he caught wind of Trevor trying to convince the girls to come with them to the strip club—yeah right—while he moved through the group and out the door.

There she was, haggling with the bouncer who was studying her I.D. as if he were going to be tested on it later. He maneuvered to her side and even though it took her a double glance, when she did recognize him, she gifted him with a brilliant smile and her full attention.

"Hi," he said quietly.

"Hi," she breathed back.

The two of them. Just the two of them. That's all they needed.

Acting on impulse, he snatched Vivi's I.D. out of the bouncer's hand. "It's a fake. She doesn't turn twenty-one until tomorrow." He pulled her away from the bouncer, away from the door, away from the crowd.

"Ahh," she gasped. "Why did you tell him that?"

"Because it's true, and you don't want to go in there anyway."

"Why not?"

"Because the music sucks, the drinks are pricey, and my buddies and I are leaving for the clichéd strip club. Unless you save me by joining me for a walk on the beach."

"Save you?"

"Yeah. Do I look like a guy who enjoys strip clubs?"

Vivi looked him up and down and laughed. "Yes. You look exactly like the kind of guy who would enjoy a strip club."

Lane looked down at his attire. Clean T-shirt, pressed shorts and flip-flops. "What makes you say that?"

"Well…you're all big and brawny and hairy and just seem to spout testosterone—"

"Spout? Testosterone?" he interrupted in disbelief.

"I just mean…you're all *man*."

"Oh really? Because the way you're describing me you'd think I was all ape."

"Oh my God, that is not what I said. At all," she insisted, giggling, as he started walking them away from the club.

"Then you might want to start clarifying before I take offense and leave you to the boring, over-loud music and high-priced drinks instead of tempting you with this," he said, pulling her in front of him and turning her in the direction he wanted.

He felt it take her breath away. The scene before them was captivating. Soothing. He had no idea there was going to be a full moon. It was just dumb luck that he'd maneuvered her to a vantage point where they could see the ocean. The moon seemed to be positioned just for them, bright as daylight, shooting its rays along the ocean, shining a wide swath of light across the water, up the beach, and through the buildings to where they stood. It was magic. Romantic. And Lane just kept right on following his instincts when he pulled her gently back to him, her back pressed against his front, bent down toward her shoulder, and leaned in to kiss her neck.

"Text your friends," he whispered. "Tell them I've made you a better offer. I've got a car. I'll make sure you get home safely and before curfew."

"Curfew," she snickered. "Fine, but I don't know the address."

"Ask them to text it to you."

She pulled out her phone from a tiny little bag hanging off her shoulder and began to do as he'd instructed. He pulled out his own phone and texted his brother.

"Staying. Vivi. Walk on the beach."

He shoved the phone back in his pocket and waited for her to finish up. The response was almost immediate. He felt the buzz against his thigh and pulled out his phone.

"Happy Birthday, Bro. If you need privacy, take my room. I certainly won't be needing it."

He texted Tray back.

"Fat chance. But I appreciate the thought."

"What?" she asked.

"What—what?" he asked back, sliding the phone in his pocket and meeting her grin.

"You're smiling."

"Am I?" He felt his smile go even bigger. "Just figuring a pretty girl in the moonlight has gotta trump a dive strip club."

"Oh, Lord."

"What?"

"I'm not sure I'm gonna measure up to your expectations."

"I have zero expectations."

"I mean a strip club has some level of…"

"Debauchery?"

"Well…"

"Depravation?"

"I was thinking excitement. You know…for male apes."

He laughed. "You don't think you're exciting?"

"Compared to a strip club, I'm probably a little tame."

"Well, let's see," he said as he started to walk them across the parking lot. "You started my day off with a good look at your backside all tied up with a pretty bow. That was exciting." She hung her head, shaking it, so he reached down and took her hand, giving it a squeeze. He laced his fingers through hers as he spoke. "You had me worried you'd died all alone on the beach from some unnatural cause. That got my heart racing pretty good."

She grinned.

"You passed out in my arms while yelling at me," he said. "That was exciting."

"Was I yelling at you?"

"You let me hold you in the water," he whispered close to her ear as he turned her toward him and crowded her against his car. Though she kept her chin down, her pretty brown eyes glanced up. "That was the best part of my day," he confessed. "Until you finally decided to show up here."

"Dinner ran late."

"Excuses, excuses."

"I'm glad you were still here."

"I almost missed you," he whispered, leaning in.

"You would have had the strip club," she whispered back.

He shook his head and went in for the kiss. "No comparison," he said against her lips—those sweet, seductive, holy-cow-I'm-kissing-her lips. Lust exploded and his body took control of his mind, sending his arms around her and his hands up into her hair. Long, curled, pretty-smelling hair. "I like your hair down," he said against her lips.

She hummed.

"It's long," he said, tilting his head to go at her lips from a different angle. "I like long hair," he said when he came up for breath.

He circled his hands around her waist and twirled them so he was now the one leaning against his father's Roadster. He spread his legs and pulled her soft body against him, going back in for a long kiss. With tongue this time.

The words, "Oh, God," tumbled out of him when she opened her mouth under his, causing him to stand up straighter and take this kissing business very seriously. He felt a shot of lust from his chest to his groin, and he groaned inwardly as the sensation engulfed him. Her kiss was wild, sexy, and so damn hot, he didn't realize he had Sleeping Beauty's ass in his hands until the third time he ground his erection against her.

Holy shit.

"I'm sorry," he said, pulling from the kiss and dropping his hands.

"Sorry? Sorry for what?" Vivi said, looking bewildered. Dazed even. So he went back in. Hell, if she was riding this thing along with him, far be it for him to put on the brakes.

"Get a room," he heard some asshole say as he walked by. Lane gave him a sneer as he clutched Vivi to him, ducking her head to his chest so Asshole couldn't see her face.

"Come on," he said, looking into her eyes when the coast was clear. "Let's head out. You told your friends you're leaving with me?"

She nodded.

"What did they say about that?"

She shrugged.

"Cat got your tongue?"

"No," she said, feeding him her shy little smile. "I'm just feeling…woozy."

"Christ, you gonna faint on me again? I thought you just had dinner."

"Ha," she barked out a laugh and moved off his body. "*You* made me woozy. That kiss. All,"—she flipped a finger up and down his form—"that. I guess a guy like you doesn't need to spend time in strip clubs when he can do all that."

"All what?"

"You know what."

"I have no idea what," he said, dragging her back into his clutches. "But I will pay you cash, right now, if you tell me what I did that got you so…woozy."

"Your moves."

"What moves?"

"Your kiss. Those hands. Your body. All those moves."

He stared at her, uncomprehending. She may as well have been speaking Chinese. "All right. Well…this is interesting," he said. "I like your moves, too. But I'm pretty sure you were well aware of that." Vivi leaned in and kissed him quick with a smirky little smile on her lips before he said, "How 'bout we take all our moves to the beach?"

"I'm yours," she replied, moving around to the other side of the car.

"I wish," he mumbled to himself following her around and opening her door.

"Nice car."

"Not mine," he said.

He got her settled, settled himself in the old hot rod his Dad had let him borrow for the trip down, and started the engine with a roar.

"I thought we'd hit the beach in front of my uncle's place. Nice lounge chairs already set up. The ones on the pool deck have cushions. We can stake a claim and watch the moon cross the ocean. The fringe benefit is having clean rest rooms close by. Oh, and a stocked liquor cabinet, in case we're there at midnight and you become old enough to drink."

She laughed at that as they pulled out onto the main road. "Apparently, I still won't look old enough to drink. That bouncer was really giving me a hard time."

"Because you definitely don't look twenty-one. You don't even look nineteen. You look eighteen, maybe."

"And you look just as old as those guys in law school."

"I'm big," he shrugged. "And hairy, as you've vividly illustrated."

"You're not that hairy," she said, laughing in apology. "You're just very…masculine."

"And you're very, very feminine," he said, picking her hand up and bringing it to his lips. "Christ, that bow on your bathing suit took my breath away, but seeing you tonight, haggling with that bouncer in this fluffy little dress—"

"Fluffy?"

"With your hair all down and curly, and then I got you in the moonlight and saw that pink stuff on your lips and those long-long eyelashes and man. Yeah, you're a girly-girl to beat all girls."

"I'm not *that* girly," she protested.

He snorted.

"I'm not."

"How long did it take you to get ready tonight?" he asked.

Silence.

Lane looked over at Sleeping Beauty, all wide awake and staring straight ahead. "How long?" he coaxed. "'Cause anything over twenty minutes makes you a girly-girl."

"Of course, it took me longer than twenty minutes. I can barely shower in twenty minutes with everything I have to wash, condition, exfoliate, and shave. It's hell being a girl." She reached over and touched his hair. "What did it take you? Ten minutes? Shower, shave, run a towel over your head, brush your teeth, and throw on some clothes?"

"I shaved for *you*," he grinned. "Wouldn't have bothered if I hadn't planned on seeing you."

"Yeah," she sulked back into her seat. "Well, why do you think it took me so long to get ready?" she admitted.

"For me?"

"Maybe."

"I just admitted I shaved for you. The least you can do is pretend you did all this," he said, pointing up and down her pretty little body, "for me."

"I'm not admitting anything," she said, smirking. "But I will say I would have been disappointed if we'd missed you guys. The restaurant was busy, and it took forever to get our large table served."

"It worked out."

"I still can't believe you told the bouncer my I.D. was fake."

"I wanted to get you alone."

Silence.

Lane glanced in her direction. "Am I scaring you?"

"No."

"You sure?"

"Yeah."

"Why aren't you talkin'?"

Silence.

"S.B?"

"I'm starting to feel a little woozy."

CHAPTER FIVE

Thank God, I'm single. The thought kept running through Vivi's brain as Lane drove them through the slow-moving traffic. "Mind if I type a quick text message?" she asked him.

"Go right ahead," he said.

Of course he wouldn't mind. He's—like—perfect.

She pulled out her phone and typed in Kevin's name and texted her in-the-moment thoughts.

"Thank you for telling me when you did. You are completely forgiven. Sorry I was so mean."

She hit send and let it go. Then she turned off her phone.

"Everything okay?" Lane asked.

"Everything's perfect," she said without thinking.

"Perfect?" he said, quirking a brow at her as he came to a stoplight.

"Yeah." She smiled right at him, not hiding a thing. "Pretty perfect."

He cleared his throat. "This afternoon you told me your life hurt."

"I did?" she asked, reflecting back. "Mmm. Yeah, it pinched. A little bit."

"Vivi, I gotta tell you that the guys were talkin', and it seems your sorority sisters shared a little bit about what you've been through recently."

"Oh." Her heart sunk and embarrassment crept in. She dropped his serious green gaze and looked out her window, rubbing her hands over her knees and rocking a bit to soothe herself. "I suppose everybody's having a good laugh at my expense." *I probably need to get used to that.*

"No. Ya know, it's titillating gossip. That's all. And I wouldn't have mentioned it except…"

"Except what?" She swung her head around and gave him a deadpan stare.

"Well, my best friend is gay. We've been next-door neighbors since we could walk, and he came out to me a couple years ago. Besides the obvious shock, it didn't really change anything between us. Which I'm grateful for, because he's a good friend. We can talk about anything. Clearly. And after I heard your story, I started thinking about Lam and the struggle he has trying to fit in socially. He's not blatant about his preferences, and he's gone on dates with some real nice girls. I don't think he's trying to deny who he is. I just think he's trying to enjoy life one day at a time."

"So, he's not openly gay?"

"No. Not yet. Working on it."

"Yeah, I think Kevin is like that. I think graduation is probably his stepping stone into living his truth. I just…you know, didn't see it coming. At all."

"I'd introduce you to Lam and you'd never know with him either. Your perspective on this would be valuable information, if you'd let me share it with him."

"My perspective?"

"How finding out he was gay made you feel."

"Hmm. Is he leading some poor girl on?"

"There's a girl who is kinda crazy about him. He has mentioned to me more than once he's concerned about her reaction once she finds out."

"Oh, well, I'm a wreck."

"A wreck?"

"On the beach today, when I saw you, the first thing I wondered was if you were gay. Because after finding out about Kevin, I no longer trust my instincts. Kevin's a great guy and a lot of fun, but I truly thought we were romantically involved. I thought he was hot for me, not hot for the guy dating my roommate." She felt herself getting angry. "You know, he may have shown me a good time, but I wanted it to be true. Be real. He would kiss me, for God's sake. He'd touch my boobs. I had no clue he was gay, and I don't mind admitting that this has really thrown me. I thought I was somewhat intuitive. Shouldn't I have been able to sense something like that?"

"You'd think so— Wait! He touched your chest?"

"Yes," she exclaimed. "And when I asked him about it, he said he liked women's breasts. Does your friend like women's breasts?"

Lane rubbed a finger over his lips, thinking. "I don't know. I never thought to ask. I would assume no, but..." He shrugged.

"Exactly."

Lane turned into a parking lot leading to an underground garage. He pulled into a numbered spot and shut off the engine. "Okay," he said, staring over at her expectantly.

"Okay, what?"

"So ask me."

"Ask you what?"

"Ask me if I'm gay."

She could feel herself blush. "I know you aren't gay."

"Really?" He smirked. "How can you be so sure? I mean, if your intuition is not what you thought it was?"

"Because," she leaned toward him, lowering her voice, "when you were kissing me, I felt a very heterosexual response."

That made him blush. His smirk turned into a shy smile, and he glanced away.

"And Lane, trust me on this. Under the circumstances, that was definitely the best part of *my* day."

He burst out laughing. "Come on," he said, opening his door. "Let's go check out that moon."

"I mean," she said, getting out of the car. "It was very...self affirming," she joked.

"Yeah?" he asked, taking her hand and pulling her along with him. "Well, for me, too."

As they entered an elevator she said, "Thanks."

"For what?" he asked, hitting button number five.

"Helping me make light of it."

He gave her one of his crooked smiles.

"I'm serious. Yesterday this all felt like pretty heavy stuff. And now…" She shrugged.

"A day at the beach will do that for you."

Yeah, a day at the beach with a testosterone-laden hottie who couldn't stop looking at my ass. One who saved the day like Superman by picking me up and carrying me into the water. That kind of day at the beach will sure do it.

The doors opened and Lane headed down the hall with purpose, a key in his hand. "I'm just gonna grab two beers. You think you can handle a beer, right?" he teased. "And maybe put a little tequila on ice. Just in case we make that midnight toast."

"I thought you were worried about getting me home before curfew."

"You'll be twenty-one in a couple of hours. Screw the curfew," he said over his shoulder.

Vivi stood just inside the doorway on a small, tiled foyer area. She could hear Lane opening the refrigerator and messing with some ice. Her eyes scanned the space, taking note of all the open duffle bags and masculine stuff lying around. But underneath the law student clutter, she could tell the place was large and furnished beautifully. "Does your uncle rent this out?" she called.

"No," Lane said, coming back around the corner carrying a small cooler. "He doesn't. It's too nice. Doesn't want any riffraff messing it up."

"I don't blame him. It's really beautiful."

"Four bedrooms and a pull-out couch, so it sleeps plenty. You should see the view from here too. Right on the ocean. Five stories up. There's a nice-sized balcony. Oh, hold up," he said. He left her standing there for a moment and came back with two beach towels. "Just in case we need 'em," he said. Vivi took them out of his hands.

"Have you stayed here often?" she asked as he locked up the door and they headed down the hall to the elevator.

"A couple family vacations. Never with a bunch of guys before. This has worked out pretty well though. One of Tray's buddies is in culinary school, so he cooks brunch, which tides us over until happy hour. Today he pulled out an antipasti platter when we came in from the beach. I'm not a wine drinker, but a couple of the guys are really into it. They opened some fancy Italian wine and we all hung out until it was time to head to dinner."

"Wow," Vivi said. "It's a whole other scene down at our place. Pop Tarts, protein drinks, cheese and crackers if we're lucky. No culinary classes at Wake Forest."

They exited the elevator and made their way across the pool deck and down the steps to the beach. Vivi took off her flip-flops and carried them once they hit the sand. It felt cool, almost cold, on her feet. A significant difference in temperature now that the sun wasn't beating down on it.

Where the pool deck had been softly illuminated, the beach was unlit except for the moon, which seemed a little smaller but just as bright as it had been a short time ago. A tall shadow indicated a stack of lounge chairs off to the side, but Lane headed past them, toward the water where a couple of chairs had been left scattered on the beach.

A gentle breeze blew off the ocean, catching the ends of Vivi's hair and tossing them around her shoulders. She unfolded one of the towels and tucked it in at the top of the lounge chair. Lane took the other towel and laid it along the bottom part, saying they only needed one chair.

Her heart fluttered.

She stood perfectly still, watching Lane work. He smoothed out the towels, opened the cooler, took out a long-necked bottle, twisted the cap off and then handed it to her. Cold, a little damp, she took a sip as she watched Lane open another bottle for himself and then step out of his flip-flops and sit down. He put his beer down in the sand, let his gorgeous, muscular legs straddle the lounge chair, and then patted the spot in between. He looked at her expectantly.

A chill ran up her spine.

When she didn't make a move, he reached out and tugged at the hem of her dress, pulling her closer. Then he put a hand on each hip and guided her into his lap, pulling her snugly against him so her back rested against his chest. He picked up his beer and clinked their bottles together before taking a long sip. She sipped, too.

"Good?" he asked, returning his beer to the sand.

She nodded.

She felt his hands in her hair, playing with it, gently stroking it, combing his fingers through it, appreciating it. He pressed his nose into the back of her head and breathed deep. "You smell good," he whispered. He gathered her hair and stroked it all over her left shoulder. "Is that okay?" he asked, as he wrapped his arms around her, shifting her further against him so that the back of her head was snuggled below his left shoulder. She could easily look up to the right and see his handsome face peering down at her.

"You're quiet again," he said.

"Mmm," she murmured, turning her face back toward the ocean.

"Most girls I know are much chattier than you."

"I'm fairly chatty," she assured him. "I've also been accused of being bossy on more than one occasion."

"You were a little bossy this afternoon when you told me to put you down."

"You didn't listen."

"Nope. I like to be my own boss." He pulled one arm from around her long enough to take a sip of beer, but replaced it as soon as he was through. Vivi sat there in the comfort of his arms, holding a beer she didn't really want, enjoying the breeze off the ocean, the rumble of the surf, and the brilliant full moon.

She turned her head and said, "This is really nice, Lane."

"Better than boring, loud music and over-priced drinks?"

"Yeah," she said, turning back toward the water. "Way better."

"I think so, too," he whispered against her ear. "You cold?"

"I'm pretty perfect," she said, relaxing into him and the night.

"You are indeed," he said.

She smiled into the dark.

"So what's Sleeping Beauty's plan for the rest of her life? What's your big dream?"

"Hmm," she said on a sip of beer. "What a compelling way to ask that question. I bet most of my friends aren't considering their big dream as they scramble to find a job. Most haven't figured out what their dream is yet."

"But you have."

"I figured out my dream when I was six years old and asked for a whiteboard for Christmas. I've wanted to be a teacher for as long as I can remember."

"A teacher?"

"Yes." She laughed. "Not very chic or inventive. But I can't imagine doing anything else. I'm looking forward to having my own classroom and working with students."

"So that bossy streak is going to come in handy."

"My personality is well-suited to the profession," she admitted.

"What grade?"

"Originally, I wanted to teach high school. Had thoughts of becoming a college professor. And I still might. But my student teaching took place in an elementary setting, and I just fell in love with those young ones. Eager to learn, eager to please. They look at you like you have all the answers."

"Well, who wouldn't like that?"

"Exactly."

"What's your favorite subject?"

"Math. I double majored in education and math, thinking that's what I'd be teaching."

"I thought I kicked ass in math, until I hit Calculus. That course kicked my ass back. Hard."

"Mmm," she said, turning to her side so she could look up at him. "I made good money off of guys like you," she quipped. "Being that Wake is a liberal arts college, there is a math requirement," she said, running a hand over his chest. "I started tutoring my second semester and built up a nice fat bank account to show for it. Which I'm going to need since teaching jobs seem to be scarce at the moment."

She tried to turn back around, but Lane stopped her. He pulled her a little sideways, up against his chest, keeping his arms circled around her. "I like to see your face when you talk," he said. "You comfortable?"

She nodded, feeling shy. Again. Lane did that to her in a way no guy had ever done. She didn't feel like her bossy self around him. She felt...pretty? Feminine? Yes, both of those. Plus a little overwhelmed. He was forthright in a way Kevin obviously hadn't been. And Lane seemed somewhat romantic. Taking her I.D away from the bouncer was forthright and suggesting a walk on the beach was romantic. Carrying her into the water today was heroic and romantic. *This* was romantic.

At the moment, she was really digging on romantic.

"Any job prospects?" he asked.

"Lots of resumes out. I've already had an interview with a school system in Atlanta. I won't know if there's an opening until July sometime."

"Is that where you're from? Atlanta?"

"No. I'm from a little town in North Carolina."

"Me, too. Where?"

"Henderson?"

"No shit?"

"What?"

"I'm from Oxford."

"You've got to be kidding," she said, sitting up.

"Nope. Our hometowns are fifteen minutes apart."

"Wilson High School?" she asked.

He nodded. "Henderson High?"

She nodded back.

"So we're arch rivals," he said.

"I guess we are." She grinned at him. "What?" she asked when he just sat there grinning back.

"Nothin'. Just thinking about how much I wanna kiss you," he said, running a hand through her hair.

Her chest tightened, and her belly flipped. Man, did this guy know how to turn her on. Her body started to heat and purr. The closer Lane and his chiseled face leaned in, the faster her head started to spin. "Take a breath," he whispered as he took the beer out of her trembling hands and set it aside. He gently pulled her around and up into his lap, draping her legs over one side of the lounge chair. "I'm just going to kiss you. Once. Then, if you like it, you can kiss me back," he whispered as he brushed her hair away from her cheek and licked at the spot below her ear.

"I'm probably gonna like it," she whispered back, feeling his hands move from her hair, one going around her middle, the other tilting her face toward his.

"That is my fervent hope," he said, licking his lips before he touched them softly against hers.

Lane's gentleness unraveled whatever tension her body held. The soft timbre of his voice. The tenderness of his touch. The slow, patient, torturous exploration of her lips with his tongue. Lane was proving to be an expert at seduction, and Vivi was nothing but putty in his hands.

Willing putty.

Eager putty.

Impatient putty.

Lane was taking his time writing a sonnet against her lips and greedy Vivi just wanted CliffNotes.

She tried to contain her yearning. She wanted him to be the one to deepen the kiss. But he'd had his finger on her woozy button all day long and right now she was at full tilt. "Lane," she whispered, and he answered the call. His tongue slipped into her mouth like a breath, and the satisfaction of feeling that intimacy, along with the release of his own pent-up moan, brought great pleasure. Her hands grabbed at his shoulders while he pulled her closer, opened his mouth a little wider, forcing her to do the same.

Soooooo different from kissing Kevin, the non-woozy part of her brain compared. The way Lane explored her mouth with his tongue, held on to her jaw gently with his hand, guided her this way, coaxed her that way. It was all so…meaningful. Like this kiss meant something to him. To both of them. There was emotion tied to it, to every little bit of it, and she felt it, thoroughly. Her body responded by going tingly in places that had yet to learn to tingle. And then it went tight, and eager, and hot, and…damp.

The longing felt good. Unique. A very pleasant reaction to Lane's kiss. But the kiss was the thing. The kiss was a connection. His kiss had her conscious mind laid out at the bottom of the woozy pool. Saturated. Sedate. Floating along in a blissful cocoon. Her body was highly engaged in the act of kissing. Her tongue, her lips, her teeth, her hands, and now the rest of her were all participating fully in kissing Lane, but her mind couldn't hold all the pleasure. Her mind was blissed out.

"S.B.," Lane whispered in between kisses. His hand ran up and down her side, pulling a portion of her attention from the deep of the pleasure zone. "S.B. Baby, I want you to do something for me."

"Anything," she whispered back, smiling shyly as he left a little space between their lips.

"Careful," he warned. "You don't know what I'm asking yet." He chuckled softly.

Dazed and happy, Vivi was surprised when he reached in his pocket and pulled out his phone.

"Give me your number."

She didn't hesitate. She rattled it off. Twice. He one-fingered the number and her full name into his data, keeping his other arm around her with a hand securely on her back. He hit "Done" and put his phone back in his pocket.

When he looked up, she took Lane's face in both her hands. "You planning on calling me?"

"Every chance I get," he said, pulling her around to face him, forcing her to straddle his lap. The kissing heated up fast, and it wasn't long before Lane started talking a little woozy himself. "Mmm… God…S.B…how hard am I gonna have to beg to get you to follow me upstairs?"

Vivi smiled against his lips, wondering why she'd ever consider not following him. That path was just gonna lead to a lifetime of "Oh, what would have happened if I had just gone?" Lane Kettering was not gonna be a regret she left on the table.

"What's upstairs?" she teased.

"Music," he said, running his hands up her thighs. "A locked door…a comfortable bed," he said between kisses. "Condoms," he admitted, and then stopped everything else as he pulled away and owned the moment, looking straight into her eyes. "You wanted somebody hot for you? Well, you might wanna start being careful what you wish for, because I swear to God I've never been hotter. You want to ask me some questions? You want to see my license? You want my blood type? Sleeping Beauty, I'll give you anything you want. But as much as I thought I could spend the entire night out here kissing you in the moonlight, I'm not lying when I say we've either got to end it here or go straight on till morning. Because I am so tangled up in you right now I know I won't have the strength to stop somewhere in between."

He was panting. And earnest. So, very earnest. And yeah, the sensible thing to do would be to leave the night right here. Maybe pick it up on the beach tomorrow. Or at least ask him more questions. But the big question—the only question—Vivi had been clinging to for days, had already been answered, in poetry.

"You want me?" she whispered.

"Want doesn't begin to do my feelings justice."

She smiled and slowly leaned in to kiss ruggedly handsome Lane Kettering from Oxford, North Carolina.

CHAPTER SIX

Lane asked Vivi to wait in the living area while he checked out the condition of his brother's bedroom. Being that Tray was the groom, and the reason for the party, he'd been given the master suite all to himself. Everyone else was sharing a room except Lane. Lane was on the pullout sofa.

"Not tonight," he said out loud while remaking the bed and looking around through Vivi's eyes. He tossed his brother's clothes in a pile, cleaned up the mess in the bathroom, straightened the towels, and then set off to find Sleeping Beauty, half expecting her to have taken off. But there she stood, pretty as a sunset and twice as sultry.

He opened the cooler he'd left by the door, pulled out the short bottle of tequila he had stuffed into the ice, and took Vivi by the hand, leading her out onto the balcony. "It's not quite midnight, but I figured now's probably a good time to tell you a little something about me."

"Yes?"

Her bright, expectant eyes and pretty smile grabbed him around the nuts. He was falling fast for all this sweet and soft, nearly desperate to get her undressed and into his arms. But he needed to slow it down, play it cool. Maybe she was a sure thing, but he surely didn't want to blow it. Not now. Not when she came from a town right next to his own. In the back of his mind, he was already formulating a plan to maneuver around the obvious pitfalls.

Her—a college graduate.

Him—not.

He cleared his throat. "May sixteenth is your birthday," he stated. "It just so happens it's my birthday, too," he said, unscrewing the top of the tequila.

"You're kidding."

"Nope. I was pretty pumped when this trip ended up happening over my birthday. Figured I'd be treated to a wild night with my brother and a team of almost-lawyers." He pulled her close and wrapped an arm around her. "I did not dream big enough. Didn't have a clue that I'd be lucky enough to celebrate with you." He put the bottle to his mouth and took a swig. Then he reached over, took a clean glass from the outdoor bar cart, and added a shot to it. He set the bottle down, picked up the glass, and tipped it to her lips. She took it in both hands and downed the shot. Her grimace was cute. Her pink painted fingertips came up to touch her lips as her eyes went wide from the fire coursing down her throat, maybe ricocheting all over her insides. That thought made him take another shot straight from the bottle.

"Were we born the exact same day?" she asked.

"No," he said, shaking his head and then coming to rest, staring her straight in the eye. "There's a two-year difference."

"Well," she said, tilting her head and smiling. "Happy birthday to both of us."

Six words. That's all they were. Six words, none of them his favorite. Yet, coming from her lips, with that sexy voice, in that breathy little way she had about her when she went all shy? A direct hit to his libido. What the hell was gonna happen when he got her in bed?

He needed condoms.

Lots and lots of condoms.

He took her hand and drew her behind him, but halfway through the condo he managed to get her in front of him and have both of his hands on her shoulders, the rest of his body pushing up against her as they headed down the hall. It was getting to the point where he couldn't keep his hands off her any longer. And man, he thought, as he laid a kiss on the curve of her neck, his lips wanted in on the action too. When they came face to face with the enormous bed, he made his excuse. "I'm gonna leave this bathroom for you. I'll head down the hall and be back in a minute."

He took the time to scramble into the bedroom his cousin Trevor was using and felt no guilt whatsoever rooting around in Trev's duffle bag until he came up with a box of condoms. Jackpot. He texted his brother saying Vivi was spending the night and told them not to be assholes whenever they came in. Oh yeah, and thanks for the bedroom. Then he used the bathroom, washed his hands and face, and took off his shirt, inspecting himself in the mirror. He sniffed both armpits and gave himself a passing grade of a B plus. Then he laughed, hoping that was considered more than a passing grade from his little wannabe teacher.

He came back to their room happy, refreshed, excited, and yakking his head off. "You know, you already gave me one of the best birthday presents ever today when I saw—Holy shit!"

Sleeping Beauty was brushing out her hair—her long, dark, silky smooth hair—standing at the end of the bed in nothing but a tiny little bra the color of the sky on the best day of his life and a matching pair of panties, all lacy, all soft, all fuck-me-I'm-gonna-blow-now.

Jesus Christ.

"What?" she asked, laughing at his expression. "You've already seen me in my bathing suit."

He stumbled back against the door he'd just shut and locked, clutching his heart, desperate for his ability to inhale to return. "Your bathing suit rocked," he said, his eyes squinting like he was in pain. Which was the damn truth. "But you, in that, like this, here, with me? Fu-ck. I mean, shit. I mean, sorry. I'm just…" He looked down at his bare feet to stop his lame-ass mouth from talking and took time for a deep inhale. "Vivi," he said, raising his head and looking into her eyes. "You are…beautiful."

Her eyelashes fluttered and her gaze dropped to the ground. Bashful Beauty had now entered the picture. Which helped put some of the wind back in his own sails. He pushed himself away from the door and walked to her, taking the brush out of her hands and turning her around, her back to him. He slowly brushed her dark brown tresses from scalp to tip, enjoying the quiet between them, letting his overzealous desire quiet back down.

"I don't have a sister," he said. "My mom is great and we get along real well, but…"

"But what?"

He shrugged, continuing to brush her hair. "Women are pretty much a mystery to me. So, you know, maybe it's a good thing you like to teach," he whispered. He leaned down and kissed her shoulder as he placed the brush on a table. "I like being the boss, but I'm open to any and all suggestions," he whispered against her ear, feeling her body rock back and settle against him. He surrounded her with his arms, nudged her hair aside to get to her neck, and started kissing his way into bed. "Lights on or off?" he whispered.

"Off."

"Did you text your friends? Tell them you're with me and that you're not coming home tonight?"

She nodded.

"And Vivi?"

"Hmm?"

"Happy birthday."

CHAPTER SEVEN

July 1ˢᵗ

"Thank God it's the first. We can text all day, right? No limit on the first of each month, right?"

Vivi stared at her phone.

Nothing.

She texted Lane again.

"Are you there? It's THE FIRST OF THE MONTH. Where are you? I miss you? I need to text with you."

Three long hours later, her phone beeped up a text.

"Sorry. Sorry. REALLY SORRY. I know it's the first of the month. I've been living for the first of the month—God, S.B. I miss you. Unfortunately, it's also a Monday, and I'm now working for my uncle's construction company down in Nags Head. The same uncle with the condo where we're gonna meet next May. Gotta stay on his good side. Couldn't be texting on the job. We start work before the damn sun comes up, but we get off early. So I'm here now. I'm all yours. Text away."

"I'm not sure I like this once-a-month texting rule. I get all wound up and worried you're not going to show up."

"I'll show. Trust me. How was Europe?"

"Incredible. I can text a few pictures if you want."

"As long as you're in them, text as many pictures as you like. I'll need them to get through the next month."

"Take a selfie. Right now. I want to see you."

"I haven't showered yet. I'm covered in dirt. You don't want to see me."

"I want to see you. NOW."

"Bossy, bossy. Hold on."

Vivi tapped her foot hard and fast, having no patience for this at all. It was her own dumb fault. She should never have agreed to his rules of engagement. But since she and Lane had decided to continue their relationship after Myrtle Beach, neither one had a moment to breathe or see each other during the summer.

Her schedule was booked with travel. Fun post-graduation travel. Some search-for-work travel. Family-vacation travel. Reunion travel. Travel for friends' weddings. The list went on and on. There wasn't a time when she planned to be in Henderson that Lane was going to be close by in his hometown of Oxford. His time was being taken up with his brother's out-of-town wedding, various out-of-town jobs, and an out-of-town summer school course. Then he'd be back at school full time at the end of August. Since it was his senior year, and she, hopefully, would be starting her own career, they decided to let their relationship ride. No commitments. No demands. Only texting on the first of every month to keep in touch. And a promise. Next May they'd celebrate their birthdays together again, right back in Myrtle Beach.

Seemed reasonable.

At the time.

Felt reasonable when they were holding each other tight, and he was kissing on her like he couldn't get enough.

Two days after they parted, it began to feel a whole lot like unreasonable. A whole week later, she wanted to Google his address and show up on his front doorstep. But then she left for Paris and a full month touring Europe, and she had to talk herself into having a good time by pushing Lane Kettering into the future. Something she could look forward to without making herself crazy in the present. And with Europe as a distraction, it worked okay.

Right now, she felt mighty close to crazy.

His picture popped up on her phone screen and she rushed to enlarge it. *Oh man*, her heart sighed. His hair was lighter, his tan was darker, his beard was scruffy, his eyes—his eyes were perfect—shiny, green, sparkling, and his smile was the same cute, smirky one that lit up her insides. Best of all, his shirt was off and he was sweaty and dirty, and…magnificent.

She typed out her response. Hit send.

"You are one dirty, dirty, man."

"If you were here, you'd be dirty too."

"I'd like that."

"Any job offers?" his text asked.

"It looks like I'll hear from Atlanta in a couple weeks. They didn't promise anything, but did call to inquire whether I was still available."

"Hmm. Atlanta."

"I know. I've applied all over North Carolina. But unless I end up in Chapel Hill, I guess we've got to stick to our plan."

"Except for Thanksgiving and Christmas. You're coming home from wherever you are then, right? I'll get to see you then?"

"I'm crossing the days off the calendar with a red marker."

"Me too."

"How are you?"

"Fine. Good. Making money. Reliving our nights together while I work, before I go to sleep, first thing in the morning, all day long."

Vivi laughed at that. Was grateful he was still so forthright. Before she could respond, another text came in.

"You mean a lot to me, S.B. You gotta promise me again that you're gonna show up in Myrtle Beach next May sixteenth."

"I promise."

"I'm going to hold you to it."

"Okay."

There was a break in their texting flow, and then Vivi's phone rang.

"I'm breaking my own damn rule," Lane said, his voice smooth and quiet. She couldn't respond, because he'd just brought her to tears. "Are you there?"

"Hmm-hmm," she said, wiping at her eyes. "I'm here, and I miss you, and I love the sound of your voice."

"That so? Hmm. Then how 'bout we amend our agreement to texting *and* phone calls on the first of every month. I like your voice, too."

August 1st

"I'm going to Atlanta. NC schools are slow to process new applicants and retire worn out teachers. I've got to go to Atlanta."

"You don't have to go if you don't want to."

"It's my dream."

"Atlanta's your dream?"

"No. The job. Teaching's my dream. Second graders. Decent starting salary. Nice school environment. Not the best school, but far from the worst. I like the principal. I'm going to Atlanta."

"For a year."

"Well, for however long."

"A year."

"We'll see."

"I can be bossy, too."

"I do remember. Fondly."

"How's my Sleeping Beauty?"

"Okay. Tired. Happy it's the first of the month and I get to spend time with you."

"Virtually."

"Are you aware Thanksgiving is less than four months away?"

"Three more first of the months."

"Any chance you're going to make it home during the next week? I've only got a week until I'm a working woman."

"Living your dream."

"Hopefully."

"You'll love it. You'll be good at it. Once you start, it'll make the time go faster. I'm hoping school does that for me. Feels like I'm sort of wishing my life away at the moment."

"Lane, you've got to enjoy your senior year. Once you're done, you're done."

"Sounds like you're missing your senior year."

"Not really. Wouldn't have met you if I didn't graduate early and go to Beach Week. Are you gonna call me?"

"Are you gonna cry?"

"Probably. But only when I first hear your voice."

"Send me a picture."

"Call me."

"As soon as I get the picture I want, I'll call you."

"What picture do you want?"

"You. In that sky blue lacy set of undies."

CHAPTER EIGHT

First Day of School

Lane entered his last class of the day, happy to find his buddy Lam already there, saving a seat right next to him. As first days went, this one had been a doozie. Football practice before classes had his body shutting down and craving a nap during his first two. Then he did his weight training after lunch. He was now down to one more class and then he'd be back out on the field. Hell, he'd have thought hauling bricks and digging ditches all summer would have kept him in better shape. Now that classes were starting, football practice was taking its toll. He needed to get more sleep. Like, right after practice.

He was too tired to do any talking, so he just gave Lam a fist bump and slouched into his chair as the classroom around him filled up. He flipped his notebook open and was making some notes about a trick play he needed clarification on—details he wanted to go over with his coach—when the teacher walked in and shut the door. He glanced up as she was making her way to the center of the room.

"Aw, fuck," he whispered, his whole body going into fight-or-flight mode. Flight. He definitely needed to fly the hell out of here. He closed his notebook and ducked his head.

"What?" Lam asked.

Lane started to get up quietly. "I gotta get out of here," he said under his breath. "Back me up, man." Lane bent his head, held his notebook up to cover his face and quietly made for the back door.

Luckily, things were still getting settled, and he managed to escape from the room unnoticed.

"Christ," he said as he headed in the direction of the front office. He had maybe a three-minute head start before everything blew up in his face.

Vivi, now known better as Miss DuVal, was enjoying her first day of school as a full-fledged teacher. On Wednesdays, her schedule held only four classes, so she was easing her way into the whirlwind of high school nicely. Get this day under her belt and she'd be ready for a heavier class schedule tomorrow.

She'd been nervous but totally prepared for her morning calculus class. The kids seemed resigned to be there. No outbursts, no spitballs. Her nerves had settled considerably by class number two, algebra, which she could teach blindfolded and with one arm tied behind her back. No nerves at all for AP Calculus, as those students were her wheelhouse, her people. She was excited about the challenge of her last class of the day, Statistics, because she'd never taught it before. Never tutored it—nothing. The principal needed her to handle it, so handle it she would. It was a condition of the offer of employment which had come in at the last minute while she was packing for Atlanta.

She'd been so busy putting on the brakes in Atlanta, and settling back into her parents' house, that the driving desire she initially had to break the rules and text Lane to tell him she was now gainfully employed by his alma mater died down. She'd wait. It would give her something to surprise him with on September first.

Mr. Liskey talked her ear off in the teacher's lounge, and she'd missed the opportunity to be in the classroom as the first students entered. She liked to greet them, somewhat individually, if she could. As the last class of the day, she knew their blood sugar was probably running low and thoughts of getting the hell out of school were running high. That was okay, because it was her plan to spend the first class dazzling them with the wonderful world of statistics and how it related to betting in Vegas. She needed something to inspire their interest.

She walked in as the students were getting settled. There was only a low hum of conversation. The room was full, but nothing she couldn't handle. She grabbed the class roster, determined to remember names and faces by the end of a full week. When she heard a scrape of a chair she looked up to see the tail end of a student exiting the room.

"Wrong class?" she asked the boy next to the now-vacant desk.

"I think so," he said. "Probably. He didn't really say."

"All right. Well, everyone, I'm Miss DuVal." She pointed to her name on the board. "In this class, you will become enamored with statistics," she said, hearing a bunch of grunts in reply. "How many seniors do we have in here?"

Seventy-five percent of the students raised their hand.

"Juniors?"

Five.

"Any sophomores?" she asked hopefully. None. "And freshmen," she said, expecting no hands and getting exactly what she expected.

"I've been asked to take roll every day. Give me a week to learn your names and faces and then we won't have to go through this so formally. Please respond by raising your hand and letting me know if you can see the board and hear me from your present seat.

"Caralee Barrett?"

"Here. I'm fine in this seat."

"Thanks. Benjamin Church?"

"Here. I'm good."

"Perfect. Tom Gallagher?"

"Here. I'd be more comfortable in the back on a sofa."

"But I wouldn't have the pleasure of seeing your face quite so well. We'll keep you right here. Ah, next is Mark Handelman."

"Here. Fine."

"Great. Sean Jacobs."

"Here. I can hear and see fine."

"Terrific. Ah, Lane…" Vivi stammered. *What?* She looked up, confused. "Lane Kettering?"

She scanned the classroom. No response.

Her eyes drifted toward the lone chair, fourth row center. She looked back at the name, a chill running down her spine. A young cousin?

"He left," came a male voice. Vivi glanced up to see that the huge, handsome, black kid sitting next to the empty chair had spoken.

"Pardon?"

"He left."

"And you are?" she asked, glancing down at her roster.

"Lambert Somers."

"Lambert," she repeated, something terrifying starting to pound in the depths of her soul.

"I go by Lam," the kid said.

"Lam," she repeated quietly. *Lam, Lam, oooh!* Her eyes locked with Lam's right before she held up a finger toward the class. Right before she marched herself out of the classroom and into the hall.

Down the long, quiet corridor was a lone figure, walking slowly with his head down. She watched him reach the end. As he turned the corner, he glanced back in her direction. Their eyes met right before he disappeared.

CHAPTER NINE

Principal Levendusky was waiting for Vivi when class let out. Somehow she'd managed to hold her shit together and teach while hoping against hope that there was some explanation other than the fact that Lane Kettering, *her* Lane Kettering, was now not just her love interest, but her student as well. Because the ramifications of that kept dancing through her head as she tried to play teacher.

I'm a teacher, dating a high school student. This is fodder for the tabloids. Ohmygod, ohmygod…

Vivi managed to quell her growing panic and focus on the job of teaching, but the moment she saw Principal Levendusky it all came flooding back. She blinked a few times while she tried to restart her heart when he stepped into the room.

"Are you here to fire me?"

Mr. L., as he was affectionately called, tilted his head and brought his brows together. "No. No, we give our new teachers more than one day to make good around here," he joked. "But it seems we have a situation I'm hoping you can help resolve." He motioned for her to join him as they walked into the hall and toward his office. "A student came in demanding to be removed from your Statistics class. His college counselor, Mrs. Hodge, insists he needs to maintain a strong course schedule for his college applications. He's a smart kid. He's applying to top schools. There's no reason he shouldn't be taking Statistics. Mrs. Hodge and the front office have looked for another equally challenging class to put him in last period, but there's really nothing satisfactory. He needs to be in your class, Vivi. I'm hoping you can talk to the boy and see what can be worked out."

"Mr. Levendusky," she started but he held up his hand.

"You need to talk to the boy," he said quietly. When she looked up at him, she saw a little smile, a twinkle in his eye.

"What did he tell you?" she asked.

"Not a damn thing, and I pressed—hard. Lane is generally not a hothead, so him being so insistent, well…I've been around young people a long time, and I'm pretty sure this isn't about Statistics. I'd like to give you a chance to talk with him first, and then I'll join the two of you. Together we'll figure out how best to resolve whatever is going on here."

Vivi sighed. She was going to lose her job. Her first-ever teaching job and she only got to experience it for one day. Lane! What the hell?

Once they were within the front offices, Principal Levendusky allowed her to proceed down the hall to his office alone. She did so briskly, wanting to get to the bottom of this. Wanting to find out for herself just what the hell was going on.

She opened the door, and there he was. His gorgeous shaggy head bent low as he sat in a chair at the side of the room. His chin snapped up when she entered, his green eyes dangerous and catching her off guard. Her heart fluttered as he stood and came at her, angry.

"You're supposed to be in Atlanta," he accused in a passionate whisper, closing the door behind her.

"And you're supposed to be a senior at UNC," she said in similar fashion. "Give me your license," she demanded.

He pulled his wallet from his back pocket while he stood way too close to her, his eyes never letting go of her gaze. He removed his license and held it directly in her line of vision. "My birthday. May sixteenth." He tapped the card. "Two years apart, just like I said."

"You're nineteen!"

He gave her a quick, short nod before he put his license away.

"I thought you were twenty-three. I thought you were at Carolina, finishing up college this year, not high school," she cried.

"So what?"

"So what?" she repeated. "So what?" she shouted, incredulous. "So now I'm technically dating one of my students and won't TMZ just have a heyday making me out to be some horrible sex offender."

"S.B., I hate to break it to you, but TMZ doesn't give a shit about you. You are not a celebrity."

"Not now. But when the local news gets wind of this, you and I will both be celebrities and not in a good way. Oh, God," she said, succumbing to panic. "Oh, God," she said, reaching out, unable to breathe, tears springing to her eyes.

"Vivi," Lane said, catching her up in his arms and helping her to sit in a chair. "You're making a big deal out of nothing. I've got this handled. I promise."

He was crouched down beside her when Vivi remembered his smell, his warm, succulent, all-male smell, and it swamped her. She wanted nothing more than to wrap her arms around him and weep into his shoulder.

"It is a big deal," she cried, as she gave in and launched herself into his arms, sobbing against him. "It changes everything."

"It changes nothing," he said, bringing her with him as he stood, running a soothing hand down her back. "I've pulled out of your Statistics class. You're not my teacher. You never were. You and I were both students when we met. I'm not letting anybody twist what we have into something salacious."

"We have to tell the principal," she sobbed.

"We're not telling Levendusky a damn thing."

"We've…we've got to tell your parents." She sniffled and pulled away.

"I'm looking forward to introducing you as my girlfriend."

"Don't you understand?" she said, dabbing at her eyes, trying desperately to pull herself together. "I can't be your girlfriend. Not while we're both at this school."

"Too damn bad. We're already involved."

"No one is going to stand for a student dating a teacher."

"Then quit."

"Quit? I can't…quit." She pushed out of his arms and walked over to grab a tissue off Mr. L.'s desk. "When this job came up at the last minute, I burned every bridge in Atlanta. Because this job is perfect. Teaching high school math at my age, with no experience, in North Carolina. This is like the Holy Grail. I can't quit."

"Well, I'd offer to transfer somewhere, but then I wouldn't be able to play football, and I need football, S.B. I've got college coaches offering me places on their teams. They want to see me playing this year and getting better. I'm not gonna get the playing time I need if I transfer over to Henderson High. Their season's already started. *Our* season has started."

Vivi felt like she'd been hit by a big wave and was caught under the surf, tumbling around, banging into the sand, not knowing which way was up. She headed for the nearest chair and sat. "Why didn't you tell me all of this?"

"What? Tell you that I was in high school, when you were ready to graduate college? Christ, S.B., you wouldn't have looked at me twice."

"You don't know that."

"I wasn't willing to take that chance. Not if you didn't ask me any direct questions. And yeah, when things started getting serious I probably should have spelled it out a little clearer. But hey, we only had three days together, so I figured why ruin a good thing. You were going off to Europe, then Atlanta. By Thanksgiving I will have committed to a college and figured I'd tell you then. Figured it'd be an easier pill for you to swallow if I had one foot out of high school."

"You're nineteen," she cried.

"Don't you dare tell me my age has anything to do with how you feel about me."

She looked Lane up and down, finding it hard to believe this was happening. He didn't look nineteen. At all. He was so big and burly, and hairy and…and tempting. She sighed. "How is it possible you're still in high school?"

He squatted down in front of her and started parting his hair on the top of his head, leaning in to show her something. "See that scar?"

"Oh my God." Vivi drew back.

Lane brushed his hands through his hair, combing it all back into place. "I'd just started first grade when I was hit by a car."

"You were hit by a car?" Vivi asked, horrified.

"Yeah." He smiled, almost as if he was proud or amused. "I don't remember it, so you know, don't worry. Apparently I was chasing a ball and ran out into the street right in front of some poor mom who hit me with her minivan."

"Oh, Lane," Vivi breathed.

"Yeah. It was bad. Really bad. Head trauma. Busted hips, legs, ribs, one arm. My spine held up pretty well except in the neck area, so I was in traction for months. I was in a coma for a week or so with the whole brain swelling thing. Like I said, I don't remember any of that. What I do remember though—vividly—was a really tough year of physical therapy. Learning to walk again. Learning to speak. Pretty much starting from scratch. I missed a year of school and started first grade all over again while still doing physical therapy. Then, because I wasn't reading well enough by the end of second grade, they decided to have me repeat that as well. My father had a real problem with me falling behind by two years. In order to placate my father, I received a special dispensation making me eligible to participate in competitive sports until I graduated. Otherwise, I would have missed the age deadline for playing football this season by three and a half months. So, thank you, Dad."

"No wonder you seem so much older. Going through all that trauma and therapy."

"And I'll have you know I am now an exemplary reader. I'm just old. For high school. Which, frankly, has given me a total leg up in the athletics department."

"Yes, but it complicates things for us terribly."

"So what? Things were already complicated with you living in Atlanta and us only texting once a month. We've just uncomplicated it."

"They're not letting you out of my class."

"It's already done."

"You need a strong course load."

"College coaches don't care about that."

"But college admissions officers do."

"Viv."

There was a knock on the door and then Principal Levendusky poked his head through. "How are we coming in here? Working things out to everyone's satisfaction?"

Lane snorted. Vivi stood up, smoothed her skirt, wiped under her eyes with her tissue and motioned the principal inside.

"Principal Levendusky, there's something we need to tell you."

"Vivi, please don't," she heard Lane say. "We can handle this ourselves."

"Mr. Kettering and I have a previous relationship," she went on, ignoring Lane.

"Call me Mr. Kettering one more time and I will describe, in complete detail, our previous relationship," Lane growled.

Vivi crossed her arms over her chest and pointedly gave Lane her best bossy-teacher stand-down look. Then she turned back to Mr. Levendusky.

"Mr. Kettering and I," she said slowly, "met at the beach last May when I was a student at Wake Forest."

"Where I seduced her into bed and fucked her six ways till Sunday."

Vivi gasped, Mr. L. slammed the door, and Lane stood there owning every word. "I warned you," he said, eyeing Vivi. "Do not pull your bossy teacher crap on me. I'm your boyfriend. Your *lover*," he emphasized. "You treat me like I'm one of your second graders and all hell's gonna break loose."

"I think we should all sit down," Mr. L. said, his voice gruff and his attitude full-on no nonsense. He moved behind his desk and put on a pair of glasses, indicating that she and Lane should sit in the padded leather chairs in front of him, side by side. He sat as well.

"Miss DuVal, how old are you?"

"Twenty-one, sir."

"Mr. Kettering?"

"Nineteen."

"And the two of you are involved romantically?"

"Yes," Lane said before Vivi could respond.

Mr. L. looked in her direction. "We are involved romantically, yes," Vivi agreed. "Although we haven't seen each other in several months, and Mr. Ketter—Lane," she corrected herself, "was unaware that I had taken a job here. I was under the impression that he was a senior in…well, elsewhere. So it was a surprise to both of us when I read his name on my class roster."

"Which is why I immediately walked out, came to the office, and requested to drop the class. I'm sure there are plenty of rules and regulations about teachers dating students, but Vivi isn't my teacher, she's never been my teacher, so we shouldn't have a problem here," Lane said.

"Unfortunately," Mr. L. said, taking off his glasses and rubbing the bridge of his nose, "that's not exactly how it works. While she's a teacher and you're a student in the same school, whether in her Statistics class or not, the rules and regulations still apply."

"What if she worked at some other school?" Lane asked. "What if she were in Atlanta teaching second graders like I thought she was," he said, throwing her an incredulous look, "and I was here, and we continued our relationship just as we planned, would there be a problem?"

"No."

"What if she taught over at the high school in Henderson? Would our dating be a problem?"

"No.

"Then this is bullshit."

"Lane," Vivi said, touching his arm wanting to calm him down.

"Well, it is. Look Mr. Levendusky, I'm not an idiot. I understand I can't announce to the community at large that I'm dating Wilson's new statistics teacher. But the fact is we are dating. We've been dating. We are here in your office not lying about that."

"As much as I appreciate the candor, Mr. Kettering, you are putting me in a very precarious position. I am under an obligation to report any misconduct by my staff."

"And what sort of misconduct are you accusing Miss DuVal?"

"I'm not accusing her of anything, Lane. At the moment I'm listening. I'm gathering facts. I'm weighing my options."

"Look," Vivi spoke up. "I'll resign. I understand about the rules and regulations, and I believe in them. And as much as I really want this job, I can't rewind the clock. I could sit here and tell you we'll break up—"

"We're not breaking up," Lane interjected.

Vivi motioned her hand toward Lane. "And he calls me the bossy one." She gave Mr. L. a sad smile.

He gave her one back.

"I'm sorry about all this," she said, standing. "I really am. I can stay on until you find someone else, or I can pack up my things right now and clear out of my classroom. I do not want to make this hard on either of you. The truth is I would never have taken the job if I'd known Lane was a student here."

Principal L. steepled his fingers and tapped them together over his desk. "Sit down, Miss DuVal. There's no need to resign, at least not yet. Frankly, with one teacher taking early retirement at the last minute and another dropping out unexpectedly for cancer treatments, I need you filling the position I hired you for and then some. And, if I may be so crass as to admit, getting you at a first-year teacher's salary really helped my budget. So, at the moment, I'd rather not lose you. On top of that, you've signed a contract for the school year. We'd have to look into how to release you from that without it marring your record or damaging your career." Mr. L. looked over toward Lane. "Who else knows about the two of you?"

"My buddy, Lam. But he's not going to say anything."

"How can you be sure?"

"He's trustworthy," Lane snapped, irritated. "Besides, he's got secrets of his own."

"Secrets of this magnitude?"

Lane shrugged.

"Hmm," Mr. L. said.

Silence fell as the principal seemed lost in thought.

"I think we should inform Lane's parents," Vivi suggested quietly.

"They already know about you," Lane said.

"They do?" she asked, pleased.

"Of course they do. Maybe not as much as our principal does at the moment, but they know I'm crazy about a girl named Vivi DuVal from Henderson. The fact that you're now my teacher will come as a surprise, but Tray will back us up."

"How is Tray?" she asked.

"He's good." Lane smiled. "Enjoying being a newlywed."

Mr. L. cleared his throat.

"Sorry," Lane said. "Vivi and I haven't actually seen each other in three months. And we only text on the first of the month."

"Well, I suggest you continue with the long-distance attitude. You certainly won't be taking Miss DuVal to the prom."

"But she just might be chaperoning," Lane said with a grin.

"Mr. Kettering, I beg you to take this seriously. For Miss DuVal's sake if not your own. Now, I have several other fires that need putting out, and you, son, should be on the practice field. Trust me, I'll take Miss DuVal up on her offer to resign if there is a hint of you becoming distracted over this matter, letting it affect your grades or your football."

"Both of those are important to me, too, sir."

"All right. Let me say for now, I understand the two of you are bringing a unique situation to my attention, and frankly, I need to do some research in order to know how to properly proceed. In the meantime, Miss DuVal, I'd like you to consult legal counsel on your own. Let's gather all the facts so we have a clear, concise picture of where we stand. Mr. Kettering, you will inform your parents about Miss DuVal's new position here at school, and I'd like to meet with them and the two of you in one week's time."

"That's very generous of you," Vivi said, standing and offering her hand.

"It's not generous of me at all. I'm simply covering my ass. In twenty-five years, this is the first situation of its kind to come up. I simply don't want to mishandle it. Mr. Kettering, you told me you're not an idiot. Prove it. Information about your personal relationship with Miss DuVal does not leave this office. Are we clear?"

"Perfectly, sir. If we could just have ten minutes alone to sort things out—"

"Two minutes," Mr. L. said, standing. "I was nineteen once. You get two. Two minutes alone. That is all."

Then he left.

Lane and Vivi gazed at each other for a moment, their faces filled with humor and disbelief. Lane reached over and clasped her dangling fingers, entwining them with his own. "Mr. L. underestimates me."

"How so?"

"We haven't seen each other in three months. I could get us both off in two minutes if I had a condom in my pocket."

She laughed and then sighed. "I'm happy to know you don't carry condoms in your pocket."

"I'm gonna start," he warned.

"Lane, this is serious."

"I know it's serious. You ought to know by now that I'm nothing if not protective of you Sleeping Beauty. So, this complete nightmare we've just awakened to, trust me, I am up to speed."

"I'm sorry," she said, leaning her head against his shoulder. "I thought you'd be psyched I was working for your alma mater. I thought it was so perfect," she sighed. "Less distance between us, seeing each other more often."

Lane choked out a laugh. "We will definitely be seeing a lot more of each other."

"Hmm. So, what? Are you some sort of scholar athlete? Star of the Warrior football team?"

"I'm the running back."

"And the college coaches looking at you?"

"Mostly in state."

She sighed. "I like football."

"Good."

"But even if your parents are able to come to terms with you dating a teacher, my father is going to have a real problem with this."

"He doesn't want his over-achieving, college-graduate daughter slumming it with a dumb high school jock?"

"Are you kidding? Dumb high school jocks are his wheelhouse."

"So we shouldn't have a problem then."

"Oh, there's gonna be a problem. A big one. He and my uncles run the Henderson High Booster Club. And they are going to pitch one big fit when they catch me cheering for Oxford's star running back."

CHAPTER TEN

Lane and Vivi had decided to Skype each other after they told their respective parents about what was going on. Other than that, they had not discussed how they were going to handle this new twist to their relationship. One hurdle at a time, Vivi supposed.

So she helped her mother, Charlotte, in the kitchen, playing sous-chef, setting the table, and suggesting they open a bottle of wine to go with her mother's delicious meal, even if it was only a Wednesday night.

Her mother, dressed for summer in a pretty pastel shift, stopped what she was doing and looked at Vivi. "You've worked one day and already you need a glass of wine with dinner? Are the kids over there in Oxford that bad?"

"Ha," Vivi spouted a laugh. "The kids are great. But one kid in particular has presented a…concern. A concern I need to discuss with you and Daddy. Trust me. A glass of wine will help this go down a whole lot better. In fact," Vivi said as she took down some wine glasses from the cabinet, "you and I may want to start now."

"Oh, dear," her mother said. "What in the world is this about?"

"Lane Kettering," Vivi said, eyeing her mother as she opened the wine.

"Lane Kettering!" Her father's voice boomed from behind her as he walked into the kitchen. "I don't want to hear that name in this household. Damn kid is playing better this year than he did last. And Henderson is on an upswing now that we've wrestled Josh McCourt into using his computer skills to finagle some offensive plays. Still, he ain't helping our defense none, and that is the concern against Wilson. With a running back like that Kettering kid, we are in trouble. Big trouble."

Jeb DuVal, always large and in charge, ended his tirade with a kiss on his wife's cheek. "Sorry, sweetie. Just came from a Booster Club meeting where Kettering was all the talk. Apparently, he broke some record in last week's game. I'm so sick of hearing about that kid. Been hearing about him and how great Wilson's football program is for the last three years. The last thing I want to hear about when I walk inside this house is Lane Kettering."

Jeb turned to Vivi and went to give her a hug. "I'd much rather hear about daughter number two's first day as a full-fledged teacher. Those heathens over there in Oxford treat you okay, sugar?"

"Heathens?" Vivi's nerves ratcheted up a notch. "Daddy...how 'bout a glass of wine?" Vivi just went ahead and started pouring.

"Wine? On a Wednesday? What are we, the Evans family? It's not like we've got it stockpiled in a fancy wine cellar like that Hale does. I tell you, we had some damn good wine the night we raided that thing."

"It's a wonder Hale Evans didn't have you and your brothers arrested," Charlotte said.

"Gotta be proactive keeping family secrets secret," Jeb claimed as Vivi handed him a glass. "So tell us, Vivi-de-bee, how bad was it for you being born and bred in Henderson and having to play nice with the riffraff over there in Oxford?"

"Daddy, since the town of Oxford is now paying my salary, it might be appropriate for you to simmer down on the rivalry/hatred bit."

"Yeah—not gonna happen, sugar plum. Your uncles and I are third-generation Hendersonians. Hating Oxford is in our blood."

"Except when they hire your company to repave their streets, parking lots, and highways."

"Except for that," he agreed with a big ol' grin.

"Jeb. Wash up. Come to dinner. Your daughter has something to tell us," Charlotte said.

Vivi watched as her mom downed half her wine and reached for the bottle to fill it back up. She toasted Vivi with the glass and drank again, eyeing her over the rim. "You're right. This is going to go down a whole lot better with wine. Go on and open another bottle and put it on the table."

"So you've figured it out?" Vivi asked, doing her mother's bidding.

"I thought his name sounded familiar when you mentioned him this summer. But being as I don't spend all my time worrying about Henderson football, it escaped me."

"Daddy's gonna freak, isn't he?"

"Deep down inside, Daddy's gonna love that you're dating the star running back no one can stop talking about. After he gets over the fact that he's playing for the devil's team, and there is nothing your father can do about it, he'll come around. Probably even brag about it."

"Oh, Lord. He can't brag about it. He can't tell anyone about it. I'm his teacher," she emphasized.

"Whose teacher?" Jeb asked, coming back into the room as her mother proceeded to spit wine into the sink.

"Lord, woman. What's got you all choked up?" Jeb said, coming over to soothe his wife by rubbing her back.

"I'm fine. I'm fine," she said, pushing him away. "Let's fill our plates so we can sit down and hear all about Vivi's first day at Wilson."

"Fine. Good. I'm starving."

Vivi let them get a few bites in before she eased into her day, talking about her first three classes and the kids in them. She talked a little about how it felt to actually be teaching, and how her nerves died down as the classes went on. She emphasized how nice the students from Oxford seemed, how respectful they were. Then she went on to say that looking back, she didn't understand why there was such a heated rivalry between the two towns, being as the people over there looked identical to the people over here.

"I mean, you and Mom aren't judgmental people. I've never heard either of you blasting somebody about their age, race, or religion. I mean, you don't worry about what's going on behind the neighbor's closed door, do you?"

"Don't kid yourself," her dad said, wiping his mouth. "We are proud Henderson do-gooders. We judge everybody on everything. That's how it's done around here."

Vivi's mouth dropped open. "Well, I know that's how it's done. I just didn't think you two participated."

Her mother shrugged. Her father kept on eating.

"Daddy, Josh McCourt, the man who is revamping your beloved football team, is *from* Oxford. That town is a stone's throw away. This rivalry thing is crazy."

"You're looking at it all wrong, Vivi-de-bee. The rivalry between our towns is a good thing. It's what makes us want to be better. It's why anybody gives a rat's patootie about anything around here. There is one football game that matters every season. The one against Wilson. We beat them, we are town heroes for the next year, regardless of our record. What games drew the biggest crowds at Wake? Carolina, Duke, and N.C State. Those are the big rivalries. Because they are right down the street. Beat those teams and it's a big, big night."

"Well, you're not wrong about that," she said. Vivi sighed and took a sip of wine. "But, I'm getting off topic, I think. So, remember the guy I told you two about at the beginning of the summer? The one I met in Myrtle Beach right before graduation. The one from Oxford?"

"The gay one, right? I didn't remember him being from Oxford," her father said, enjoying his meal.

"No, Daddy. That was Kevin. From Wake. He broke up with me, right before the beach trip, which is where I met Lane."

"Lane?"

"Lane," she restated.

"Lane, from Oxford?"

"Correct."

"Not Lane Kettering from Oxford. Not the thorn in my side who has chewed our team up one side and down the other for the past three years."

"The very same, I'm afraid."

"I don't understand."

"Well, when Lane told me he was a senior this year, I mistakenly thought he was a senior in college. I assumed he went to Carolina because he was wearing a Carolina T-shirt. But that's just where his brother went to law school. It turns out that Lane is a senior at Wilson. And not only is he the very same running back that you seem terribly obsessed with, but now he's also a student of mine. In my Statistics class."

"Let me get this straight," her father went on, seemingly searching for control. "This boy lied to you?"

"No, Daddy, he didn't lie. I…jumped to conclusions."

"He's in high school for Christ's sake," he shouted.

"Yes, he is. But I didn't know that for the past three months. Since I was going to Atlanta, we agreed to keep our relationship light. He was going to tell me about still being in high school when I came home for Thanksgiving and saw him."

"So he lied to you."

"He's two years younger than I am. He thought if I knew he was still in high school, I wouldn't be interested."

"Well, you're not. Interested. Are you?"

"Daddy. Of course, I'm interested. And when you meet him, you'll understand why."

"Meet him? I just told you I didn't want his name mentioned in this house. I sure don't want the kid traipsing through my kitchen dragging around all his championship trophies, rubbing his victories in my face."

"Oh, Lordy, Jeb. This has nothin' to do with you," Charlotte said. "Now, hush up and listen to Vivi. This thing is serious."

"Serious? How the hell can it be serious? The kid is in high school, for Christ's sake."

"Regardless of how serious Lane and I are, what Mom is talking about is the seriousness of the situation I have now found myself in. If word gets out that we are romantically involved, it would ruin me and damage Lane's reputation as well. Could hinder his chances for getting into college."

"Sugar, what the hell are you talkin' about? That boy could get kicked out of school tomorrow, take his GED, and be welcome on any college football team in the country. He's that good."

"Jeb. You're missing the point," Charlotte said.

"What?"

"Your daughter is now, inadvertently, romantically involved with one of her students. If people find out, it's going to cause an ugly scandal."

"Hmm," Jeb said, leaning back in his chair, thinking.

Vivi looked over at her mother. "Please tell me my own father is not plotting a way to release this knowledge at just the right time to get Lane kicked out of school before they play Henderson?"

"Jeb?" her mother queried. When her husband just kept on thinking, she shouted, "Jeb!"

"Okay, you're right," he said. "Wouldn't be sporting like."

"Daddy!"

"Sugar plum, I'm kidding. Your reputation is just as important as the comeback of Henderson football."

When both mother and daughter stared at him, Jeb spread his arms out wide and said, "What?"

"Have you lost your mind?" her mother asked.

"I'm just saying—"

"Stop it, whatever you are saying. You sound like a damn fool."

Jeb looked over at his daughter. "I apologize. The Boosters have been all caught up in this football thing. I'm not thinking straight." He took a hearty swig of wine. "Okay then. You met the running back from hell at the beach. Now you're his teacher. What's the problem?"

When Vivi's mouth dropped open, her mother said, "I'll handle this," and turned her attention to her husband by folding her hands under her chin and addressing him directly.

"Remember Miss Osmiss?"

"Miss Osmiss?"

"Yes, Miss Osmiss. Young, pretty—"

"The hot English teacher in eleventh grade."

"Right."

"Who could forget her? There were plenty of rumors that she and a number of guys on the—" Jeb looked at his daughter. "Oh, shit!"

"I believe we've finally got his attention," Vivi's mother said to her before she went back to eating.

"What the hell happened with this Kettering kid in Myrtle Beach?" her father shouted. "Jesus. We need a lawyer."

Vivi blinked, startled. "We only need legal advice, Daddy. To figure out where things stand now."

"We need a lawyer to force *Lane Kettering* to sign a nondisclosure agreement." Jeb's fist came down on the table. "He's in high school, Vivian Leigh. What the hell were you thinking?"

"I was thinking he was twenty-three. I'm telling you, Daddy, he doesn't look, act, or speak like a high school student. His vocabulary is equivalent to an English major's."

"Vocabulary. I'll bet. Do you have any idea the kind of shit guys like him talk about in the locker room?"

"Lane's not like that."

"I've got news for you, sugar. They're all like that. Now you're going to need to quit this job before this blows up in your face."

"Principal Levendusky isn't letting me quit. At least not for another week. I signed a contract. He needs me. And he is aware of the situation. Lane and I told him at the end of the day."

"What the hell did you do that for?"

"So he understands our relationship started before I was hired. That it has nothing to do with me being a teacher and Lane being a student. That's why I'm telling you. That's why Lane is telling his parents. So all of you will know the truth and can back us up."

"Oh, we're gonna back you up. Your uncles and I will be driving over to Oxford to have a little chat with Mr. Fancy Words and his father."

"Daddy, you're not getting my uncles involved. In fact, you can't tell anyone. You're just going to have to trust Lane and me to keep our relationship handled."

"Your relationship? There can be no relationship."

"There already is a relationship." Vivi's heart was racing a mile a minute. She realized right then how hard it was going to be if she had to give up Lane. Even in the middle of this…pickle.

When her father said nothing, she said, "I want you to meet him. You may think you know the running back, but I want you to meet Lane, the man."

"He's not a man, Vivian Leigh. He's a kid. Hell, you're just a kid. Two kids with raging hormones."

"Piper Beaumont," her mother interrupted. "I met her at your Aunt Genevra's wedding Saturday. She's dating Vance Evans, and if I remember correctly, she's a lawyer who defends college students. Call her. She'll be able to sort this out for you."

"Have her draw up a nondisclosure agreement as well," her father said.

"And shall I have her draw up one for you too?" Vivi asked her father. "I'm not sure I can trust you with this news around the Boosters."

"Aww, Vivi-de-bee, darlin'. I already admitted it wouldn't be sporting, didn't I?" Mother and daughter both sipped their wine, eyeing Jeb. "I'm not going to say anything," he shouted.

"Okay," Vivi smiled. "Thank you. Now, tell me. Just how good is this running back from hell?"

CHAPTER ELEVEN

The conversation at the Kettering table went down a little differently.

After Lane's brother Tray laughed his ass off over the phone when Lane called to tell him about Vivi showing up as his statistics teacher, Lane was resigned to getting it all out in the open by telling his parents over dinner. His parents were notoriously conservative, God-fearing people. A little bit prudish maybe, considering their taste in film. Had he brought Vivi home as his girlfriend, Lane didn't think the age difference between them would raise an eyebrow. She looked younger than he did, for Christ's sake. But now that she was his teacher, well, he feared that might make it an entirely different story.

And let's face it. His parents were the ones who needed to understand how all this went down the most. If his parents were behind his relationship with Vivi, the rest of the world could go fuck itself.

Yeah. Not exactly the attitude to drag into dinner table conversation.

He ate his fill quickly because he was starving and wasn't sure he'd have the stomach for eating after this conversation. Then he jumped in with both feet.

"This girl I met at the beach with Tray, back in May? Vivi DuVal from Henderson? She's twenty-one."

His father, a well-known property and casualty insurance broker in the area, still had his tie on, although he'd loosened it up a bit. "An older woman," he said, looking up and smiling at Lane. "Nothing wrong with that. Is she in school?"

Lane choked on his response and fidgeted in his chair. "She was. She just graduated from Wake Forest. A year early."

"A year early? She must be driven," his mom said.

"Well, she's smart," Lane said, not knowing how to proceed. His parents kept eating. Finally, he said, "Tray met her. He liked her."

His parents nodded while continuing to eat.

"I like her. A lot."

Both his parents' heads popped up. *Well, looky there. I've got their attention now.*

"Will we get to meet her? Is she living in Henderson now?" his mother asked.

"Yes," Lane nodded. "To both of those."

"How does she feel about you being in high school?"

Lane rubbed his hand along the table, hedging. "She was surprised. When she found out. Today."

"She didn't know?" his father asked.

Lane shook his head.

When the silence drew out, his mother prompted, "Lane, darlin'?"

He sighed and sat back in his chair, picking up his fork and playing with the food left on his plate. "Look. I'm crazy about her. I met her on the beach the first day we were there, and she was sassy and sweet and real, real pretty. We spent the next four days together, even celebrated our birthdays together because hers is the same day as mine."

"Interesting."

"Uh-huh. So, we sort of jelled. She thought I was older because I was with Tray and his buddies, and I didn't tell her any differently because she was getting ready to graduate from college and I didn't want her to run away screaming. Once I found out she was from down the street, I started hoping maybe there was a way we could see each other again. She had a job offer in Atlanta. I figured I'd tell her I was still in high school when she came home for Thanksgiving. By then I'd have one foot in college and hoped that when she discovered our age difference, it wouldn't much matter."

"You said she found out today."

"Yeah. She found out when she walked into the Statistics class she's teaching at Wilson and read my name on her roster."

"She's…a teacher?"

"Yep. My teacher."

His parents looked at one another and then burst out laughing.

Good Lord, it was like dealing with Tray all over again. "I'm glad y'all find this amusing. I really am. But unfortunately, it puts Vivi and me in an awkward situation."

"Oh, Lane," his mother said, dabbing at the tears of mirth in her eyes. "This must be horrible for you."

"Well, I'm sure not laughing my ass off about it like you and Tray. He thinks this is the funniest damn thing to ever happen."

"What did…Vivi?…do?" his father asked.

"She asked to see my license. Ripped me a new one for lying to her. Which I did not do," he claimed. "I told her there was two years between us. She just…misinterpreted which way."

"She kick you to the curb?"

"Not yet. She got over the age difference pretty quick. But the fact that we are so far apart in school years is probably going to weigh heavily when she has time to stop and think about it. Today she was more worried about her career. She's been wanting to be a teacher since she was six years old. And for some odd reason, she doesn't think dating a student is going to look good on her résumé." Lane smiled. "She insisted we tell Principal Levendusky so he was aware we were already involved before she ever graduated from college. She was also insistent I tell the two of you, so you know that I'm not being seduced by my statistics teacher."

That made both his parents sit up.

"Yeah," his mother said on a long sigh. "I'm not really wild about my baby boy making out with his teacher."

"I don't know," his father said, thoughtfully. "I would have loved to have been seduced by any number of my teachers. I sort of had a thing for teachers."

His mother reached over and smacked his arm. Then she squinched up her nose, thinking, and said, "You know. I sort of did too. There was this professor in college that I was sort of desperate for—"

"La, la, la, la, la," Lane said, holding his hands over his ears. "Waaaay too much information, Mom. And as far as you are concerned, Vivi DuVal is my girlfriend, *not* my teacher. I'll get her to come over and meet y'all as soon as we can figure out how to manage the minefields that now surround us. She doesn't look like a teacher. She looks like a girl. A nice girl. A nice girl from an upstanding Henderson family. So if there's any seducing going on, you can be sure I'm the one doing it. Which is probably not sitting well with her father right now. She's telling them all about us too." Lane stood to leave.

"Hold on," his father said. "How serious is this?"

Lane glanced over at his mom quick, before eyeing his dad. "Serious enough that Principal Levendusky wants to meet with you two, me, and Vivi next week. Since our relationship is preexisting, he's gotta do some research to see where this puts us regarding all of the student/teacher rules and regulations. Cover his own ass."

"So if whatever happened between you two at the beach got out now?"

"Well, right now I'd be a hero in the locker room and Vivi would lose her job."

He watched as his parents digested that information.

"Okay," his father said. "We'll meet with Principal Levendusky and Vivi. Let him know we've got your back and hers."

"How are you holding up?"

It was the only thing Lane knew to ask. He'd been sitting on his bed staring at his computer for the past thirty minutes, gathering his courage to Skype Vivi. Because after the chat with his parents, the reality of the situation had started to sink in and he felt defeated.

Vivi was a smart girl. A college graduate. Had landed the perfect job to start her career. He was probably six years behind her if he was redshirted next year. Which was a possibility. That's how it worked. And if he was lucky enough to stay healthy, stay good enough to play Division I football while attending college, he may not come out with a degree even then. She'd probably figured all this out by now. Probably realized he wasn't going to be worth the risk.

Maybe it was a good thing they'd stuck him back in her Statistics class. At least he'd have a year of face-to-face contact, giving him the opportunity to talk her back into a relationship.

"Wait," he said as Vivi started to open her mouth. "Before you say one word, and definitely before I sit in your classroom tomorrow pretending I haven't had my hands all over your smokin' hot body, I need you to commit to me one more time. We meet in May back in Myrtle Beach as planned. No matter what happens between now and then."

"Okay," she said, tilting her head and giving him her little Sleeping Beauty smile. Soft, easy, sweet. Her hair was up, her neck was bare, her lips were plump and tempting.

Yeah. This situation was surely going to kill him.

"I'd be relieved, except now I'm just thinking about how bad I want to kiss you."

She leaned into the screen, whispering, "How bad do you want to kiss me?"

He growled.

She laughed. Then she stopped and bit her lip. "Are your parents freaking out? Planning to call the authorities?"

"S.B., get real. You heard Mr. L. If you were teaching Statistics over at Henderson High, this wouldn't be a problem. And although I fantasize about pressing a lot of things against you, legal charges is not one of them. We don't have a problem."

"I hope you're right. I have a call into a lawyer my aunt knows personally. We'll get to the bottom of this. Seriously, Lane, what did your parents say? You did talk to them, didn't you?"

"I said I would, S.B. And after they were done laughing at me, and sharing their own nightmare teacher-crush stories, they came to an understanding about how this affects you and your career. They get it. They've got your back. If anything should ever break, they'd be telling the true story, sticking up for the both of us."

"I truly appreciate that—because let's face it, your parents could be having a fit over this…" She stopped. "Are they?"

"No. No. They are looking forward to meeting you. Which I think should happen sooner rather than later. Under the circumstances."

"Yes, and I need you to meet my father and get him to chill out. Little did I know the name Lane Kettering was going to flip him out even before he found out about us."

"What do you mean?"

"To hear him talk, you are the devil incarnate. Not because of anything to do with me, but because you have single-handedly defeated the Henderson High football team three years running. They are all talking about you over here. Plotting their revenge."

"And here you are ratting them out. I think us secretly dating and you living over there in Henderson is gonna work out well for me after all. You can pass whatever information you hear my way."

"It's not like my dad's the coach. He just runs the Boosters with my uncles. Who, by the way, he was threatening to rally up and head on over to Oxford to have a chat with you and your father, forcing you to sign a nondisclosure agreement."

"Jesus, Viv. He doesn't need to do that."

"I know. I told him so. Once he meets you, the real you, not the high-school-running-back you, he'll trust you more. Right now, he's yelling about how our raging hormones will bring down disaster."

Lane couldn't say anything to that. Because he was thinking the same thing. He couldn't see much of what Vivi had on, but every time she sat back or shifted, he got a glimpse of the pale-pink, low-cut tank top she was wearing, and how it hugged her chest. Which was very obviously braless.

"S.B., what are you wearing?"

"My pajamas," she said, pulling at her top and looking down at herself. "Why?"

"No reason." *Except seeing you sitting on your bed, wearing next to nothing is making me think with my dick—which is clearly a bad idea.* He cleared his throat. "So, let's talk about the real elephant in the room."

"What's that?"

"You. Presiding over the Statistics class I'm being forced to take."

"Ah. You can't even say the words, can you?"

He shook his head.

"Okay. So, I'm guessing the bossy part of you is having a hard time thinking about the bossy part of me giving you a grade."

"I'm acing the damn class. That's a given. If I've got questions, if I'm not following, I will talk to you about them outside of school. You can tutor me all you want one on one. But the thought of being one of your students, I gotta tell you, I have not come to terms with. So, you're gonna need to cut me some slack for a little bit until we see how this is going to go."

"So...what exactly does that mean?"

"It means if I show up wearing sunglasses, it's not because I'm being an ass. It's because I'm trying to distance myself."

"Okay. I...didn't...realize this was going to be so...painful for you."

"Can anybody hear me?"

Vivi leaned closer to the screen and started to whisper. "No. My parents are watching TV, I think. I locked my bedroom door just in case, so no. I don't think so."

Lane licked his lips and slid a hand over his face, trying to figure out a way to not sound like such a horny teenager. Fuck it. "S.B., if we had never met, you would have walked into that classroom today and I would have been attracted to you. Maybe I would have thought you were older than twenty-one because you're a damn teacher. Whatever. But I would have taken one look at you, even all buttoned up in teacher clothes, and I would have started daydreaming. Fantasizing. Now, the reality is much better than that. You're my girl, and I'm crazy about you. And, you gotta know that every night since we've been apart, I...I lie in bed and replay our first night together, or our second night together, or our very, very, very long third-night-and-into-day-number-four together. Until I feel... well, satisfied. Understand?"

She was blushing. Bright pink. Hand over her mouth. *Yeah, she got the picture.*

"So, you standing up in front of the classroom with those kinds of memories in my head...concerns me. On top of the fact that I hate the idea of being in a student/teacher relationship with you when we already have what we have. It's weird, it's unnatural, and it makes me feel like I'm less."

"Less what?"

"Less. Just…less. Less in control. Less an equal partner in this relationship. Just less in your eyes." God, he was sounding like such a fucking baby. And damn if all of a sudden he didn't want to start crying like one too. The emotion welled up in him so fast he was afraid he wasn't going to be able to hide it. "Viv, I've…I'm gonna go."

"No," she shouted. "Lane, please. I'm sorry. I hear you. I get it. I do. Now that you spelled it out it makes perfect sense. So, yeah. I'm not gonna be your teacher, okay?" she said obviously trying to soothe him. "Our relationship is our relationship. In my mind, you're sitting in my Statistics class because you're there to support me, a first-time teacher. I'm not looking at you as a student. I'm not teaching to you. I'm not calling on you. Wear sunglasses. Write a damn novel while you're sitting in my class, for all I care. I'll just like seeing you there. Because I'm crazy about you too. And you're my boyfriend, even if I can't brag about it for a while. You can give me some feedback on how I'm doing. Let me know what the kids in the class are thinking. Help me fine-tune my skills. I need that. It'll be good for me to have you there. But, yeah, I get it. I don't want anything to change between us either. Okay? I'm crazy for the brawny guy on the beach who didn't take any of my shit and then picked me up and carried me into the water, saving my day, my week, my…happiness. I don't want to date a student. I don't. I want you. Although…I am sort of excited about dating a running back."

Lane let out a chuckle, falling in love even as he saw the writing on the wall. "Vivi," he whispered sadly.

"Lane, don't. Please, don't. Just, let's see how it goes."

"You're going to be grading my papers!"

"Maybe you can grade your own damn papers while we are secretly watching Sunday Night Football together."

"All right," he relented. "Okay. This may work out yet. But Sleeping Beauty needs to understand what a hot-button issue this is for me."

"Yeah. I think I got that when you told my boss you seduced me into bed and fucked me six ways till Sunday."

"Shit. Sorry about that."

"Might want to play it a little cooler next time."

"Don't play teacher with me," he warned.

"Got it."

"Bossy pants, I'm not sure you do, but I am willing to give it a try. Now, go…put on some clothes. I'll see you tomorrow. In that Statistics class I'm sitting in on to give you a first-year teacher critique."

Right. That oughta go over real well.

CHAPTER TWELVE

It was hard to ignore the Warriors' star running back. One, he sat in the dead center of her classroom, towering over everyone except Lam, who sat right next to him. Two, he looked terribly conspicuous wearing his sunglasses. Terribly conspicuous and totally hot in a bad-boy, I'm-king-of-all-I-survey sort of way. Three, he was *her* Lane, and her body hadn't forgotten how his hands felt when they had stroked over every square, trembling inch of her. Her woozy factor shot into the danger zone the moment he sat down at his desk.

Oooo-kay, so now she had a very clear understanding of what Lane had been talking about.

Her heart rate sped up, her stomach was practicing specialty knot-tying, and her body had decided to go soft in all the most notorious places. She touched her brow and found she was sweating. Sweating! She reached for the water bottle on her desk and downed a swig. Unable to face him or the other students at the moment, she turned her back to the class and went to the board in a haze. This was not how she had planned to start things off today.

Then the thought seized her: Was Lane now staring at her ass? Was she going to have to teach this class with Lane staring at her rear end every day? After he'd seen her naked rear end and naked everything else? Was he sitting there, thinking about what she was thinking about up here? She felt herself go hot all over. Started feeling a little dizzy. Dear Lord, this was going to be so much harder than she thought. She literally couldn't think outside of the fact that she and Lane had been naked together and he was sitting in the middle of her classroom surrounded by his peers.

"I'm sorry," she said, turning and facing the class with what she was sure looked like wild eyes. "I'm just going to…ah…" She placed her hands on her desk and let her head hang. *Get a grip and do it fast.* "Yeah, if y'all would talk quietly among yourselves for a moment, I'll be right back."

As she headed for the door, she heard a hum start up in the room. Putting one leg into her bossy teacher pants, she shouted, "Quietly," just to prove to herself she could.

Ohhhhh…Myyyyy…God, Vivi thought as she shut the door and turned, leaning into the first locker she saw. The metal felt cool against her forehead, soothing the burn of her inflamed skin. She forced herself to take deep breaths. In. Out. She could do this, she told herself. She needed to be professional. She and Lane had already discussed this. He was here to observe. She didn't want him to think she wasn't up for the job. She…she—the slow breaths were helping her calm down—she could do this. For Lane. Show him she could teach, anywhere, anything, anytime. Even if he had dragged his hot football body into her classroom looking like he just rolled out of bed after their long, long night together.

That is so not helping.

She heard the rear door to her classroom open and close. Felt him move up beside her and fiddle with a lock a few feet down.

"You having another panic attack, S.B.?" he said quietly, not looking in her direction.

She nodded her head, still leaning against the locker. Feeling like she was going to cry.

She was surprised when the locker Lane had been toying with opened. "You've got this," he said into it. "They're just a bunch of high school kids in that room," he said. "Not one of them knows a damn thing about you. And they don't care anyway. They're just looking forward to getting out of school today and the pep rally tomorrow night. Something like that. You need to get their minds on statistics. That's your job. And I know you're good at your job because I've heard talk from your AP Calc class. They like you. You teach to their level. You make it easy. That means," he snickered, "you are damn good at this teaching gig. So, you can do this."

She turned her head to look at him. "I can't do it with you in the classroom," she whispered.

He stared into his locker. "I'm not going to look at you. I'm not going to think about you. I'm going to be drawing plays in my notebook to talk to the coach about at practice. Ignore me. Do your job."

He closed the locker and headed back in the door he came out of.

Okay, so who was the teacher now? Vivi wiped at her eyes, sucked in a couple breaths, and pinched her cheeks. She'd go in and take roll. She'd get back to her lesson plan. Ask a few of the kids why they wanted to learn about statistics. How they hoped to utilize it in their lives. Then she'd get to the lesson. She could do this. She loved doing this. This was who she was.

And after a few stutters and a couple of surreal moments, it went okay. Maybe even started heading toward well.

She was able to ignore Lane for the most part, but she did notice him smirk whenever the rest of the class would laugh and that somehow made her feel better. He wasn't completely tuning her out. She didn't really want him to have to do that.

When the bell rang and class was dismissed, she noticed Lane stayed in his seat while his buddy, Lam, made his way to the front of the classroom. When everyone was gone, he held out his hand and said, "I'm Lam."

She smiled an easy smile, appreciating the gesture of friendship from her boyfriend's confidant. "I'm Vivi," she said, offering the same as she shook his hand.

"Nice to meet you," he said. "I've got my buddy's back." He turned briefly, looking over his shoulder at Lane. "Which means I have your back too," he said, bringing his attention back to her. "I'm hard to miss, so if I'm here in the classroom with the two of you, no one is going to think anything of it, you catch my drift? I plan on being a communications major in college, so I figure facilitating communication between two people during the school day should be right up my alley. And I understand you are aware that I've got secrets, so, as far as I'm concerned, we are all in this together."

"That's nice of you, Lam. I appreciate it."

"Here's a note," he said, handing her a folded piece of notebook paper. "You read it. Write whatever you want. Don't sign any names. I don't read it. I deliver it. Then I get rid of it. Understand?"

She nodded, sort of in awe. "Okay," she smiled, looking over at Lane. "This does feel old school, but I like it."

She opened the note. There was an A++ and a smiley face. She took it to her desk, pulled out a pencil, and wrote XO. Then she folded the paper and handed it back to Lam, who put it in his pocket.

"I'm probably going to stay after class most days. Maybe need a little clarification on statistics now and then. My buddy, Lane, he'll probably stay with me too. We're tight like that."

"Anytime," she said. "And Lam, thank you. For all of it."

"No problem, Miss DuVal." Lam smiled his big smile and wow, did she see why the girls would be after him. His whole face lit up.

"Good luck on the field tomorrow night," she said. Vivi watched big Lam maneuver through the chairs and out the rear door. She watched Lane unwind his athletic body from the desk, books in hand, and follow Lam to the door. He took off his sunglasses, looked her right in the eye, and then blew her a kiss.

Her heart stopped, and she leaned back against her desk.

This was wrong on so many levels, but right on the only one that mattered. The level where her heart sat, trying to beat its way out of her chest.

Day 2 of her teaching career.

Day 100 of loving Lane Kettering.

"Vivi?"

Principal Levendusky's voice startled her out of her reverie.

"Yes?" she answered, standing up straight, running a hand over her brow. Nervous she'd been caught daydreaming about Lane, she looked over to see Mr. L.'s head sticking inside her door. "Yes, sir. Come in. Please."

"Just wanted to check on you. See how your Statistics class went."

"Fine. Fine." She started to laugh and then looked at him in earnest. "It wasn't easy. I nearly had a panic attack. But I promise I'm going to give you your money's worth and more."

"I'm sure you will. Mr. Kettering gave me a thumbs up, so I'm assuming you two are finding your way with this so far."

"So far, yes. I'm sure the novelty of being in the same school all day will wear off and feel more routine than it does at the moment. I've also taken your advice and am seeking legal counsel so that Mr. Kettering and I are clear on where we stand with the Department of Education's rules and regulations."

"I'm pleased to hear it. I'm sure we'll all come to an agreeable arrangement. Frankly, right now I'm banking on that because I have a request. We are in serious need of a new faculty advisor for our cheerleading squads. Ms. Goznell in the English Department has been doing it so long now she just phones it in. And there was an incident last Thursday, surrounding the JV football opener. Suffice it to say, I need someone who is willing to be a little more hands on. And probably someone who understands better how high school girls think and what kind of trouble they can get into. I definitely need someone who understands social media. Most of all, I need someone who may be able to derail a few bad ideas before they get started.

"As the faculty advisor, you'd be responsible for overseeing practices, try-outs, and any special events in which the cheerleaders partake. When I met with the captains of the Varsity squad, I asked if they had any suggestions for an advisor. One of them mentioned you."

"Me? How do they even know about me? I just got here."

"Stacey Collins is in your calculus class, and she likes your style."

"My style?"

"Those were her exact words."

"I wonder what style she's talking about. I'm not sure I've actually developed a style."

"You have something Stacey likes. And she's got a good head on her shoulders."

"I'm not particularly athletic. I don't have to teach cheers or anything, right?"

"No. Nothing like that. You just oversee and direct."

"All right. I'll do it."

"Terrific. Now, I'm going to throw you right into the lion's den. The vice principal is having a mandatory meeting and will be reading them all the riot act. I'm going to walk into that meeting, introduce you as their new advisor, and then leave."

"The lion's den, uh?"

"Yes. You up for this?"

Vivi figured she owed Mr. L. for being so understanding. She also thought if she could handle teaching a class with Lane sitting there making every nerve in her body tingle, this would be a piece of cake.

Oh, how wrong she was.

The Vice Principal's office was packed with girls. Twenty-two of them to be exact. And they looked scared. Really, really scared. No one made a sound as she entered in front of Mr. L. No one smiled. A few of them glanced at her, but their focus ultimately drifted to the principal.

"Ladies," he acknowledged. "This is Miss DuVal. She's volunteered to be your new faculty advisor. Since she has more expertise with social media than Ms. Goznell has, I'm hoping she might be able to direct you all a little better. Because in case Vice Principal Baker hasn't made himself perfectly clear, one more incident like this, one more *rumor* about another incident like this, whether true or false, and there will be no cheerleading squad at Wilson. We are enjoying the benefits of a winning football team. We don't want to overshadow that with an ugly scandal. So knock it off!"

With that, Mr. L. turned, walked out, and slammed the door behind him.

"Hmm," Vivi said. The word scandal echoing around in her brain. "I'm coming in blind. Where is Vice Principal Baker?"

"Hasn't come in yet," said a pretty blonde with bright blue eyes.

"Stacey?" Vivi questioned.

"Yes. I'm in your calculus class."

"Right. You recommended me for this job?"

"I hope you're okay with that."

Vivi just nodded, looking over the group of girls. Athletic, each attractive in their own way, looking just like girls did when she was in high school four years ago. Some were dressed down, some were dressed up. All of them wore makeup, some applying it more appropriately than others.

"How many of you are seniors?" she asked.

Seven raised their hands.

"How many juniors?"

Seven more raised their hands.

"How many sophomores?"

Six.

"Freshman?"

Two.

"Why only two freshman?" Vivi looked to Stacey.

"It's competitive. Generally freshmen have to wait to make the squad."

Vivi nodded.

"So, what happened?"

Everyone one of them shrunk down and looked away. Except for Stacey, who surveyed the lot of them and stepped forward with her cell phone.

YouTube was opened, and a boisterous video played showing young girls very clearly dressed in Wilson cheerleader uniforms strutting their stuff up and down the aisle of a bus loaded with dirty, sweaty, victory-drunk football players. To the best of her knowledge, it appeared this was a wet T-shirt contest without the wet T-shirts.

"What is this?" Vivi asked. Not who is this? Because she really, really didn't want to know. Faces were not shown as the camera was focused on the girls' bust lines.

When no one said a word, she looked at the name of the YouTube account. "Bitchin' Bros? Who is Bitchin' Bros?"

They shook their head in unison.

"It's Wilson's version of Gossip Girl. Or they wanna be," Stacey said. "No one knows who it is."

"But you can narrow it down now to someone on this bus," Vivi said, incredulous. Then she shook her head. There were probably a dozen videos or more of what went on during that bus ride. Those videos could have been shared through texts, emails, Instagram, whatever. Having one of them end up on YouTube was inevitable. Clearly, these girls either didn't care, weren't thinking, or worse... wanted to be exposed like this.

"Ladies," Vivi started, pouring on her bossy teacher persona. "How many of you plan to attend college some day?"

They all raised a hand.

"How many of you have aspirations to hold a job and make some money?"

Every one of them raised their hands again.

"How many of you want that video shown at your wedding rehearsal dinner in front of your grandparents, parents, and future in-laws?"

No one raised their hand.

"Yeah. I didn't think so." Vivi eyed them all up. "I want the Varsity squad on the right side of the room, and the JV squad on the left."

The girls shuffled and stood, eleven on each side. Vivi faced the Varsity squad. "Stacey? Are you the captain?" Stacey nodded. "I'm going to ask you a question, which you will answer for your squad. I expect the truth. If I find out differently, tonight, tomorrow, or six months from now, everyone loses their position. Understood?"

Stacey nodded.

"Did any foolishness go on during the bus ride last week to or from the varsity game?"

"The varsity game was here at home last week. No bus ride."

Vivi breathed a sigh of relief.

"All right. Going forward, if cheerleaders have not been forbidden from the team buses, I expect y'all to sit in your seats and handle yourselves in an appropriate manner, which will be further discussed at a later date. I'm going to dismiss this squad to wait in the hall for me, if you don't mind."

They filed out without a word. Vivi followed them and shut the door before turning on the eleven remaining underclassmen. She tilted her head.

"This...video might seem tame in today's world and none of your faces were clearly shown. But it sends a very clear message about who you are. Maybe you didn't all participate, but as a team, a squad, you're all tainted by this. So, because words don't teach, and my real fear is that the next video you find yourselves in online won't be quite so tame, I'm going to require all eleven of you to show this to your parents. Tonight. I want you to hear what the people who love you have to say about this kind of behavior being broadcast around the world before it becomes some college admissions counselor turning you down for your first-choice school. Get y'all thinking a little bit harder about your actions in public in this day and age of social media. I'll need a phone call from either your mother or your father tonight. No messages left. I want to speak to them directly. It'll give me a chance to introduce myself."

She made them get out their phones and add her as a contact, giving them both her home and cell phone numbers. Then she required them to send her their contact information. Once she was sure she had everyone's, she said, "If I don't get one hundred percent parental participation, you girls, along with the Varsity squad, will be banned from the pep rally and the game tomorrow night." She watched their mouths gape open. "Understood?"

She eyed every one of them. They were embarrassed. They were angry. They were hating their new faculty advisor. Until Mr. Baker stepped in and Vivi told him she had the situation under control. Then they all breathed a sigh of relief.

How bad was this Mr. Baker? Vivi wondered.

Once he backed out of the room, Vivi quietly suggested they all take a look at their social media pages, accounts, etc. this evening and delete anything that might raise the eyebrows of their parents, college admissions counselors, or job interviewers.

Vivi thought it might be in her best interest to double check on that as well.

CHAPTER THIRTEEN

"What the hell happened with the JV coaches?" Lane asked Vivi as they Skyped that evening.

"Why? What did you hear?"

"The JV game was canceled, and there are rumors that the coaches are going to be fired."

"Oh. Wow. I'm sorry to hear that," Vivi said, and meant it.

"What do you know?" Lane asked.

"What do you know?" she replied.

"I asked you first."

"I asked you as a student who has probably heard a rumor or two already. I'll share if you share."

Lane was quiet. Too quiet. His face was serious, and he was obviously disgruntled.

"Lane?"

"I'll share if you share? What is up with that?" he asked.

"I don't know. I'd just like to get your take on things before I tell you what I know. I was made the faculty advisor for the cheerleaders today and—"

Lane cut her off with a long whistle.

"What?"

"Now that's gonna be a job."

"Are you kidding or serious?" Vivi leaned toward the computer screen, trying to read him better. She didn't like talking to him this way. She couldn't read his facial expressions well enough, and she really missed touching him.

"Serious. Some of those girls…well, actually some of those girls are really nice. Stacey Collins is crazy smart. Normal. I guess a lot of them are no big problem. But a few of them?" He whistled again.

"Yeah. I got the picture—in video form—this afternoon. Seems the young ones got themselves into a bit of trouble."

"And now the coaches are getting fired?"

"They were on the bus. They should have put an end to that kind of nonsense before it even began."

Lane shrugged. "They won."

"What's that mean?"

"It means that the bus ride gets rowdy when we win. Especially if it's a big win."

"So how rowdy does the bus ride get?"

"You don't want to know."

"I kinda do. I need to know what I'm up against. Principal Levendusky wants me to shape these girls up or he's firing the squad, so to speak."

"S.B., stuff happens on those buses all the time. That video of the JV squad strutting their stuff is nothing compared to the crap that has gone on in previous years. And really, it was no big deal. No reason for good coaches to be fired over dumb teenage stuff."

"Lane?"

"Yes?"

"Do you have a passcode on your phone?"

"I do."

"Do you have any pictures of me on your phone?"

"You know I do."

"You need to delete them. Now. I hadn't thought about it before, but if someone gets a hold of your phone and sees our text messages, our pictures…"

"Yeah. Okay. I get it."

"How 'bout your Facebook page, or any other form of social media?"

Lane shook his head. "I don't know. I'll check. I'll take care of all of it, I will."

Vivi tried not to panic.

"Lane, did you forward any of my pictures to...to Lam or anyone?"

All the lines on Lane's face went taut. "S.B.? Are you asking me if I took that picture you sent me in your underwear and texted it to all my friends? If I posted it on social media? What the hell kind of a guy do you think I am?"

"Lane, please. It never even occurred to me until today. Until I was standing in front of twenty-two women practically my own age and giving them a lecture on how social media can come back to haunt you."

"And you think I'd do that to you?"

"No."

They stared hard at each other through the magic of the internet.

"Good," Lane finally said.

As much as she really, really wanted to, Vivi instinctively knew better than to say one more word on the subject. She did trust Lane. She was crazy about Lane. This was not Lane's fault. So she bit back her concerns and changed the subject. "How was football practice?"

"Fine. We're ready. You coming to the game tomorrow night?"

Vivi blinked. "Why wouldn't I be at your game?"

"Because you're acting a little crazy."

"I am?"

Lane sighed. "Yes. You are."

There was a long pause where the two of them just sat and stared at each other. A sadness overwhelmed her as she started to realize she was making life difficult for him without even trying. Vivi reached out and touched a finger to the screen. Lane touched his finger to hers.

"Lane—" she started, the sinking feeling she had pouring into his beautiful name.

"Unh-huh. No," he insisted. "You're tired. You're under stress. Go get some sleep, Sleeping Beauty. Lam will have a note for you at the end of class tomorrow. Sweet dreams," he said, before he closed his laptop.

Lane flopped back onto his bed and growled as he rubbed his hands over his face.

He was dating a fucking teacher.

Day two and the ramifications were worse than he could have imagined. Day two and he was being interrogated by the faculty advisor to the cheerleaders about what goes on inside of the team bus after a big win. Day two and he needed to close down every account he held on social media. Day two and he had to delete his all-time favorite picture.

Of Vivi.

In her underwear.

The same underwear she'd greeted him in on the night he was never gonna forget. Back when she was just a co-ed, warm and sweet and shy. Back when his biggest challenge was working his way into a kiss under a full moon, on a beautiful beach, and convincing her to celebrate their birthdays together. Back when he didn't know his way around a woman's body anywhere near as well as he was going to four days later. Back when Vivi taught him everything he longed to learn through her sighs and her moans and her pleas and her tears.

He'd hit the bedroom light that night and kissed her lips in short, sweet kisses. He felt the tender skin of the curve of her waist under the glide of his fingertips as he slowly maneuvered her backward toward the king-size bed. She sat down abruptly when it hit the backs of her legs, and he knelt on the floor in front of her so her pretty face was perfectly level with his to renew their kiss. While her hands found his hair, his hands found her knees and spread them so he could edge his way in closer, his fingertips drifting slowly up her silky thighs to the edge of that sky-blue lace she wore. His thumbs met in the middle and felt her heat and dampness as they stroked over the lace. He wasn't tentative. The tequila shots had made him bold. Made him want. And he definitely wanted her naked beneath him.

He kissed down her neck, and she must have liked that because she let her head fall back so he'd have plenty of flesh to work with. He got to that soft little spot right before her collar bone and sucked the skin of it into his mouth. Sucking on Vivi satisfied a longing he wasn't even aware he had, but it also further stimulated his desire to lay his naked body down over hers.

His hands stroked up her back and both of them went to work removing her bra. No fooling around trying to finesse it open with his fingers, he had it unhooked and sliding from her shoulders in a few short seconds.

And then there was flesh. Soft, pliant, luxurious flesh to fill his hands, to mold with his fingers, to drop his mouth down onto and tease that tantalizing stiff peak with his tongue, drawing it right into his mouth. God, he loved sucking on her flesh. There was something so satisfying about having a piece of her in his mouth. He lost himself in the feel of it. Sucking harder because he wanted to. Needed too. But when he heard her moan, he brought himself back from the deep and released her, asking if he'd hurt her.

Vivi panted no. No, he hadn't hurt her. At all. She insisted she didn't want him to stop, so he laid her upper body flat on the bed, leaned his lower body against her and went back at it. This time he continued to satisfy his own need to suck, and nip, and squeeze, and…suck, but now he was paying attention to how his need drove hers. It kind of blew his mind how his own pleasure ratcheted up a notch with every little response he drew from her.

He began to follow his instincts, to do exactly what he craved with his hands and his mouth while listening for, and feeling for, her response. And the more he did that, the more responsive Sleeping Beauty got. And the more responsive she got, the bolder he became. When the thought first struck him, he didn't second-guess a thing. He went down to his knees, slid her little panties off her legs and put his mouth on skin so baby smooth it made him groan. She was bare except for a tiny little triangle pointing the way to heaven, and his tongue enjoyed the sensation of her silky, fleshy outer lips before the rest of his mouth wanted in on the action. He feasted on Beauty in a way he never before imagined. He'd barely gotten started when she went off. Big. He felt it and heard it in a way that really got his attention.

He liked that she came. Was proud that he did that. Yet, it sort of surprised him, because he'd just started figuring things out down there, and he wanted to figure out more. But when he lifted his head and looked up her glorious body, the tan lines from her bikini brought home the fact that he had a naked woman stretched out before him. His cock immediately bitch slapped him and told him it was time to stop fooling around, pull out a condom, and get the thing on. His brain couldn't argue with any of that logic.

He grabbed the condom from his pocket as he unzipped his shorts and pulled them off, along with his boxers. He stood for a moment gazing at the miracle lying on the bed. Sleeping Beauty was talking. He knew it because he saw her mouth move, but hell if he heard a word through the pounding in his chest, in his head. In his dick. He watched as she rolled over and crawled up the bed, pulling the comforter and sheets down and crawling underneath. Her ass was just as tempting without that little blue bow, causing him to open the condom packet with his teeth and sheath himself. He crawled onto the bed, throwing sheets and blankets out of his way to get to his Beauty.

Naked, not sleeping, Beauty.

Tempting, delicious, shy little smile, Beauty.

He kissed her as he positioned himself between her legs, and God love her, she wrapped those feminine little limbs around his hips, giving him nothing but a green light and an easy angle to work with. He probably should have kissed her again. Probably should have taken more time, but his brain had stopped functioning and his hand was guiding his cock into the soft, sweet flesh that was primed and ready to take him in. He wasn't any bigger than the next guy in the locker room, but next to her body, he seemed large, felt huge when the tip of his cock squeezed itself into her opening. He wasn't breathing when he backed out and tried it again, going a little deeper this time. Three more tries and he was in deep enough to use both hands to prop himself up. He held his weight off Beauty as he rocked against her, slipping in a little easier every time.

He grunted. He sweated. He closed his eyes. He felt every damn sensation as her body welcomed him, cocooned him, made him want to burst into tears at the incredible pleasure it gave. He mumbled something, wasn't even sure what it was. Appreciation in some form or another. And then he was in deep, as deep as he'd ever been, and he was afraid to move. Afraid to break the spell of how good it felt to be connected to Vivi in such an intimate, amazing, life-affirming way.

He was sure that nothing in his life was ever gonna be better than this.

And then he started to move.

He hadn't thought about it. It was a simple instinct that just took over, and that's when everything went on autopilot. His arms wrapped around Vivi, his hands slid down to her hips, pulling her against him while he went up on one knee for leverage. He ground himself deep and hard and fast, and holy shit, he felt his balls tighten. The pleasure became excruciating, and *please let that condom hold*, he came hard, and long, and deep, and wide.

His body shook, vibrating with his release, which went on and on. He drew in a ragged breath, hung his head between Vivi's neck and shoulder, and groaned into the mattress.

When his awareness started to return, he felt Vivi's hands soothing him along his back, felt her body soft and easy beneath him, and felt himself easing up inside her. He really didn't want to move, would have preferred to stay right there, but getting rid of the condom was probably time sensitive. He turned his head and kissed her neck, told her how amazing she made him feel and begged her not to move while he took care of business.

When he came back to the bed, he pulled the rest of the condoms out of his pants pocket and set them on the bedside table. Then he tackled Beauty with his hands and his lips, causing her to laugh and tackle him back. He managed to get her underneath him again, kissing her silly until he got a little serious and pulled back to look at her sweet smile.

"Teach me something," he said as he brushed the hair from her face. He leaned to his side so he could look at her, give her some breathing room.

"Like what?"

"How you like to be touched."

Beauty blinked at him.

"Here," he said, as he slid his hand down over her tummy and tickled the flesh around that tempting little triangle of hair.

"Hmm," she sighed, her eyes drifting closed.

He couldn't help but smile as her body relaxed into the mattress, relaxed under his hand.

"You're doing just fine," she said as he touched her lightly, skimming his fingertips over the silky skin of her inner thighs, gently caressing the coveted area between her legs. He pulled her right leg closer to him, and then cupped her sex with his hand, rubbing in slow, small circles.

He dropped his head to the pillow and whispered in her ear. "Do you like that?" he asked.

"Mmm."

He felt her pelvis push into his hand.

"Why did you do that?" he asked against her ear. "You want more pressure?" She nodded her head, and he gave her what she wanted. "Like that?"

"The heel of your palm," she whispered, and he realized, yeah, that's where her hot spot is, as he applied a little more pressure at the top of her sex, which freed up his fingers. Without any thought at all, his middle finger slipped between her lips and circled around the entrance to heaven.

He wondered what would happen if he just let that finger slide right up, drift over her clit, so he tried it, and yeah, the little moan she made told him it worked like a charm. He did it again, licking the skin of her neck before whispering, "You like that?"

"Mmm."

"Feeling a little woozy?" he teased.

She opened her eyes and smiled at him. "Definitely woozy."

He leaned over and kissed her mouth, his finger stroking up and down the length of her sex. "Is this the magic spot?" he asked against her lips, his finger finding, studying, laying claim to the precious nub where she'd wanted more pressure.

He felt her smile against his lips. "That's the spot," she whispered.

"What about this?" he asked, his finger sliding lower, dipping into her body up to his knuckle.

"That's good too," she replied, eyes shut, concentrating.

His finger slid back and forth between the two. Then he wrapped his leg around hers and tugged it, spreading her open for his exploration. It wasn't long before he noticed her hips moving, reaching for his fingertip when he was coming up to meet her clitoris. That's definitely where the action is, he thought, enlightened, since it wasn't where the action happened for him at all. He stopped his finger right on her sweet spot and watched her face as he stroked it slowly. He felt her leg muscles contract and tighten as he rubbed and circled, pressed a little harder. Then he realized other muscles like her stomach and her butt were clenching as she moved ever so slightly against his finger.

He pressed his mouth against her ear again, not wanting to break her concentration, for surely she was concentrating. He just wanted to know on what. "S.B., this is hot for me. Watching you. Making you move. Talk to me. I want to know what you're feeling and where you're feeling it. You claim to be a natural-born teacher, so please, teach me."

"Mmm," she said, licking her lips, her eyes remaining closed. "I'm…I'm feeling really, really good," she whispered and then cleared her throat. Her voice was stronger when she spoke again. "I'm feeling…engorged, right there. Right where you're touching me. Like all my nerve endings are congregating at that one spot. Like everything from my waist down is focused on that area."

Lane was content to know that. To understand that. And then she went on and taught him something he never would have figured out on his own.

"When it gets to this point, I can feel my body opening, my muscles contracting and releasing, expanding, getting ready for you. So as the sensations heighten where you're touching me, I start to feel an emptiness—a longing—building at the same time in an entirely different area."

"Jesus."

"It's perfection, really," she said. Her face grimaced just a bit, he felt her body tighten and move against his finger. He applied more pressure, shortened his stroke, and flicked over her clit faster.

"Yes," she said. "That's it. Just like that, Lane."

Something about hearing his name caused his dick to jump. He felt her body tightening beside him, underneath him. He couldn't believe when she spoke again.

"As all my focus is climbing to the pinnacle, to release, right where your finger is, below I am aching with need. The need of your body inside mine."

"How do we do that?"

She bit her lip. "Put on a condom."

"Now?" Things were going so well, he didn't want to stop. He didn't want to interrupt her pleasure. He wanted to follow through, watch her come.

She stilled his hand with one of her own. "I'm okay," she said. "Take your time. I'm being selfish right now, trust me."

He wasn't sure how any of this was selfish on her part, but he wasn't planning to argue now that his dick was hard and getting back inside her sounded like the best idea ever. So he sheathed himself clumsily, hating condoms at the moment. Then he turned back to his side, hooked her leg back up just like he had it, and kissed her as his finger went back to work. First up and down the length of her sex, then focusing on her clit. It was starting to make sense in his head. To feel more natural. But he wanted badly to finger her now, just to see what would happen. So he did. He took a slow stroke down and pressed his middle finger slowly into Vivi as deep and as far as he could go. He felt her soft, moist walls clench around his finger as she groaned.

"You like this too," he claimed. He moved his finger in and out.

"Yes," she breathed.

"But not as much?"

"I need one first, then the other."

He kissed her cheek, pulling out, going back to the lesson plan to give her what she needed.

"Lane," she said, her pelvis bucking against his finger now, "as soon as I come, I'm going to want you inside me."

"I can do that," he assured her.

"I'm…oh—hmmm, I'm really going to need you inside me. No…fooling…ummm…arounnnd."

As he watched, her body tensed up, her lips and eyes squeezed shut, her head bent forward, and convulsions started somewhere deep as she came. He didn't think she'd want him to stop, so he just kept on going, doing what he was doing, rolling toward her, separating her legs further to get his body in between, rubbing her clit over and over as he positioned himself at her entrance, until he was overwhelmed with his own need to feel her convulsing around his cock. As he laid himself over her sweet body, he pulled his hand away from her and used it to guide him inside.

"Mmmm," she hummed her approval, as she writhed and seemed to come all over again. It was amazing to be inside of her, her body milking his, propelling him to move and move fast before it all became too good and he didn't get to move at all.

His body against her body, his hands clasping her hands, bringing them over her head as he kissed her and told her how awesome it felt to be inside her like this. What a gift her body was to him. Hot, slick, sexy, sweet, beautiful.

Back in his parent's house, Lane rolled off his bed to clean himself up.

Yeah, he just remembered why dating a teacher wasn't such a bad thing after all.

CHAPTER FOURTEEN

When Lam handed her a note at the end of class, he told her she was to keep it safe. She opened it up and found a simply drawn heart inside.

Her own heart melted all over the floor.

Lam stood in front of her while Lane sat in his chair in the middle of the classroom.

"Lam," Lane said. "My brother, Tray, and his wife, Lindsey, are coming to the game tonight. I bet you didn't know that Miss DuVal is a good friend of Lindsey's."

"I am?" she said to Lam.

"Apparently," he replied with a raised brow and a sly smile.

"The two of them will probably want to sit together at the game tonight. Next to my parents," Lane went on. "Give my brother a chance to introduce my parents to our statistics teacher."

"Who wouldn't want to meet our statistics teacher?" Lam said, grinning at Vivi.

"For some reason," Lane said as he stood, sounding very put-upon, "my mother is overly eager to meet our statistics teacher. And since Miss DuVal and my sister-in-law are so close, she'll probably be invited back to the house after the game."

"Sounds like a plan," Lam said out loud, but the expression on his face raised the statement to the level of a question.

"Lam, I'll enjoy seeing Tray and…Lindsey again," Vivi said, wondering how this would play out in such a public setting.

"Miss DuVal?" Lam asked.

"Yes."

"Have you noticed that you are the only one in the entire school wearing lavender today?"

She smiled. Embarrassed. Day three and she stood out like a sore thumb because no one told her that on game days everybody wears the colors.

"Probably show a little team spirit if you'd put on the black and red tonight. I've got an extra jersey you can wear."

"What would people say if I was wearing your jersey, Lam?"

"Miss DuVal, all the girls wear my jersey. You'd just be hopping on the band wagon."

"She's not wearing your jersey," came the disgruntled voice of Lane.

Vivi smiled and whispered to Lam. "Tell him I wouldn't dare."

"Okay," he whispered back.

She grabbed Lam's hand once she saw Lane had left the room. "Who wears his jersey?" she whispered.

Lam shrugged. "Far as I know he's never given one away."

Her brows lifted. "Really?"

Lam shrugged.

"Play well tonight," she said.

"That's a Wilson Warrior guarantee," he claimed before leaving the room.

Vivi called her cousin Lolly on the way home from school.

"I need something to wear to the football game at Wilson tonight. It has to be black and red, and I need to look really good in it. What have you got?"

"I've got tons of red. My favorite sundress would show off your cleavage."

"I'm a teacher at Wilson. Can't have too much cleavage falling out."

"Come on over. We'll figure out something."

Vivi's dress-designing cousin fixed her up brilliantly in a fun little red dress with black piping and a lacy hem. She might not feel like she could wear it in the classroom, but on a warm summer night, it was perfectly appropriate for a young new statistics teacher to wear to the high school game. It was also perfectly appropriate attire to wear while meeting her boyfriend's parents. A bonus.

On her feet were black patent kitten-heel sandals. Her hair was up in a ponytail because it was too hot to wear it down the way Lane liked. She dolled it up with black and red ribbons like she saw her cheerleaders had this afternoon. She wanted to sneak Lane's jersey number into the ribbons but didn't dare. Plus, she didn't have any idea what his number was.

That thought stopped her. Lane and all the other football players had their jerseys on today. He sat in her class with his jersey on, but she was so afraid to look at him closely that she had no clue what number he wore. She was all about numbers, and yet, she didn't know his. She was all about statistics these days and hadn't a clue about his. For a guy she was so crazy about, she had a lot to learn.

Vivi was happy to learn that her parents would be attending Henderson's game that night—out of town—so she didn't have to worry about her father showing up with any nondisclosure agreements for the Warriors' running back. The cheerleaders in question had all managed to get their parents to call her, so the pep rally had gone on as planned. Afterwards, she'd warned the JV squad she would be attending the game tonight not so much to watch over the Varsity squad, but to monitor their behavior in the stands. It was a great cover for her to attend the football games. She wondered if Principal Levendusky had thought of that.

She checked in with Stacey and the other varsity girls when she arrived. They'd heard what she'd done to the JV group and treated her with the utmost respect. They went over their standard operating procedures for a home football game with businesslike precision and then told her how they would share bottled Gatorade and cookies with the visiting team's cheerleaders during half time while the Warrior Marching Band played. Vivi approved.

And then she smiled when Stacey invited her to join them.

These girls just needed a little guidance. Someone who took an interest in what they did so they wouldn't run amok. Vivi pulled out her phone and texted Lolly, wanting Annabelle Devine's number. The Keeper of the Debutantes over in Henderson could probably give her some good advice about coaching the cheerleaders in Oxford.

She turned from where she stood on the track running around the field and looked into the stands that were starting to get very crowded. She hadn't seen Tray Kettering in over three months and wondered how she was ever going to find him in this crowd. That caused her to turn back toward the field and look for Lane as the teams warmed up. With helmets on, they all looked the same. Not knowing his number was really starting to irritate her.

"Vivi," someone called. "Vivi DuVal," she heard distinctly as she turned around, searching for the source. A pretty blonde in a red T-shirt and black shorts waved as if she knew her.

Ah. Lindsey.

Yes, there was Tray, handsome as ever with his light brown hair and almost-as-gorgeous-as-Lane's green eyes. He was shorter than Lane and just as handsome in a less rugged, more academic way. Okay, maybe he wasn't as handsome as his little brother, but no one was as handsome as Lane in her opinion, so there was that. She made her way over to the first row of the stands where they beckoned her, Tray's hands all over his bride. Lindsey leaned over the railing and down toward Vivi.

"I'm Lindsey, your new best friend," she said. They both laughed at that.

"Yes," Vivi said, coming around and up the steps. "I heard I had a new best friend."

"Fancy seeing you here," Tray said, mirth glistening in his eyes. "I had heard you'd be teaching second graders in Atlanta and wouldn't know the truth about Lane until Thanksgiving."

"Best laid plans," she said, shaking her head.

"How's it going?" Lindsey asked.

"It's…going," Vivi said. "It's a bit surreal, I will say that. In fact," she looked at Lindsey with a little desperation, "I could really use somebody to talk to about all this, so…you know, I might put this new best friend thing to good use."

Lindsey took pity on her and pulled her in for a hug. "I love my brother-in-law," she said against her ear. "You can trust me with whatever you need to."

Vivi just nodded, feeling a little lonely at the moment, realizing she really didn't have anyone to confide in. Realizing for the first time she couldn't tell anybody about her amazing boyfriend, Lane Kettering, superstar running back for the Wilson Warriors.

"You ready to meet Mom and Dad?" Tray asked. "Might be good to get it out of the way now. Once the game starts, they'll be focused on Lane and stop badgering you with questions."

"Sure," she said, brightly. Feeling everything but.

"They sit up in the parents' section. Same seats every game. They've saved seats along the bench in front of them for the three of us. Let's go."

Vivi grabbed Tray's arm as he started up the bleacher steps.

"You gotta give me a heads up," she pleaded. "How are they feeling about this?"

Tray gave her a gentle smile and stepped back down to her level. "Just be you, Vivi. Just be the girl Lane fell for at the beach. There's not a set of parents around who would object to you."

Wow.

When Tray started up the steps, Vivi looked over at Lindsey and said, "I can see why you married him."

Lindsey smiled. "He's the best."

Vivi followed the two of them up to the top third of the bleachers where a man who looked a lot like Tray stood right beside the aisle with a sweet, expectant smile on his face. Next to him was a tall... mom.

"Dad," Tray said, "This is Vivi DuVal."

Vivi put her hand out to shake hands. "Nice to meet you, Mr. Kettering," she said. Her voice was shaky. Shy. Her emotions were nearly swamping her when Mr. Kettering put a second hand on top of hers and looked her in the eye.

"I'm so pleased to meet you, Vivi," he said sincerely. "Let me introduce you to my wife, Bizzy."

Hearing that name brought on a smile, remembering the first hour she and Lane had ever spent together. She shook hands with Bizzy Lane Kettering and tried not to gush, "I'm so happy to be meeting Lane's parents."

"Vivi, darlin'," his mother started, her eyes lighting up now that they looked her up and down. "Why don't you sit between me and Rex for a few minutes before the game starts? Let us become acquainted before we give you back to Tray and Lindsey. All right?"

Lane's mom was so sweet and so gracious she put Vivi at ease right away. "I'd like that," she said, and meant it.

They squeezed her in between them, and as they all got settled, Tray asked who would like a soda or a hot dog and then went off, leaving Lindsey to sit by herself in front of them. Mr. Kettering patted his daughter-in-law on the back. Lindsey smiled over her shoulder at him, but didn't turn around to join their conversation.

The Ketterings asked her about where she lived in Henderson, how she liked Wake Forest, why she decided to graduate early, and how she liked teaching at Wilson so far. All very typical first-time-meeting questions. The conversation flowed. They were trying to put her at ease, and it was working. When the marching band took the field to play the National Anthem, Lindsey looked behind her and patted the seat next to her, indicating that Vivi should move down. Mrs. Kettering leaned over and whispered that they'd talk more after the game. Vivi took that to mean she was welcome to sit next to Lindsey.

"You need to know something about the Ketterings," Lindsey said, leaning close to Vivi after the anthem played.

"What's that?"

"They are very superstitious when it comes to Lane's games."

"Okay."

"Seriously superstitious."

"As in…?"

"As in there was no way they were going to let you sit between them all night. As in, they sit in those same seats for every game, along with all the other parents of the players. As in, your relationship with Lane lives or dies by how well he plays tonight."

Vivi laughed. Until she realized Lindsey was not laughing.

"Are you serious? If he doesn't play well it's my fault?"

"They haven't lost a game in three years."

Vivi blinked. "And this is my first game."

"Exactly."

Vivi's stomach grew tight. "How good is this other team?"

"Worst in the league."

"Oh, thank God," she said relieved.

"You should be good."

But the way Lindsey said it didn't make her feel any better. Then she had a thought that made her feel even worse. She leaned in to Lindsey.

"Swear to God you will not repeat what I'm about to ask you."

"I swear," Lindsey said.

"What number is Lane?"

Lindsey burst out laughing. "What kind of a girlfriend are you?"

"I didn't even know he played football until Wednesday. The same day I found out he was still in high school."

"Oh my God," Lindsey said, shaking her head. She looked over at Vivi and then leaned in close. "All I can say is the sex must have been pretty darn good."

Vivi burst out laughing, nodding her head for Lindsey, remembering just how good the sex had been.

She let her eyes scan across the numbered jerseys for...? "What number did you say he was?" she whispered to Lindsey.

"I didn't say."

"Oh. Well, what number is he?"

"I'm not telling you."

"What do you mean, you're not telling me?"

"I'm not telling you. Trust me. The offense is taking the field. Just watch, and pay attention."

Watch and pay attention? All right, she thought. It wasn't like she was going to turn around and ask the Ketterings what number their son wore.

Vivi had one sister and six cousins. Only one of them was a boy, and he played baseball, because baseball was king in Henderson. But Vivi's father and her uncles had played football in both high school and college, so she grew up a fan. And she lived in North Carolina where the ACC was king and you cared about college sports. So again, she was a fan. And Lane was a running back. Which meant that he ran with the ball. And since he was being recruited heavily, it meant he probably could run fast and score touchdowns. So when the first play of the game was a short pass to number eleven, who caught the ball on the fly and then turned on the power boosters to run down the field, stiff-arming one defensive player and eluding two others all the way into the end zone, Vivi began to feel woozy.

She stood while everyone around her cheered and yelled and clapped and whistled. Stood and watched as number eleven was pounded on by his teammates as they congratulated him. Stood and watched as he came to the sidelines, got a high five from his coach, took off his helmet, and looked into the stands.

Right at her.

Lane Kettering had just run eighty yards for a touchdown on the first play of the game. And then he'd looked for her.

CHAPTER FIFTEEN

It'd been three months, fourteen days, and something like thirteen hours since Lane had last had his hands on Vivi. So after the locker room celebration was over, and he'd politely answered all the local media's questions, and after he and his dad had met a new college scout from South Carolina, Lane had one thing on his mind. One thing only.

He had his cell pressed to his ear as he walked toward his car. "Where are you?"

"I'm at home."

"Vivi, you're supposed to be at my house, waiting for me."

"I know. I'm sorry. I just…"

"You're just what?" he snapped.

"I'm just…feeling a bit…woozy."

That had him stopping in his tracks. "Woozy?"

He heard a big sigh. "Seven touchdowns' worth of woozy."

Lane Kettering stood there, in the dark, speechlessly grinning from ear to ear.

"You scored *seven* touchdowns," she breathed.

"New school record," he said.

"Who scores se-ven touchdowns?" The way she said it made it sound like she was in the throes of an orgasm. "I…I couldn't trust myself. Lane, I'm not kidding. All I could picture was you walking off that field and me throwing my arms around you and tackling you to the ground. In front of everyone. I had to get out of there."

Lane chuckled. "Give me your address. I'm coming to you."

"You're not coming to me. I won't be able to keep my hands off you."

"I'm counting on that. Now give me your address." Lane put her on speaker and started Googling Jeb DuVal.

"Lane, we haven't talked to the lawyer yet. This is a bad idea."

"S.B., there's nothing your hands can touch tonight that they haven't already touched before. This teacher crap is all just semantics."

"Semantics that may ruin my career."

"So we have a very slim window of opportunity we need to take advantage of. Because until Mr. L. or someone in authority tells us we can't continue a private, physical relationship—we can. Besides," he lowered his voice and smiled, "I scored seven touchdowns."

"Laaaaannne," she wailed.

He really did like tempting Vivi. "Hold on. I'll be right there."

"Where are your parents?" Lane asked as he followed Vivi into the family room.

"I told you my Dad is head of the Booster Club right? Well, he and my uncles are all fired up about Henderson's new offense after their big win last week. So he and my mom went with my aunts and uncles to watch them play Swain County in Bryson City."

"Bryson City? Isn't that five hours away?" He couldn't hide his grin as he began backing her up against a wall.

"Lane," Vivi reached out and stiff-armed him. Shaking. Shaking usually meant things were going in his favor. Lane looked at her hand pressed against his chest then quirked a brow. "Yes, Bryson City is five hours away," she said trying not to smile. "My parents aren't coming home until tomorrow."

"And why am I just finding this out now?" he smirked.

"Well, I don't want to get you in trouble by keeping you out after curfew," she teased.

"I set a school record tonight," he said, removing her hand from his chest. "Pretty sure my parents are going to overlook curfew."

"Maybe not if they knew you were with me. Unchaperoned."

"It's been fourteen weeks since I've been able to touch you. To kiss you," he said, moving in, wetting his lips. "I'm going to take advantage of being unchaperoned."

He let himself go then. Both hands on both breasts, his mouth all over hers, his knee shoved between her legs, and man, it was better than he remembered. Definitely better than his fantasies. Because after a moment's hesitation, she was matching his enthusiasm play for play, getting her hands underneath his shirt, shoving it up his chest, making him stop what he was doing so he could pull it off over his head.

"Seven touchdowns," she said, panting.

"School record." He pulled her mouth back under his.

"You are reee-aally good," she said against his lips.

"You taste really good," he countered. "I wanna unzip your dress."

She turned around and pulled her ponytail out of the way.

"Jesus Christ, S.B. I thought I was gonna have to beg," he said, unzipping her dress, watching as she stepped out of it before she turned around and held it up in front of her.

"I think you're probably right," she said.

"Good. About what?"

"That we have a narrow window of opportunity. Thank goodness Piper Beaumont didn't want to meet with me until Monday."

"Who's Piper Beaumont?"

"The lawyer. She suggested you be there too."

"Whatever you want."

"Lane, if she tells us we need to…stop…"

"Stop what?"

"Stop this," she said, flipping a hand back and forth between them. "Then, we're going to have to stop."

"I will prepare for the worst."

"Okay," she said. It sounded a little panicky to him.

"S.B. please, just let us be us one last time. Before all the student/teacher bullshit starts. We are the same two people we were in Myrtle Beach. And thankfully, three months apart hasn't changed anything. We're still crazy about each other. Right now, we're alone. In your home. In Henderson. Just you and me. Safe. Okay?" he asked, ducking his head, looking her in the eye, moving back in slowly. He desperately didn't want her putting her dress back on.

"You scored seven touchdowns," she breathed.

"For you. I did that for you."

"For me?"

"Uh-huh." He stepped in, wrapping his arms around her waist. "I mean, I had fun doing it. The Spartans aren't playin' their best these days, so I figured I might be able to take advantage of that. But I did it for you."

"I don't understand."

"If I had my best game ever, which I did, my parents could have no objection to me dating you. In fact, they are so superstitious, now that I've set a school record, they're probably going to insist we keep dating." When she laughed at that, he backed her up into the wall. "If I had my best game ever, which I did, Principal Levendusky wouldn't worry that I'm being distracted from football or my grades." He pulled her dress away from her and dropped it to the floor. "If I had my best game ever, which I did," he said as he started to kiss her shoulder, "the recruiting staff from my top colleges in North Carolina will get serious about signing me before the rest of the country comes knocking on my door."

"What does that have to do with me?"

"You don't want to date a high schooler forever, do you?" He kept kissing her neck.

She smiled and shook her head no.

"Didn't think so."

"You scored seven touchdowns."

"You keep saying that," he whispered against her ear as his hand snuck inside the back of her panties and squeezed her silky soft derrière.

"Because I got woozy when you scored the first one."

That had him pulling back and looking down into her eyes. "Woozy?"

She nodded slowly.

"And then it got worse when you scored touchdown number two."

"Go on."

"And after touchdown number four, all I could think about was that time we were in the ocean and you took my hand and put it down your—"

He had to shut her up or he was going to blow. He put his hands against the wall and leaned in, taking control of her mouth. Her hands were on his belt buckle and unzipping his shorts before he realized what was happening. When she snuck her hand down his pants, he hummed against her mouth, pressed their bodies together with her hand caught right where it belonged, and started to move against her.

He…

Did not…

Last…

Long.

"Jesus, Viv," he panted against her neck. "I'm sorry. I just…"

"Scored seven touchdowns," she said with a smirk.

He laughed, stepping back. "Yeah." He reached over for a bar towel and cleaned off her hand and arm and then cleaned himself off. "I scored seven touchdowns and it took seven seconds for you to get me off."

She wrapped her arms around his neck and kissed him hard. "We don't have all night this time. Your parents are going to expect you home at some point. What I did right there? That was for me. Please tell me you have a condom."

"S.B. I believe I told you the other day I was going to be packing at all times. I was not lying about that." He pulled a black packet from his shorts and held it up for her to see.

She stared at it. Like a deer in the headlights.

"S.B.? What are you thinking?"

"I'm thinking you walking around with a condom in your pocket and me knowing about it might be a little too much temptation."

"I think we'll be able to handle it."

"I don't. I was so hot for you after your third touchdown I would've done you on the fifty-yard line."

"Keep talking," he said as he picked her up and carried her to the oversized couch. He sat back and let her straddle him.

"My body is crazy for you," she said, exasperated.

He laughed and divested her of her bra. She didn't even notice.

"You can't carry condoms in your pocket," she insisted.

He stopped listening because his hands had found their way to her breasts, which stood out against the rest of her tanned body, milky white and looking like they were lit up by the light of the moon. He couldn't wait to get his mouth on one so he tossed her on her back and followed her down.

"Lane," she breathed as he sucked her nipple and half her breast inside his mouth. God, he loved filling his mouth with her. His hands had a mind of their own and were taking off her panties even while he was stretched out on top of her. Even as he feasted on her flesh. He rolled to his side and tucked a knee around her thigh, opening her up to his fingers.

"Holy shit," he said, releasing her breast. He couldn't help himself. He went right for the money, slipping his finger deep inside. "S.B. You are so ready."

"I know," she whispered, smiling at him when he looked up to see her face. "That's what I've been tryin' to tell you."

"Fringe benefit from my best game ever?"

She nodded.

"Christ, I love football," he said, sinking his tongue into her mouth.

He made her come, quick and dirty, because he remembered every little detail about her body and had been longing to prove that to himself for three months and more. On top of that, he was so turned on by her being so turned on that he was ready, willing, and able to drive home touchdown number eight. He was hearing the crowd cheering in his head. Or maybe that was the Tonight Show they'd left on. Whatever.

"I've missed you so much," he said, pulling her up and shifting her around so she was straddling him again. "Like this. Just…mine. All mine," he said, handing her the condom packet before he stood her up on her knees so he could push his shorts and boxers off, down his legs, and kick them to the floor. "Seeing you in the stands tonight…" His hands were all over her, pulling her forward so he could kiss her. "I love that you're here instead of Atlanta."

"You do?" she said, sighing against him in relief. "I feel like I'm causing us a lot of trouble."

He plucked the condom packet from her hand and tore it open with his teeth. "No doubt I'd prefer you teaching statistics over in Henderson, because then we wouldn't have to go through all this bullshit…" He stood her up again and sheathed himself. "… but I swear to God, you are so worth it."

"You've got me naked on your lap. Of course I seem worth it."

He put his hand behind her head, brought her mouth to his, and soothed her with a kiss. "Not gonna lie. I'm pretty jacked about having you naked on my lap right now."

"Mmm," she said, "then make this good because this is the last time we are doing this in my parents' house."

"Stop being bossy."

"It's an occupational hazard."

He grinned against her lips as he positioned his cock at her entrance.

"What?" she asked on a breathy sigh as he eased her down on to him.

"Nothing," he whispered.

"Tell me," she insisted, head thrown back, eyes closed.

He debated, and then just couldn't help himself. He slid his thumb over her clit as he kissed her neck and said, "I'm screwing the teacher."

Damn if she didn't burst out laughing.

He stopped everything.

"See, right there," he said, looking into her eyes, brushing the hair off her face, "that's why I know you're the one for me."

"What?"

"You're putting us first."

Her hands came up and caressed his face. Then she touched her forehead to his. "Maybe I shouldn't be. But you're my hero," she said, kissing his lips. "In every sense of the word. You saved me that day on the beach. My life expanded when you walked into it. And now you're letting me tread all over your territory and ruin your senior year. And I get to watch you score touchdowns. It's hard not to put us first. Us really works for me."

"Mmm." He brought her hands down from his face, pushed them behind her and placed them on his knees. "If this is how you plan on ruining my senior year," he said, his fingers and eyes coasting over the soft curves of her body, "you just go right ahead and do it. I will plaster a smile on my face and do my best to suffer through."

"Seven touchdowns," she whispered.

He sucked one of her breasts into his mouth, and she started to move on him.

"You are so fast," she said, eyes closed. "What's that feel like? Running eighty yards for a touchdown?"

He sat back, put his hands on her hips and let her set the pace, watching through heavy lids. "It's fun," he said, licking his lips because his voice was coming out rusty. "Sometimes it feels too easy. Sometimes," he said, really thinking about putting it into words for the first time, "it feels like I'm Superman."

Sleeping Beauty smiled with her eyes closed, rocking her smoking hot bod against him. Thank God she'd taken the edge off him earlier, because letting her ride him, giving her what she wanted, what she needed, felt like pure heaven.

"What did it feel like for you, S.B.?" he whispered, stroking back her hair. "What did it feel like for you to watch me score seven touchdowns?"

"That's easy," she said. "I felt like Lois Lane."

CHAPTER SIXTEEN

On Monday evening, Piper Beaumont, looking all sunshiny in yellow, with untamed curls and bright blue eyes, met with Vivi and Lane at a small coffee shop situated off route 85 between Henderson and Raleigh. She started the meeting by asking for a dollar.

"A dollar?" Vivi wondered as Lane pulled out his wallet.

"We'll call this a retainer," Piper said. She nodded a thank you to Lane and took the bill. "Being that you're Genevra's niece and Lolly's cousin, I'm putting the two of you on the Friends and Family plan. Money has to be exchanged so you may talk freely to me, as your attorney, and I am obligated by law to keep whatever you say confidential."

"So you think I need an attorney?" Vivi's voice held an edge of panic.

"I think you were right to call me. I think your situation is unique and completely understandable. However, if somebody had it in for either one of you, the way the law is written regarding student/teacher relationships, they could make your life a living hell."

"But I'm nineteen," Lane protested. "Our relationship started months before Vivi was offered the job at Wilson."

"And if Vivi was working at Henderson Bank and Trust, there would be absolutely no reason for you two not to enjoy a romantic relationship. But this student/teacher thing is another matter entirely."

"We understand that," Vivi said. "Of course, we understand that."

"I don't understand it," Lane protested.

Vivi sent him a sweet smile and bumped him with her shoulder. "Of course I understand it as a teacher. But since our relationship started prior to our current situation, and with Lane being over eighteen, how bad can this possibly be?"

"There are two criminal statutes you need to concern yourself with."

"*Criminal* statutes?" Vivi asked, concerned.

"The Indecent Liberties with a Student statute—"

"Indecent Liberties with a Student?" Vivi repeated, horrified.

"And the Intercourse and Sexual Offense with Certain Victims statute," Piper finished.

"This is bullshit. There is no victim," Lane argued.

"Regardless of the student's age, those statutes state that a teacher less than four years older than the student would be committing a Class A1 misdemeanor. Punishable by jail time, public service, house arrest, etc. Under the circumstances, I could get you off with a hand slap at the most. However, if convicted, Vivi would then be required to register on the North Carolina Sex Offender and Public Protection Registry."

Vivi started to shake. Her eyes started to water. "Oh, God." She couldn't breathe. "I'm...I'm a sex offender?" Feeling claustrophobic, she turned her whole body, struggling to get out of the booth. Piper jumped out, crouched down in front of her, and shoved Vivi's head between her legs.

"You're not a sex offender," she soothed. "Those laws are designed to protect children from predators. Lane certainly isn't a child, and you certainly aren't a predator. You're just caught inside the technical language right now. If this ever went before a judge, I would defend you and would get you off. I promise. Breathe."

Vivi popped her head up. "But the damage would already be done."

Piper shoved her head back down. "That's why it's good we're talking about this now. So you and Lane both understand the seriousness of the situation."

"I feel sick," Vivi groaned.

"Beauty," Lane cooed, pulling her hair back from her face and holding it behind her. "You're fine. We're fine. We've got this."

"We don't have this," she protested from between her legs. Vivi looked up into Piper's blue eyes and confessed. "I couldn't keep my hands off him Friday night. He scored *seven touchdowns*," she cried.

Piper bit her lip and winked at Lane as Vivi put her head back between her knees. "I understand. I'm crazy about Vance Evans and if somebody told me I couldn't touch him I'd have my head between my knees too."

"Oh, Lord. You two are ridiculous. If anyone should be crying here, it's me," Lane said. "I'm the horny teenager for God's sake. Vivi, this is nothing we can't handle. It's eight months until graduation, and we thought we were going to be in separate states anyway. The law says we can't have sex. It doesn't say we can't be crazy about each other." He looked up at Piper. "Can I kiss her?"

"Kissing on the mouth is not against the law. By either party. However, Lane, obviously it wouldn't do either of you any good to be seen kissing."

"Obviously. What else isn't against the law?"

"What else do you have in mind?"

"Skyping?"

"As long as it doesn't involve indecent or lewd acts."

"Can I touch her?"

"That's a gray area I wouldn't advise getting into."

"But if she trips and falls in the school hallway right in front of me, I could help her up, right?"

"Of course. You can touch any part of her body that's not considered sexual. Her hand, her arm, her elbow—Look, let's be realistic. As long as the two of you aren't caught with your pants down in a compromising position, you're fine. But rumors and gossip, well, that will take the two of you down a whole lot faster than a judge or jury will. So play the part of indifferent teacher and student for the next eight months and play it really well. Figure out a way to have fun with it. Y'all are too young not to be having fun. Just lay off the sex and everything will work out fine."

Vivi raised her head and took in a deep breath. "Lane needs a beard."

"Excuse me?" Lane said.

"You need a girlfriend." Vivi sat up and took in some deep breaths.

"That's not a bad idea," Piper agreed.

"I've already got a girlfriend, thank you," Lane reminded them. "And under the circumstances, she's pretty much a handful. The last thing I need is another one."

"It would fend off rumors and gossip," Piper said.

"There are no rumors and gossip."

"Yes, but it would completely divert all attention away from the two of you. It would go a long way to keep any rumors from getting started."

"*We* are going to go a long way to keep them from getting started. Trust me. We will not be caught with our pants down."

Piper moved back into her side of the booth. "Who knows about you two?"

"Our parents," Lane said as he rubbed Vivi's back. "The principal. And my buddy, Lam. And Lam's not going to tell anybody because I'm keeping an even bigger secret for him."

Piper's eyes widened. "Hmm. Must be some secret."

"Well, it's not going to send anybody to jail."

"Oh, God," Vivi moaned, crossing her arms on the table and dropping her head onto them.

"I'm sorry, S.B.," Lane said. "Come on, lighten up. I'm not letting anything happen to you. You gotta know that by now."

Piper's eyes darted between Vivi and Lane before coming to rest solely on Lane. She smiled at him. A warm, personal smile. "You love her," she stated with fascination.

Vivi saw Lane's face pop up to look at Piper. "How could I not?"

Piper tilted her head and gave Lane a look as if to say "aww." She started nodding her head, smiling at the two of them. "So the fact that you're not going to be getting any for the next eight months?"

Lane raised his hands in the air in wonder. "Will be exactly like it was before I met Vivi. Geez. Do I look like the kind of guy who can't go without sex?"

Piper laughed. "You look like a guy who doesn't need to. You look like a guy who has girls hanging all over him."

"The kind of guy who enjoys strip clubs, right?" Vivi chimed in.

"Definitely," Piper said. "Though I may be painting all good-looking men with a broad brush at the moment. Vance, I just found out, has quite the reputation. Pretty sure it started when he was in high school."

"Mmm," Vivi said. "I've heard stories."

"I'd love to hear them. But, maybe we better get Lane graduated before you and I start down that path." Piper reached into her yellow leather tote, saying, "Okay, when are we meeting with this principal?" She pulled out a pad of paper and pen.

"You don't have to do that," Vivi stated half-heartedly. She'd actually love Piper and all her sunshine to have her back when she faced Principal Levendusky.

"Oh no. I'm all about falling in love at the moment. I mentioned Vance Evans right? So, I've just joined your team. Now, tell me everything your principal knows."

"We told him the truth," Lane said. "That we met at the beach, have been dating long distance for months, and as soon as I saw Vivi enter the classroom, I left to drop the class."

"Does he know that you've been intimate?"

"Ah, yeah. I sort of let that one out of the bag."

Vivi rubbed a hand over Lane's. "He knows. That is why he asked me to contact a lawyer. I guess so we'd come to this conclusion on our own."

"But he didn't suspend you? Until this matter was resolved?"

Vivi shook her head. "He needs me."

"How does he need you?"

"I was offered this job because he's down two teachers and nobody else can teach statistics. And I'm cheap. Beginning-teacher's salary and all that."

"Huh. We can work with that."

"What do you mean?"

"We want him on your team, too. We'd like him to sign an acknowledgement that you came to him immediately, as soon as you were aware there was a conflict of interests. That way, he's on the hook for being aware of the circumstances surrounding your previous relationship. If push came to shove, he'd have to testify to it.

"In return, Vivi, are you willing to sign a statement acknowledging your pre-existing relationship with Lane, saying you are aware of the statutes we've talked about here, and will refrain from a sexual relationship until he is no longer a student at Wilson?"

"We can still kiss, right?" Lane asked.

"You may kiss her. On the lips, in private. Like you'd kiss your grandmother or your sister." Piper said.

"You just killed that for me," Lane grimaced.

"Vivi, you don't have to sign this," Piper said. "I'd just like to offer your principal a reason to sign the acknowledgement and give him peace of mind. This is your call."

Vivi looked to Lane.

"Sign it," he said. "You've wanted to be a teacher your whole life. No way am I standing in the way of that."

"See, when you talk like that, I'm very tempted to jump you."

"It's already on the calendar, Sleeping Beauty. May sixteenth. If I don't jump you first."

CHAPTER SEVENTEEN

After the mortifying meeting with Principal Levendusky and Lane's parents where Piper used her lawyer speak to announce that Vivi and Lane would refrain from having a sexual relationship while he was a student, September flew by. Lane was busy winning football games and visiting colleges. And as he predicted, out-of-state schools had started to show up. It seemed like he could go just about anywhere.

Vivi was busy creating lesson plans, grading papers, fending off advances from Mr. Liskey—the very cute, very preppy, thirty-year-old geometry teacher—and getting to know her cheerleaders.

Most of the girls were ambitious, a few were really sweet, a couple had a terrible case of foul language, and several seemed boy crazy. Vivi didn't want to throw stones. She was boy crazy too—crazy about Lane Kettering. She had even gone so far as to use his latest football stats in her Monday Statistics class lesson plan. If she couldn't touch him, she could at least hold up his record-breaking season for everyone to see. So, when the girls she was advising got to discussing boys, and dates, and clothes for their dates, and boys, she let them.

On the last Monday of the month, instead of their regular practice, both the JV and Varsity squads met in Vivi's classroom. She told them she'd arranged for a special guest speaker, Annabelle Devine, well-known in Henderson as The Keeper of The Debutantes.

Because of Annabelle's passion for adhering to old school etiquette, Henderson's debutantes were well known for their grace and charm, not to mention their kick-ass parties. Annabelle also held a paying job as the Mid-Atlantic Field Representative for her national sorority. She had a real knack for getting and keeping coeds out of trouble.

The moment Annabelle walked into the room, she had the girls' undivided attention. Fresh, sophisticated, and completely feminine in her beautiful white dress and long, flowing red curls but powerful in her presence and attitude.

It was an etiquette lesson on manners and grace, and the benefits of being very, very selective about the boys you date. Vivi's cheerleaders ate it up. She noticed they all sat up a little straighter the more Annabelle talked.

Annabelle went on to discuss the main topic Vivi had asked her to address. Giving examples of the trouble some of her sorority sisters had gotten themselves into over the years and the ramifications it had on their personal lives and their careers.

The girls were full of questions at the end, asking Annabelle everything from how debutantes were chosen, to the dos and don'ts for getting into a sorority. They asked about handling sticky social situations, turning down dates gently, and even wanted to know Annabelle's opinion on how to ask a guy out. Vivi was surprised when they asked about handling their parents more effectively. This led into a lively conversation about what to tell your parents and what not to tell your parents.

That was a bit of an eye-opener.

Annabelle concluded by challenging the girls to consider what their dream job might entail. She suggested they start thinking about their interests, talents, and passions now, and how those could be turned into a satisfying career. She gave herself as an example, and then led into the new business enterprise she was taking on with Vivi's cousin, Lolly—The House of DuVal—exclusively designed debutante gowns and party dresses. Then she gave out her business card.

Vivi had to hand it to her. No moss would ever grow under Annabelle's feet.

The next day, the *Annabelle Effect* took hold. Vivi noticed the change in her cheerleaders right away. They came to school better groomed with their uniforms mended, cleaned, and pressed, and conducted themselves with a little more sophistication. She didn't know how long all that would last, but figured it would serve them well at present since the nominations for the Homecoming court were about to commence.

It was two weeks later when Vivi realized Homecoming was going to be her undoing.

She tried to stay calm, breathing in and out, as she drove home late one Thursday afternoon in the middle of October. Things with Lane had been good—really good considering—since that second game of the season. Now, six wins later, the two of them had fallen into an easy pattern of quick glances during the school day, notes at the end of class, and long Skyping sessions at night. A small shell had mysteriously appeared on her desk September first, with "8 Months" written on the interior with a very fine black Sharpie. Another shell had been added to it on October first, counting down to "7 Months."

She'd left them right where he'd placed them.

The two of them had barely kissed twelve times since their rendezvous after the seven-touchdown game. Lane was busy. Really busy. Busy with coaches and football and schoolwork and the press. And she was busy, too. Busy figuring out the politics of being a teacher, preparing lesson plans, tutoring students, grading papers, and keeping the cheerleaders in line. Vivi was satisfied with how things were going in all areas of her life. She did hold a secret hope that over the Thanksgiving holiday, she and Lane might be able to meet somewhere out of town—maybe in Raleigh, maybe at his brother's home in Charlotte—and spend some quality time together without the risk of being exposed. They couldn't have sex, of course, but she missed being his girlfriend twenty-four hours a day.

However, now she feared the writing was on the wall after six weeks of keeping their relationship quiet. It happened innocently enough. She was checking in on the JV squad cheering that afternoon and decided to drop in on the Varsity girls to see how the new pom-pom routine for Homecoming was shaping up. She caught wind of a conversation between the captains, the girls she counted on to be frank with her regarding all things. She just didn't want to be in on this particular one.

"I really want Lane Kettering to ask me to Homecoming," pretty brunette Olivia said to Stacey. "We are working on term papers together in English, and he's really been…"

Vivi held her breath.

"…helpful. He's not a dumb jock. I mean, I know he's no saint, but," she grinned, "if I were his date, I wouldn't want him to be anyway. So, I'm trying to gently hint we'd have fun together."

"Well, he's got to go, right? He's on the court." Stacey said brightly. "I haven't seen him with anybody else, so maybe you should just ask him."

Vivi's heart started racing, and her feet followed suit. She got the hell out of the gymnasium and went straight to her classroom where she began to talk herself down. Olivia could ask Lane to Homecoming over and over and Lane would say no. She knew it. She trusted him and his feelings for her and she…*deep breath*…knew this was not going to be a problem.

Knew this was nothing she had to worry about.

She was a teacher. She just needed to get her head back into that game. Pull it out of the high school drama that was happening around her—none of her business anyway—and remember who she was. And that worked…right up until she remembered her conversation with Lane at the beach. The one where she insisted he enjoy his senior year—in college—without the burden of a long-distance relationship. This is why they had agreed to limit themselves to texting the first of every month. So Lane could enjoy his senior year and she could focus on beginning her career. Then they would meet in Myrtle Beach again, a year later, to see where things stood.

Well, crap, she thought as she packed up her tote and headed to her car. It was still Lane's senior year—albeit in high school—and really, when better to be engaged in a social life? Especially if you were the freaking star running back and looked like Lane Kettering?

"Ahhh, damn," she sighed as she stopped completely, staring at the side of her car but seeing nothing at all. This was really gonna hurt.

She held it together until she got home and told her mom not to call her for dinner. She claimed she had a migraine and was going to lie down. And she did. Under her covers. Her head buried under her pillow so no one could hear her sobs.

She had to let Lane go. Maybe not for good, but certainly for now. And that thought just made her sob harder.

She didn't want to let him go. She depended on Lane's level head to sort things out, loved his enthusiasm about football and life, loved how he took care of her even in the most subtle ways. They felt so perfect together. Had from day one. He was easy to be with. Fun. Kind. And oh, man, how he turned her on. The thought of some other girl enjoying the Lane Kettering she knew…

Heartbreak.

Frantic, sobbing, heart-wrenching, this-is-so-not-fair, anguish.

A half-hour later, the pendulum swung over to selfish, impractical, jealous, I'm-not-letting-him-go-and-no-one-can-make-me resolution.

Tough shit if this was his senior year. And tough shit if Annabelle would suggest she watch her language. And tough shit if O-liv-i-a wanted Lane to take her to Homecoming.

Get your own damn boyfriend and keep your grubby hands off mine.

Vivi dried her eyes, resolved.

Until she wasn't.

The pendulum swung back, and she started to cry again.

Her senior year in high school had been a really, really fun time. She had come into her own and participated in everything. She'd have hated to miss any of it, especially if she'd had to watch it from the sidelines.

Lane had already been voted onto the Homecoming court. It wasn't like he could skip the dance. As Mr. L. so indelicately put it, it wasn't like Lane was going to be taking Vivi to the prom.

Even if she'd stayed for a senior year at Wake Forest, he wouldn't have taken her to his prom. Or Homecoming. Or anything.

They might be two years apart in age, but from the angle she was looking at their relationship right now, they seemed to be years apart in life. And she never, ever wanted Lane Kettering to look back on his life and feel like she'd robbed him of something as significant as his senior year in high school.

Yeah, Vivi saw the writing on the wall and could no longer avoid it. Their relationship had to end, and her heart knew it was going to end badly.

Lane tried reaching Vivi through Skype at nine o'clock. He tried again five minutes later. At ten after, he picked up his phone and texted her.

Nothing.

Bossy Miss DuVal was punctual. Every time. All the time. No exceptions.

Something was amiss.

He went downstairs, pulled out a bottle of smartwater, grabbed a handful of miniature Reese's cups his mom had bought to give out on Halloween, and headed back upstairs.

Nothing on the computer. But a text on his phone said, *"Give me a minute."*

Sure. As long as his statistics teacher showed up in that skimpy pink tank top she slept in, she could take all the time she needed. He'd thought about giving her one of his jerseys but was afraid she'd actually sleep in it, and he'd have to stare at that during their Skype sessions instead of her tits. So, that was a no go.

He propped himself up against the pillows on his bed and sat back, eating his candy and thinking about nothing. Literally nothing. His computer screen flashed and there it was. The sight he waited for all day. The sight he dreamt about at night. Sleeping Beauty's dark hair hanging down over her shoulders, framing his favorite part of her body. Well, next to her ass in that crazy thong swimsuit with the bow. But he didn't like to think about that at night. That image kept him awake and hard way too long. And he couldn't think about her naked breasts. Christ, that night he had her naked on his lap was a distraction he rarely let himself indulge in. Everything about that night was perfect. The game. The girl. The sex. He'd managed to do the one thing he'd been trying to do since Vivi had given him that first lesson about her body and what it needed. With her on top moving how she liked, and his fingers free to give her what she needed, and his hair-trigger response already shot, it was magic. The two of them reached simultaneous combustion.

Lane was in a sex-hazed fog, not hearing a thing Vivi was saying, staring at her chest until he noticed it was heaving. Up...down. Up...down. Not normal. Definitely not normal as his eyes drifted up to Sleeping Beauty's pretty face and his heart plunged right into his stomach.

"You've been crying. Why were you crying? What the hell happened?"

"Lane." She barely got his name out before she started leaking tears.

"What?" He gripped the screen of his laptop, fruitlessly trying to angle it so he could see more. "What's going on?" He'd never seen her cry. Hated hearing it when he called her on the phone that first time. Really hated seeing it now. It about broke his heart.

His protective instincts kicked in. He'd fix it. Whatever the hell was going on over there, he'd fix it. He was incapable of letting Vivi DuVal feel pain without doing everything in his power to stop it.

"S.B. Whatever it is, I'm going to..." Okay, maybe he couldn't fix everything—if her father had a heart attack, he wasn't going to be able to fix that. But he could be there for her, so that's what he promised. "...Hold your hand through it."

She grabbed a tissue off camera and turned her head, as if he couldn't see her body convulsing in sobs.

"My God. What happened, Viv? You've got to tell me."

"Nothing," she said, working to get herself together. "Nothing," she said, sniffing in a deep breath, trying to get control. "I'm sorry. Nothing happened. I mean, nothing *bad* happened. Not like I'm making it look like." She took a couple deep breaths, dried her eyes, and then settled herself down. She finally looked into the camera and tilted her head. Eyes bloodshot, cheeks tear streaked. Still, she gave him her sweet little smile.

"Hi," she said.

"Hi," he whispered, so sad for whatever was hurting her.

"Lane, I've been thinking."

Why did those words strike fear in him? His instincts told him to interrupt her now. Not to let whatever she was about to say get started. But curiosity got the better of him. He held his tongue.

Her next breath came out shaky. "Olivia Thompson wants you to take her to Homecoming. And I, well, I think you should do it."

"Really?" His eyes sprung wide. "Is this your way of telling me you'd like to try a three-way on May sixteenth?"

"What? No! Of course not."

He laughed at her horrified expression. "Then why the hell would I take Olivia to Homecoming? I've already got a date lined up."

She blinked at that. His Sleeping Beauty. Her mouth parted in surprise. "You do?"

"Yep."

After a lengthy silence. "Can I ask who?"

"May as well. Everybody else is all up in Lane Kettering's business. I think I'm trending on Twitter."

"So...?"

"I met this cute girl from Henderson over the summer. Henderson High School. She's agreed to be my date. Of course, she's going to come down with the flu or something that night and won't be able to make it. I'll have to attend by myself. Which, you know, will give me an excuse to leave early. Unless there's a cute first-year teacher chaperoning. Then I'm going to talk Lam into asking Mrs. Kerry to dance, so I can dance with you. In public."

"You can't dance with me in public."

"I can dream."

"But wouldn't you like to attend the dance with an actual date?"

"You know I would. Are you planning to quit so we can go public? Because really, as long as the Warriors stay undefeated, no one is gonna care about anything else."

"They'll care."

"Yeah, well, I'm getting to the point where I don't care," he grumbled.

"Lane. Here's the thing. We originally agreed to keep our relationship light so you could enjoy your senior year. And then I messed that up by taking this job at Wilson. So," she sighed.

"So what?" he snapped.

"So, I think we need to go back to that original plan. I mean, I know me being here is going to make it awkward, and I'm sorry about that, but being crowned Homecoming King without a date is sort of anticlimactic. I don't want your senior year to be anticlimactic."

"I don't give a shit about being Homecoming King. Frankly, it's downright embarrassing, and my teammates will tease the living shit out of me if I let them put a crown on my head. The only reason I'm showing up is because my mother would have a fit if I didn't, and I need to placate my mother if I want to keep making out with my statistics teacher."

"That is my point. None of this is easy for you. None of it is fair."

"You're telling me. I'm dating the hottest girl in the school, but I can't tell anybody."

He watched her give in to a laugh.

"Come on, S.B. We've managed pretty good so far. Hell, it's been fairly easy after those first few days."

"Yes. It has. But now we're facing Homecoming. And as much as I appreciate that you've already worked out your…story, this is just the tip of the iceberg."

"Don't borrow trouble, Viv. One day at a time. That's how we're going to get all the way to graduation."

"But is that really how you want to live your senior year?"

"What choice do I have?"

Her eyes started leaking again.

Oh, no.

"Lane, I'm afraid I've re-thought this…"

"No." Hell no. Sleeping Beauty was not breaking his heart because Olivia Thompson wanted a damn date to Homecoming. He cut her off by slamming his computer shut and then got himself dressed. If they were going to have this conversation, they were going to have it face to face.

The pounding on her front door probably sounded a little frantic to whoever was inside. He was definitely feeling frantic, so you know, whatever. The truth was he felt like he was clinging to happiness by a thread, already sunk waist-deep in a marsh pit of despair. Because as great as his senior year was going right now, a championship season would not be nearly as much fun if he couldn't share it with Vivi. So here he was, late on a school night, way over in Henderson, banging on her front door.

And in keeping with how things were going for him at the moment, Vivi's father was the one to open that door. Of course he was. At least Lane assumed the big hulk of a man standing there glowering at him was Jeb DuVal. They'd yet to be introduced.

"Mr. DuVal. I'm Lane Kettering," he said, sticking his hand out, looking him in the eye like he wasn't scared to death of the man.

After a surprised look and a slow perusal from the top of his head all the way down to his Nikes, Jeb took his offered hand and shook it. "Little late for a school night, isn't it? Come on in."

"Yes, sir. I apologize for that. It's just that…well, it seems…your daughter, sir, she's upset, and I've—"

Just then, both men turned their heads toward the loud clamor they heard bounding down the staircase. Vivi stopped abruptly in the middle when she saw the two of them together. Lane took in every detail of his willful Sleeping Beauty, standing there in next to nothing, holding the railing, leaning forward in her pink tank top, displaying waaay too much cleavage.

"Geez, put on some clothes," he barked, right along with her father.

Vivi stood up and placed a hand on her hip, completely affronted. Then she rolled her eyes before turning and heading back upstairs.

Mr. DuVal patted Lane on the back. "I think you and I are going to get along just fine. Let's head into my den and have a little chat."

CHAPTER EIGHTEEN

When Vivi stuck her head inside her father's den and saw Lane and her dad talking in a congenial fashion, she breathed a sigh of relief. Then she walked in, fully dressed—like she was on her way to work for God's sake—pissed off at both of them.

"Do not give this boy a hard time," her father said as he rose to leave the room. "He's got an undefeated season going. He doesn't need to be distracted by any of your silly nonsense."

"Silly nonsense? Daddy!"

"Don't "Daddy" me. This boy has come all the way from Oxford, raced over here because you are upset, when he should be tucked in bed getting his sleep for the game tomorrow night. If he isn't at his best, you're going to be the one to blame."

"Since when do you care if the running back from hell is at his best?"

Her father turned to Lane. "My apologies, Lane. Good luck tomorrow night."

"Thank you, sir," Lane said, standing.

Her father walked out and closed the wood-paneled double doors behind him.

Vivi looked up at Lane, nervous. It was the first time since she'd met him that he wasn't greeting her with a smile. Right now, he looked dead serious and as old as she'd originally thought he was.

"I see you and my father have bonded," she said, hoping to lighten his mood.

"You have a problem with that?" His beautiful voice was flat. Harsh. She shook her head no and let her gaze drop to the floor. Unable to form words. Unable to look him in the eye.

But Lane Kettering was nothing if not resolute. He stood his ground and waited her out. When she finally gave in and glanced up, she saw his fingers twitching, his jaw tight.

"I know you have feelings for me," he stated.

"Of course I do." It came out as a whisper. So she cleared her throat and said, "I'm crazy about you."

"Then please, start acting like it. Stop overthinking what's happening here and just go with it. And give me some damn credit for knowing my own mind."

"That's not what this is about."

"That's exactly what this is about. Do you think my senior year would be more enjoyable if you were in Atlanta? If we were still texting once a month? If you still had no idea I was a senior in high school and I had that hanging over my head? Hanging over our relationship?"

She hadn't looked at it that way.

"The only regret I have about my senior year is that we are stuck in this charade, which I agreed to solely so it wouldn't put a black mark on your dream. Your career. Because…because I love you, S.B. So if you think selflessly breaking up with me is going to improve my senior year, you're dead wrong. It would ruin the most fun I've ever had, except for those four days with you at the beach. It would take all the fun out of our undefeated season if I couldn't look up into the stands and see my girlfriend, knowing I'm getting her hot by scoring touchdowns."

She moved into his arms then. Buried her head into his chest and wrapped herself around him. "I'm sorry."

"You should be. Geez. You scared the shit out of me tonight. Made me come busting in here, having to meet your daddy while I'm all worked up and worried you're gonna dump me."

She lifted her head. "What the hell was that with you and my father?"

Lane rubbed her back. "I think he liked that I told you to put on some clothes. He definitely respects the way I run with a football."

"Lane, are you sure about this?"

"Did you cry all evening because you were planning to break up with me?"

She shrugged.

"Are you doing this because of me? Or are you trying to protect yourself? Because if that's the case, we can—"

"No. This is not because I'm afraid for myself. I'm afraid you'll end up resenting me. Holding you back from doing everything you want to do."

"Uh-huh. See, you love me. Even if you don't know it yet."

Oh, she knew it.

"So let's settle this once and for all. One day at a time, you and I, together. You're not going to be my teacher forever."

"No, I won't."

"I'm starting to think Ms. Beaumont was right. We should be having fun with this. I shouldn't be wasting this opportunity."

"What do you mean?"

"I am now going to start bucking to be the teacher's pet."

CHAPTER NINETEEN

Lane Kettering was not fooling around. Well, Vivi supposed that he was indeed fooling around—but in a very serious way. He showed up for her Statistics class the next day with sunglasses off and his game face on. He raised his hand, answered questions with surprising flourish, and every few days would switch his seat with the person in front of him until he was sitting in the front row, dead center, three feet away from where she regularly stood.

Vivi moved her desk directly in front of him, needing some sort of boundary between them in the classroom.

Lane just smirked.

Homecoming came and went. The cheerleader's new pom-pom routine was applauded, the Warriors came out victorious, and Lane's story about his date taking ill at the last minute held up, leaving him to be fawned over by girls and boys alike all night. He did not win Homecoming King but his buddy Lam did. And Lam ate it up with a fork and spoon. He not only paraded around with the crown on his head all night long, he wore it all day Monday at school.

Being the newbie teacher, Vivi had been roped into chaperone duty and was happier for it. It was the perfect opportunity to keep an eye on her cheerleaders while at the same time having a super-secret date with the hottest guy in the room.

It was the first time she'd ever seen Lane in a coat and tie, and man, did he look like he had stepped out of *GQ*. It was also the first time she really understood the term "eye candy," because her eyes did nothing but eat him up all night. She eventually had to relegate herself to a place in the shadows where she would be less likely to be caught watching him and just enjoyed the show.

It was that night Vivi began to realize how deep Lane's kindness ran. She watched as he was continually interrupted, asked to dance, patted on the back, or knocked none too gently on his arm, over and over. Every time he would turn and give the perpetrator a smile and sometimes a handshake, but always his undivided attention.

Vivi couldn't help but notice that a lot of female eyes followed him wherever he went and how oblivious he seemed to it. He didn't ask anybody to dance, but never turned down a girl who got up the courage to ask him. Of course, being the perfect boyfriend, he made sure to seek Vivi out with his eyes and send her a wink.

He stayed behind at the end, volunteering to help clean up. The rest of the teachers couldn't get out of there fast enough, so it was easy to be the last two the custodian ushered out the door. Mr. Leonard, the janitor, asked Lane to walk Miss DuVal to her car, worried for her safety, and Lane promised he would with the utmost sincerity.

Lane talked Vivi into a date on Halloween night since the two of them could venture out—in Henderson at least—under the disguise of costumes. Vivi wanted to go as Lois Lane with him as Superman, but Lane insisted she dress up as Sleeping Beauty since that was her nickname and how he'd seen her—asleep on the sand—before she ever opened her eyes. He requested she wear a blue thong underneath her costume to commemorate the occasion of their first meeting. But there was no way she could talk him into dressing up as Prince Charming in tights. She laughed hysterically just thinking about it as they Skyped one night, which didn't help her case any. When she tried to ply him by promising sexual favors on May sixteenth, he said he'd be getting sexual favors on May sixteenth no matter what he wore.

Damn if he wasn't right.

Because he came to pick her up dressed in a football uniform. His *own* football uniform. He might not have had on his shoulder pads, but the name Kettering was spelled out clearly across his broad shoulders. A Warriors ball cap took the place of his helmet, football eye black had been applied under his eyes, two days' worth of beard was on his face, and he held a pair of dark sunglasses in his hand. He looked crazy hot and old enough to play in the NFL. As her eyes moved lower, she noticed his uniform pants did have the pads stuffed inside, so his lower body looked exactly like it did when he ran for all those touchdowns.

Vivi's woozy factor hit high and hit hard.

"Where the hell do you think you're going dressed like that?" she asked.

"Sleeping Beauty," he said, eyeing her short, sexy version of the Disney princess's gown. "Do you think the real Lane Kettering would be foolish enough to show his face in Henderson during an undefeated season? I might get a few beers thrown at me, but I guareen-damn-tee ya nobody is going to think you're dating 'that running back from the devil's team.'"

Vivi blinked. Then started to laugh. He was right. Probably. Maybe. Oh hell, she didn't care because he looked so damn hot in that uniform, and she had never had the chance to put her hands on him while he was wearing it. Never even got close enough to drool over him like she was doing now.

At Henderson's local hangout, The Situation, there was a packed house where it turned out Lane became an unlikely hero. Once the rumor started that he'd stolen Kettering's jersey so the "goddamn-son-of-a-bitch" wouldn't have it for the upcoming game against Henderson, everybody wanted to buy him a beer. He turned them all down—for her he told Vivi as he backed her up into a dark corner. Wouldn't do to be caught drinking underage *and* kissing his beautiful statistics teacher.

Which he did. Kiss her. A lot. Out by the lake, late that night. And not like he'd kiss his grandmother. For the first time, Vivi was tempted to call Principal Levendusky from her cell and quit.

Miraculously, that "son of a bitch Kettering" managed to find his jersey in time for the Henderson game the following weekend. This was an away game for Wilson, putting Vivi in a whole lot of hot water since she was surrounded by family and friends while wearing the black and red of the Warriors. She had to remind everyone that she was now a teacher at Wilson and was supporting her students.

That explanation didn't sit well with anybody. Except her father who kissed her cheek.

Lane did not have his best game. The defense was gunning for him and him alone. He was tripped, pushed, held, and had his helmet ripped off twice. Henderson lost more yards on penalties trying to stop Lane than they would have if they'd just let him run the ball. And while all the focus was on Lane, the Warrior's quarterback was left to throw long for three touchdowns and carry the ball in for two. It seemed Henderson's defense had forgotten that there were other players on the field.

The Warriors finished their regular season undefeated.

Three shells now sat on Vivi's desk. November brought with it the home field advantage for the first two playoff games and the Warriors put that to good use. The opposing teams weren't pushovers. In both games, the score was tied or close to it going into the fourth quarter. Vivi's stomach was a jumble of nerves, not only because the games were so close, but because her parents were now sitting in the stands with her, right in front of the Ketterings. Cheering for Lane and the devil's team. It was a surreal experience.

Her father drew a surprising amount of attention. His paving company did a lot of business in Oxford so he was well known for that. Apparently, he was just as well known for his high school antics back when he was a Henderson football player. Vivi was amazed and appalled to learn that her father was the one, in every game he played against Wilson, to throw the first punch which inevitably cleared the benches. She was even more amazed and appalled that he seemed proud of that fact.

When asked why the hell Jeb DuVal was sitting in the Warriors' stands, he almost outed Lane and Vivi in his pride over Lane's football prowess. Thank goodness, Vivi's mother was paying attention and spoke right over Jeb as he started talking about his daughter's boyfriend, claiming a long-standing friendship with the Kettering family, indicating them seated behind the DuVals.

Vivi breathed a sigh of relief over that and the final score of both games.

Although Vivi had confided in her older sister, Jacey, that she was dating Lane Kettering, none of their DuVal cousins, aunts, or uncles had been allowed in on the secret. With so many relatives, it was too much of a risk. If word leaked out into the gossip stream in Henderson, it would surely work its way over to Oxford. So Lane wasn't able to attend the huge DuVal family Thanksgiving Hale and Genevra Evans hosted at their palatial estate, but he did pick Vivi up bright and early the next morning and drove the two of them out of town.

They were sitting in a booth, enjoying an early lunch in downtown Raleigh when Lane asked Vivi how she was enjoying living her dream.

"My dream?" She blinked. "Oh, you mean, teaching."

"Unless you've been secretly harboring a dream about abstinence."

"No, no. Abstinence I could do without. Of course, secretly dating the star running back of the Warriors is like a dream come true. Turns out I'm pretty good at living my dreams."

Lane smiled before taking a bite of his bacon cheeseburger. He swallowed, wiped his mouth with his napkin, and asked, "What about your dream of graduate school?"

"For some reason, I've been solely focused on the date May sixteenth. Haven't thought too much beyond that."

"Apparently The University of Notre Dame has a highly rated Masters in Education program."

Vivi sat back. Shocked. "Notre Dame?"

Lane nodded his head.

"Notre Dame in Indiana?"

Lane nodded his head again.

"In the middle of nowhere, Indiana where it snows and is cold and miserable all winter?"

Lane laughed. "Yeah. Notre Dame."

Vivi slammed her palms down on the table. "Why the hell would I want to go to—" She stopped herself abruptly. "Football," she breathed. "Lane? What are you saying? Is this about football? Is Notre Dame recruiting you? Are *you* going to Notre Dame?"

Lane's smile was full of excitement and pride and hope and eagerness when he said, "That's my dream."

Vivi immediately burst into tears. "Oh my God. I'm horrible," she sobbed. "I have never once asked you about your dream. I have never once asked you about your dream school. And you've done nothing but support my dream from that first night we met." She shook her head sadly. "Lane, I am not worthy of you. I thought you wanted to play football in North Carolina. Please," she said, reaching over, sniffing, pulling his hand into both of hers, "start from the beginning and tell me all about your dream."

So he did.

Lane had a big dream, and it poured out of him. Easy, happy, excited. He told Vivi how he didn't mention Notre Dame on purpose. How he didn't mention it to anyone except his dad. She found out he'd been a Notre Dame fan for years. It started when he was eight, because he liked the mascot—the leprechaun—and they had worn green jerseys the first time he'd seen them play. He became a die-hard fan when he researched all their football lore. Had seen the movie Rudy a dozen times at least. But Notre Dame recruited the nation's best, so he never anticipated one of their recruiting coaches showing up, wanting to meet Lane Kettering in Oxford, NC.

"I asked him how my name came across his desk, and he told me that Josh McCourt, a computer-science teacher at Henderson, had sent them a video tape. Very professionally done, with all my highlights from past years and the seven-touchdown game that started this season."

"Josh McCourt? I think he's dating my cousin, Molly."

"So the plot thickens, right? Because I don't know this Josh McCourt. But my brother does. Apparently, Josh is from Oxford and was a few years ahead of Tray at Wilson. He's now part of the football coaching staff over in Henderson, but that still didn't explain how or why he put together a video of me and sent it to Notre Dame."

Vivi was wide-eyed. "Oh my gosh. Did you call Josh and ask him?"

"I did. Well, my father did. He called Josh to thank him on my behalf and came to find out that one Jeb DuVal, head of the Henderson High Booster Club, mentioned me to Josh in an effort to get him to help the defense defend against me. So Josh gathered film and started looking at what I could do. He liked what he saw, and being as he felt a little badly he was helping Wilson's arch rival try to defeat his alma mater, he decided to ease his conscience by making a recruiting tape of me and sending it out to the top twenty football programs in the country."

"You are kidding!"

"I am not," Lane laughed. "S.B., your father had a hand in making my dream come true. I signed a letter of intent yesterday at the Thanksgiving table."

"Oh my goodness, Lane. Lane! This is…amazing. I'm so happy for you."

"I'm happy for me too. Even if I'm going to the middle of nowhere Indiana where it snows and is freezing all winter."

"Ahhhh," Vivi groaned, hanging her head and laughing. "I'm sorry. So sorry. I didn't mean it. I just, I didn't know. Forgive me."

"Sleeping Beauty, you can make it up to me by at least looking into their graduate programs. Because as much as I'm getting used to you being my statistics teacher, I've got a big fantasy in my head that goes right along with my football dream. One where you and I are finally on equal footing—students together on the same campus."

Vivi tipped her head to the side and sighed, looking at the gorgeous, rugged, sexy, beard-scruffled man in front of her. "If you stay healthy, I could have a masters and a doctorate by the time you graduate."

"Always good to have a dream," Lane said with a smile.

CHAPTER TWENTY

The Annual Devine-Kampmueller New Year's Eve Ball held at the Henderson Country Club was the premier social event of the season. Vivi didn't want to miss it, but she didn't want to go without Lane either. So she asked "her attorney," the newly married Piper Beaumont Evans, to ask her husband, Vance, to ask his buddy at Henderson Country Club—one cute-cute Harry the Bartender—to hire Lane to work that night.

With all the gossip being bandied around Henderson about Darcy Bennett's wedding, Annabelle Devine's engagement, and her Aunt Genevra's enormous baby bump, Vivi mistakenly thought that no one would notice Lane Kettering. It turned out he was the biggest celebrity of the night.

Everyone had seen him play and heard he'd signed with Notre Dame. The fact that he was no longer a threat to Henderson's team made him embraceable, one of their own, even. The boy next door, so to speak. Vivi was disgusted. Sort of. She really didn't mind all the men shaking his hand and wanting to hear his stories, but the girls— oh my. You'd think they'd never seen a gorgeous, sandy-haired, green-eyed, gifted athlete before. Where Lane seemed to be old hat when he walked the halls of Wilson, he was the hot new guy in Henderson. And there was competition from women way older than Vivi lining up to get his attention. Not to mention the screaming, giggly, totally annoying, high school girls who did not stop knocking each other out of the way to order a non-alcoholic drink from Lane. Because that's where Harry had put him. Right behind the teenagers' bar.

Thank you, Harry.

Vivi huffed and puffed and left the bar area so she wouldn't be caught staring at Lane. She sighed, wishing she'd had the forethought to realize that while all of Henderson was here at the moment, she and Lane could have been anywhere else in town, together, and no one would have been the wiser.

In an effort to make the best of a bad situation—one that she herself had created—she danced, had pictures taken with friends and family, and then circled up with Lolly and all of her DuVal cousins to dish the latest gossip.

Vivi was dying to tell them about Lane and had drifted off into a fantasy of finally being able to share that news with them come May when her youngest cousin Tinley—a senior at Henderson High— arrived in their midst and announced that Lane Kettering would be giving her a ride home that night.

Not. Likely.

Annnd over my dead body, Vivi thought.

But the rest of the DuVal cousins thought this was the best idea ev-vver. Oh, they gushed, what an adorable couple the two of them would make. And wouldn't it just be fabulous if Tinley started dating the gorgeous rock-star quarterback from across town?

Across town? When did Oxford become "across town?" And Lane wasn't the damn quarterback for God's sake.

They went on, saying Tinley would then be bringing Lane to all the DuVal family functions. And wouldn't that be fun to have him there where they could all drool over him, and feel his bulging biceps, and…

No. No, that would not be fun.

At. All.

Vivi needed to derail this. Fast. She couldn't let her cousins get excited about Tinley and Lane when she wanted them to eventually be thrilled about Vivi and Lane. But the thought of telling seven women between the ages of seventeen and thirty her biggest secret and then expecting the news to be kept quiet—she didn't trust it could happen. Didn't trust that it wouldn't unintentionally derail everything she and Lane had sacrificed to keep their relationship under wraps. So she kept her mouth shut. When one of them began to ask the inevitable question of, "Vivi, you teach at his school. Do you know Lane?" she backed away pretending she hadn't heard.

Vivi strolled out of the ballroom, into the spacious hallway separating it from the bar and grill area, deciding she needed a few moments of quiet. She headed to the right and down a set of stairs toward the locker rooms located on the lower level. At the end of the stairs she sat down, feeling defeated.

Her beautiful new ball gown was green. Like the Irish leprechaun Lane loved. Her hair was down and curled because he loved that too. She fingered the pretty gold and green-enamel shamrock pendant he'd given her for Christmas.

They were fine, she told herself. Another four months, give or take a few days, and it would be over. This pretending. Pretending she wasn't crazy about one of her students—pretending she wasn't committing the ultimate taboo. Just the thought of it made her head hurt. She tried to be a good person. Lane was the ultimate good person. The two of them didn't deserve to be tangled up in semantics, with the possibility of inadvertently tying everyone else around them up in semantics.

Tinley.

Of course, she'd be interested in Lane. Hadn't she heard that Tinley had been caught running around the boys' locker room at Henderson High before the school year even started? Tinley was no better or worse than some of her boy-crazy cheerleaders.

She's just like me, Vivi thought. She couldn't blame her seventeen-year-old cousin for finding nineteen-year-old Lane desirable. He was very desirable.

But to Vivi, he was so much more.

She heard pounding on the steps behind her. Startled, she jumped to her feet and turned just as Lane leaped down the last four steps and looked her over head to toe, surprised, concerned, worried even.

"What?" she said, trying not to notice how gorgeous he was in his rented tuxedo shirt with the shirt sleeves all rolled up. His bow tie was askew and his hair was unkempt, but perfectly so. His eyes were glistening, his heart pounding by the pulse of the vein in his neck. He looked around them, listening up and down the hallway, licking his lips.

"Harry told me there was an emergency down here."

"An emergency? What kind of emergency? I haven't seen anything. No smoke. No fire. No burst pipes."

Lane cocked his head and fastened his gaze onto hers. "But you're here. At the bottom of the steps. Right where Harry told me to look. Are you the emergency?"

"I'm hardly an emergency," she said, flustered.

"But you're here. Alone. In the dark."

"It's not that dark."

"Vivi, the party is upstairs. And you're not. What gives?"

She shrugged her shoulders and turned to wander farther down the hallway. Lane followed behind. "I just…I just needed a little space. I…" She turned and told him the truth. "My cousin, Tinley, announced to all of us that you are driving her home from the party tonight."

"Who's Tinley?" Lane looked confused.

Vivi smiled. "My cousin. She's a senior at Henderson. Apparently the newest member of the Lane Kettering Fan Club, and I'm guessing she's plotting a way to get you to drive her home."

"Fat chance," Lane said. "I'm here solely to intercept whoever tries to kiss you at midnight."

"Is that why you agreed to do this?"

"Why else?" he laughed.

"I don't know. I guess in my head I pictured this all differently. But the truth is I just wished it could go differently. I wish we could be here, together. Dancing."

"Hmm," he said, tilting his head toward the side. "Maybe I can make that wish come true." He pulled a key from his pocket and held it up. "Harry said this might come in handy." He took Vivi's hand and led her down a corridor, where the music from the band got louder and clearer. He pushed the key into a lock and opened the door leading into a small exercise room. He turned on the light, looked around at the treadmills and weights and then looked up at the ceiling. "Hold on." He dragged over one of the weight benches, stood on the top of it and opened a vent in the ceiling. The music from above flowed through. He smiled down at Vivi. "Emergency thwarted."

"I'm not the emergency."

"I'm pretty sure you are." Lane jumped down, walked over, and hit the lights. Then he locked the door from the inside.

Vivi's heart stuttered. "Lane," she whispered. His name came out full of emotion. And she realized it right then. She, indeed, was the emergency.

"We're just going to dance," he said quietly, moving in her direction. "You don't have to worry. We aren't going to break any rules. Just…dance. And I might kiss you," he said, taking her into his arms. "You know, the kind of kiss I'd give my grandmother."

Vivi laid her head against his chest, feeling such gratitude. Another case where he changed from a nineteen-year-old high school jock into her perfect hero. "Lane, you always, always know just what I need. I love you," she whispered.

"Well, now you've done it."

Vivi tilted her head up and peered at Lane. "What?"

"S.B., I've waited eight long months to hear you say those three little words. Kissing you like my grandmother just isn't going to cut it." His hand slid up into her hair. But she stopped him from leaning down to kiss her with a hand against his chest.

"This cannot be news to you," she said.

"You have never said the words."

"Because I'm a teacher," she insisted.

"None of those statutes said you couldn't tell me you love me. So, say it again," he demanded. "And then shut up and kiss me…like I'm…your brother."

They both started laughing.

"Oh—this is ridiculous," Vivi said as they moved to sit side by side on the weight bench. She leaned her head against his shoulder. He took one of her hands and started playing with her fingers.

"It's not going to last forever, Viv. I miss kissing you, I do. You know, like I want to. I really miss touching you in all those places I can't touch you. Because a lot of those places are soft and sweet and smell good. Just thinking about those places gets me hot—and makes me think about when you get hot. Hot and woozy. And then, you know, it's like the snowball effect because I just get hotter thinking about how hot you get and…okay, this isn't helping." Lane took a deep breath and blew it out. "What I'm trying to say, is that having to keep our hands to ourselves has forced me to appreciate you in ways I might have missed otherwise. I know this student/teacher thing is painful in a lot of ways. I mean for me, at first, I had to work hard not to let feelings of inferiority damage our relationship. Because being younger than you bugs the shit out of me anyway, and then add the teacher crap on top of that…"

"You like being the boss," she said.

"I do. I really do. I especially like being the boss of you." He laughed. "But I got over myself and finally joined your class in mind as well as body. And lo and behold, under all your curves and curls and lips and that sensational ass, there's talent and poise and generosity and wisdom. You teach…all of us," he said. "Every single one of us. With you, it's like no man is going to be left behind. You're the Marine Corp of math teachers. You love the subject. You want us to love the subject. And if you can't get everybody to love the subject, at least you work them into some form of appreciation for it. I was sitting in class the other day laughing at one of your jokes, looking around the class seeing everybody awake, attentive, and engaged in a seventh-period Statistics class. And I thought to myself, that's magic. You bring the magic. And then I thought about how great school would be if all teachers had your magic."

"Maybe all teachers start out with magic."

"Maybe. Maybe they start out more enthusiastic their first year than the next. Or maybe their lives get busy or start to hurt and the magic drifts away. I don't know. But what I'm trying to tell you, Vivi DuVal, is that this situation you and I are in? It's not all bad. I get to watch you do your thing and get to know a side of you I never would have if you weren't teaching at Wilson this year."

"And I've had a helluva time watching you do your thing, number eleven. All the way to the semi-finals of the playoffs."

"Where we got rolled."

"Definitely a bit of a shock."

"At least we lost to the champs."

"Wilson's best team ever. Division Champs. And how many personal school records?"

"Are you trying to coax me into kissing you, Miss DuVal? Because there are rules about that. The girl I love and I are rule followers, so I suggest—"

Vivi shut him up with a kiss.

A loud banging echoed from the door.

"Shit," Vivi whispered.

"Don't panic," Lane whispered back. "It's probably just Harry."

"Lane?" came Tinley's voice as bold as ever. "Lane Kettering, are you down here?" The doorknob rattled, but the lock held. They heard Tinley move off further down the hall, knocking on the men's locker room door. "Lane?" she hollered. It sounded like she'd opened the door and stuck her head inside.

"That's Tinley," Vivi whispered. "The one planning on you driving her home."

"Maybe you should introduce us. Explain our situation."

Vivi shook her head. "It's not that I don't trust her. I'd just rather not entangle anybody else up in this charade if we don't have to."

"Okay. Well, here's the key," Lane said. "I'll go out first and sneak back upstairs, if I can. If I can't, I'll tell her I was having a smoke."

"You don't smoke!"

"She doesn't know that."

"Oh. Okay."

"Lock yourself inside and wait until you are absolutely certain the coast is clear," he said.

"I'll go out the side door down by the parking lot. Then I'll come back in the front. I'll be fine," Vivi said, resigned. "This is so stupid."

"S.B." Lane chuckled. "It sure isn't boring. Come into the bar when you get in. Flip me one of your smiles so I know you're okay."

"Don't let Tinley grab your ass," Vivi grumbled. "I'm not sure she has a lot of boundaries."

Lane pecked her on the cheek, assuring her he could handle himself. They moved to the door, where he stuck his head out and looked both ways. Then he left.

Vivi locked herself inside.

CHAPTER TWENTY-ONE

"Holy Shit!"

Lane smacked his back up against the wall, startled by a busty blonde as he stepped around the corner. So this was Tinley. Quiet, sneaky Tinley. "Jesus, you scared the hell out of me," he shouted. "What the hell?"

"I've been looking for you, Lane Kettering. What are you doing down here?"

"I'm working," he said as he stepped around Tinley and moved toward the stairs.

"Doing what?"

"Checking on the heat."

"Oh." He heard Tinley and her heels follow him up the stairs. "Well, is the heat okay?"

"Yep." Lane hit the top of the stairs and started dodging people to get back to the bar.

"Why are you running?" Tinley yelled at him.

He turned, not wanting to draw attention to them, and waited for her to catch up. "I'm working," he said. "Is there something I can do for you?"

"Yes," she said. "You can give me a ride home when you're done working."

"Why would I do that?"

Tinley blinked up at him. Stunned. Clearly, no guy had ever turned her down before. Lane didn't find that hard to believe, but he did find it amusing. So he folded his arms in front of him and glared at her, hard. "Cat got your tongue?"

"I don't understand the question."

She wasn't lying. She clearly did not understand why a guy like him—my God, what the hell was it about his looks that made him appear to be such a dog—wouldn't be chomping at the bit to drive her home.

"I'm not interested in you," he said before turning and heading back to the mixed grill. Harry waved him over to the adult bar, thank God, and handed him an apron.

"Keep your head down and start washing glasses," Harry said.

"Happy to," Lane said.

"You can't serve alcohol. You're not twenty-one," Harry said.

"Got it." Lane turned around, and there she was. Miss Tinley DuVal, seating herself at the bar. "Harry? Can you sit at the bar if you're not twenty-one?" he asked, hoping to get rid of Tinley.

Harry glanced in Tinley's direction. "She's a member of the club. She can sit wherever she wants. She can even drink alcohol. We just can't serve it to her directly."

"What?"

"Membership has its privileges," Harry shrugged.

"I'm pretty sure her parents are the members."

"So it's up to them if their underage daughter has a sip of alcohol or not."

"Good Lord. No wonder people love it over here in Henderson."

Harry chuckled. "They're good people. Pretty sure you've already realized that though."

Lane looked Harry in the eye. "I don't know what you're talking about."

Harry nodded his head at the smoking hot vision decked out in green walking in the door. "Busted," he said under his breath. "How did you know about *the emergency*?"

"I've got a knack for that sort of thing," Harry said. "Go play your game."

Lane nodded, wiped his hands on the apron, and headed in Vivi's direction. "Miss DuVal," he said, placing a napkin in front of her.

"Happy New Year, Lane," she said, smiling her sweet Sleeping Beauty smile as she seated herself on the barstool next to Tinley. "Have you met my cousin, Tinley?"

Lane looked over at Tinley. "Not formally, no."

"Tinley, this is Lane Kettering. He's in my Statistics class at Wilson. Lane, Tinley is a senior at Henderson this year."

"Do you have a girlfriend over there at Wilson?" Tinley asked.

"I have my eye on somebody," Lane said, smiling back at Vivi. "What can Harry or I get for you two?"

"Champagne," Vivi said.

"Me too," Tinley insisted.

Harry put a glass of champagne in front of Vivi.

Lane gave Tinley a Coke.

"What's this?" she sputtered.

"Rules are rules," Lane told her. "I'm a rule follower," he said proudly. Then he winked at Vivi.

"What's going on with you two?" Tinley asked.

"Nothing," Vivi said. "He knows you're seventeen. You're not getting any alcohol out of him no matter how fast you bat your eyelashes."

"Then order me a shot of rum, Vivi. I'll throw it in my Coke."

"No way. I'm a rule follower too."

"Since when?"

"Since the end of my first week as a teacher," she said, sipping her champagne. "It's an occupational hazard."

"It's made you boring," Tinley sighed.

"It has, indeed," Vivi agreed.

"But she's a helluva statistics teacher," Lane defended.

"You aren't doing her any favors," Tinley said, rolling her eyes. "What could be more boring than teaching math?"

Lane wasn't paying any attention to the words coming out of Tinley's mouth at that point because trouble had just walked in the door and was eyeing Beauty.

His Beauty.

Trouble in the form of light hair with swagger, making a million dollars from the looks of it. That tuxedo was no rental. Neither was his Rolex. Trouble's eyes stopped on Vivi's back and remained set on his target as he strolled forward, reaching a hand out to gently touch her shoulder, turning her attention away from Lane.

"Harv?" he heard Vivi say. And then a breathy, "Oh my goodness," came out of his girl.

What the fuck?

Vivi moved off the bar stool and into Trouble's arms.

Lane stood there, paralyzed, watching, as things went from bad to worse. "Harv," she squealed as Trouble pulled her tight against him and kissed her on the lips.

Oh, hell no.

Vivi pushed away from *Harv*, but she didn't slap his face. Not like Lane had hoped. She just stood back, asking a lot of questions, acting like Harv wasn't six seconds away from being tackled by a running back.

Lane felt a nudge on his back. He looked over his shoulder at Harry, who pointedly looked toward Tinley, who was staring at Lane, open-mouthed.

"What?" he snapped at Tinley.

She leaned up over the bar and accused, "You like her."

Lane's eyes glance over toward Vivi and Harv before coming back and landing on Tinley. "Who the hell is he?"

"Harvard Michaels. Vivi's ex-boyfriend."

"Oh." Lane blinked, feeling a little relief. Then he squinted his eyes. "I thought his name was Kevin."

"Kevin was her boyfriend from Wake, who, it turns out, was gay. Harv Michaels is her boyfriend from high school. Big time baseball player who went off to Stanford and did all right. Definitely not gay."

"Jesus."

Just then, a pretty vision of hope sailed into the picture. Lane and Vivi's attorney, Piper with her yellow blond curls and bright blue eyes held the arm of a man Lane recognized. Vance Evans, coach of the Henderson High baseball team. They interrupted Vivi and her ex's reunion—thank God—with Coach Evans hugging Harvard-the-pompous like he was a long-lost child.

Vivi took that moment to turn toward Lane and send him a pitiful look. He scowled his displeasure and went back to washing glasses. Out of the corner of his eye, he watched as Vivi moved off with her ex and the Evanses, heading to the ballroom. He glanced at his watch—not a Rolex—and was happy to see it was nowhere near midnight. If he had to watch that Stanford asshole kiss his girl again—"

"What's the story?"

Lane turned and found Tinley had moved down the bar, closer to him.

"Story?"

"You and Vivi." Tinley's attitude had gone from flirty teenager, to drill sergeant. "And don't insult my intelligence. I saw what I saw. So unless you want me blabbing about what I saw, because clearly it would make for some great gossip in this town, I suggest you fill me in on the details. Fast."

Lane glanced over toward Harry, who subtly nodded as he pretended to be busy making a drink. Lane took that as a go-ahead.

"I'm interested in Vivi," he said once he'd moved over closer so no one could hear them. "She won't go out with me until I graduate, so I'm biding my time."

"There's probably some big rule about students and teachers."

"There are a lot of big rules about students and teachers. So, unless you want to get your cousin fired, I suggest you keep whatever you think you saw to yourself."

"What I saw was you flipping out that Harv Michaels is back in town."

"I could give a shit about Harv Michaels."

"Isn't Vivi a little old for you?"

"Aren't you a little young for me?"

"Hmm. Okay, point taken. Still. You're waiting around for *her*? When you could have any girl you want?"

"She is the girl I want. Your cousin is beautiful and smart. She knows she has a lot of talent, but knows she's not perfect, either. She's easy, and fun, and funny, and…Jesus! I really shouldn't be telling you this."

"But you have. So, here's how we're going to play it."

"Play it?"

"Let's go dance."

"I'm working."

"Harry," Tinley called. "Can I drag Lane out on the dance floor?"

Harry looked at both of them, thoughtfully. Then he directed his words to Lane. "Put on your jacket, go comb your hair, and blend in with the guests. And you," he said, looking at Tinley, "keep your hands to yourself."

"What is that supposed to mean?" she huffed.

Harry stalked in closer. "You want to help out True Love, I'm all for that. But if you're doing this to mess with your cousin's happiness, then no, you can't drag Lane out on the dance floor."

"Fine," she grumbled at Harry as Lane went to put on his jacket. "But how do you know this is true love?"

"How do you know it isn't?"

"Touché," Lane said, as he came up behind Tinley and took her hand to lead her over to the ballroom.

They walked into a party that was going full tilt. The dance floor was packed, and the band was rocking. Tinley took control and moved them into the center of the crowd where Lane tried not to be too obvious about looking for Vivi.

"Don't worry," Tinley said. "As soon as we spot them, we'll work our way over in their direction."

"How do you know they're on the dance floor? He could have her backed up against the wall somewhere," Lane said, trying not to let the thought panic him.

"Harv Michaels likes to dance. And Vivi's good at it. That's probably the reason he sought her out. Relax. Have fun. You're just a kid for heaven's sake. You having a crush on some teacher seems like a waste."

"She's not just some teacher."

"Fine." Tinley held up her hands and danced around him. "I'm not trying to change your mind or anything." But when she backed into him, Lane wasn't so sure about that. He pushed her off.

"Just. Dancing," he scolded.

"You need a cover. A beard."

"I've done okay without one so far."

"Yes, but if anyone other than me saw the look on your face when Harv kissed Vivi—trust me—your secret would be out."

Lane couldn't disagree. This Harv Michaels and his Rolex had changed the game. Raised the stakes. Lane reached out and took Tinley's hand, twirling her under his arm. He pulled her closer as they danced. "Apparently Vivi was Kevin's beard in college. She definitely didn't like it."

"Yes, but I'm volunteering. Because I love my cousin." Tinley smiled a cheesy smile up at him.

"Hmm. Not sure I believe that."

"We DuVals are close."

"What's in this for you?"

"I get to tell everyone I'm dating Lane Kettering."

"No. Do not blast that we are dating all over Facebook."

"Then you'll come to my prom. As my date."

"Not in a zillion years."

"Your prom, then. You're going to need a cover at your prom. You certainly aren't going to take Vivi."

If he'd heard that once, he'd heard it a thousand times. "Fine. As long as you know I'm not interested in you. If you want to play the part for Vivi's sake, okay. I, ah, am going to need a prom date," he sighed. "Someone who won't flip Vivi out."

"Like you just flipped out over Harv?"

Lane just glared at her.

"I'd be happy to be your prom date," she smirked. "But you need to come over to Henderson High and ask me to it in some big, showy way."

"And let your boyfriend and his gang beat the shit out of me. No, thank you."

"If I had a boyfriend, would I be going to the prom with you?"

"I hope not. There they are," Lane said, pointing in Vivi's direction. "What's your plan?"

"We maneuver ourselves a little closer to them. When a slow song starts, I'll break in to dance with Harv, which trust me, will not be a hardship. That's when you grab Vivi. Now that the two of us have been seen together dancing, no one will think anything of it if you're suddenly dancing with my cousin."

"Humph."

"Trust me. This is good. Better than doing dishes, isn't it?"

"It is," he said, finally giving in and giving Tinley a smile. "Thanks. I think."

There was no slow song. The band was not going to play a slow song. They had the whole party up and moving, so why would they mess with success and kill the crazy party vibe they had going? But Tinley and Lane had moved closer to Vivi. When Lane managed to catch her eye, she grinned at him and seemed happy, maybe relieved, even if they were dancing with different partners. Harv wasn't pressing his attention, so to speak, but swinging Vivi around in jitterbug fashion no matter what song was played. Lane may be no match for Harv on the dance floor, but come hell or high water, at midnight—in about ten minutes—he'd be showing off some moves of his own.

"Kiss Harv at midnight," he told Tinley. "*Really* kiss him. See if you can distract him enough that he forgets about Vivi. And I promise, when it comes time, I'll make a grand public display of asking you to prom."

Tinley's smile was conspiratorial. "I'm only seventeen and he's like twenty-three. A kiss like that might cause a big Henderson scandal."

"Even better," Lane said.

Tinley shrugged. "In for a penny. I'll give it my best shot. Maybe *he'd* be willing to give me a ride home," she scowled.

"Maybe your father or uncles will be willing to give you a ride home," Lane suggested.

"Oh my God. Vivi can have you. You are way too straightlaced for me, Lane Kettering."

Lane laughed. "That's what I've been trying to tell you."

When the countdown to midnight came, Tinley performed beautifully. She pulled Lane over toward Vivi and Harv so that the four of them formed a small circle. She introduced Harv to the star quarterback of the Wilson Warriors—yeah, she had no clue—and then shoved her way between him and Vivi just as the confetti flew. She laid a kiss on Harv the likes of which can only be seen in the movies. Lane grabbed Vivi's hand while the massive crowd was otherwise engaged and dodged through the couples and out of the room. Harry pointed toward a large butler's pantry between the bar and the kitchen and that's where they headed. It was small, quiet, secluded, and Lane would have bet money Harry was now standing guard at the door.

The excitement, the energy, the adventure of it all just poured into their kiss. His hands in her hair, her hands around his back. For the first time in two months, their tongues collided, and the pleasure was so intense it sent off warning shots throughout both of their bodies. They pushed apart, panting.

Lane stared into Vivi's desperate eyes, feeling the same impulse to let themselves go. They were on the verge of breaking the rules. They both knew it. And Lane could see Vivi was struggling with that as much as he was. If he took one step toward her to reengage, he could have her. Right here, right now. Maybe not full-blown intercourse, but he didn't trust himself to stop, even if he wasn't carrying a condom in his pocket.

"Harry, open the door," Lane said.

The door cracked open.

"Wider, please."

The door swung open all the way. Harry was gone.

"I wouldn't have done that," Vivi stated, panting, her eyes wide and horrified. "I didn't want to do that," she said, going into her patent panic attack.

"That's my job, S.B. Saving your ass. It has been since we met. I don't plan to start letting you down now."

"Lane."

"Tell me you love me."

"I love you."

"Good." He smiled. "The new year is looking very promising. In fact, I've already locked in a prom date."

"Tinley?"

"Ah-huh. She caught me plotting to kill ol' Harvey-boy and figured us out pretty quick. Well, not *all* of us. I just told her I was crushin' on my statistics teacher pretty good and had plans to ask her out as soon as I graduate. She claims to want to help. Did a pretty good job of blocking Mr. Rolex from getting his lips on you again." After a moment, Lane said, "Is that guy going to be a problem?"

"No. No, absolutely not. I'm sorry you were stuck watching that reunion, but we're friends. Just friends. If I'd been able to, I would have introduced the two of you right away. He would have probably gotten a kick out of me dating a football player. It wasn't his sport."

"So I hear."

"Harv's a little too Hollywood for me. In fact, he and Tinley might really hit it off."

"Isn't she a little young for him?"

"Are *you* throwing stones?"

Lane laughed. "I guess not."

"Thank you, Lane."

"For what, Sleeping Beauty? Being your guy?"

"Being my guy under these oppressive circumstances."

"Hell. Suddenly I'm dating two of Henderson's infamous DuVal cousins. I look at it this way. If you and I don't work out, I'll probably have enough fodder to write a damn book."

Vivi laughed. "I wish that wasn't so true."

CHAPTER TWENTY-TWO

It was the first week back at school after the holidays when the news broke all over Wilson that Lane Kettering was dating Tinley DuVal from Henderson High.

It came in the form of Tweets, Instagram pictures, Facebook posts—Tinley had gone ahead and changed her relationship status to "in a relationship" and changed her profile picture to the two of them dancing at the New Year's Eve Ball. When that had been taken, Lane hadn't a clue. But from the continuous buzzing from his cell, Lane surmised Tinley DuVal had to be the queen of social media, an expert at getting her message out. And her message was being heard clearly way over in Oxford.

There wasn't one person who didn't mention it when they spoke to Lane that day. He was stuck answering questions he couldn't answer. Stuck "in a relationship" with a girl he now wanted to strangle. When he wrote his note out to Vivi, he said he wanted to kill her cousin and needed her phone number to do it. Then he dialed up Tinley and had a shouting match while walking up and down the middle of the football field in thirty-two degree weather so no one could hear him.

He was livid when he called Vivi that night.

"Well, what did you expect?" Vivi said. "She's in high school."

"What the hell is that supposed to mean? I'm in high school. Hell, you're in high school!"

Vivi laughed. "I really don't think about you being in high school, Lane. I'm sorry," she soothed. "You're so much…more full-blown than a typical high schooler. You're older. You have your act together. You aren't a selfish ass, and you think before you do dumb stuff. You are also acing my class."

"I told you I would," he grumbled. "And that's easy compared to the rest of this bullshit. I feel like I am being swallowed up by the rest of this bullshit, and I don't have football to distract me anymore."

"Well, what's your spring sport?"

"I don't have a spring sport."

"Well, why the hell not? As fast as you run? Are the coaches around here insane? They should be reeling you in to being a fucking pinch hitter for the baseball team. If you can catch a football on the fly, you ought to be able to swing a damn bat."

"What the hell is up with your language, Miss DuVal?"

"Sorry. I'm feeling worked up. And I'm sort of addicted to cheering for you. Secretly. So, fix that will ya? I need something that's going to keep me going until graduation."

"Okay, well, Monday I'll talk to the lacrosse coach. It's a new sport. Nobody's that good at it. How hard could it be for a gifted athlete like myself?" He laughed.

"My thoughts exactly. So what happened with Tinley?"

"Well, she finally came out and told me that she was sorry she outed us on social media, but she had to. Because now I'm *her* beard."

"Excuse me?"

"Yeah. Apparently, you were right, and Hollywood and Tinley did get along rather well on New Year's Eve. Too well. And your uncle is not at all thrilled about it because Hollywood is six years older than she is."

Vivi couldn't say anything, she was laughing too hard.

"I'm glad you're finding all this amusing. Now Tinley wants me to go meet your damn uncle and pretend to actually be dating her, when your father knows the truth—that I'm dating you. You need to talk to him about this S.B. I am not risking your father's wrath over Tinley's nonsense."

"Oh, Lane," she sighed. "This is getting to be a little more complicated than we planned."

"Tell me about it."

"Well, hasn't Harvard left town? Why is this still a problem?"

"Apparently Hollywood is talking about moving back to Henderson. There's some project going on that he wants to be involved in. So he and Tinley are not calling it quits. Or at least, Tinley is hoping that once she graduates, they'll be able to date out in the open."

"Hmm. Sounds like a couple I know."

"And frankly, if that jackass is moving back to North Carolina, I wouldn't mind him being tangled up with Tinley. Keep his damn mouth off you. That is why I am catering to your cousin's whims. She needs my help, and on top of that, she knows too much. But right now so do I, so I've got her cooperation. Or, she's got mine. Something. It's all very debatable."

"More fodder for your book," Vivi teased.

"You are not kidding. You and your cousins are like…a mess."

"You're the reason I'm a mess," she shouted. "You and your suntanned abs. You think I needed some he-man walking into my life and fixing every little thing for me back at the beach?"

"Yes."

"Well…you're right. And you've done that and more. And I love you for it," Vivi said. "I'm snuggling down under my covers, wishing you were here."

Lane had been pacing around his bedroom freaking out up to that point. But when he heard her words, he stopped fast, letting everything settle around him. He pulled off his shirt, toed off his shoes, relinquished his pants and joined her in bed. "You remember what Ms. Beaumont said, right?" he asked Vivi. "We couldn't Skype sexy, but there were no statutes about talking sexy."

"Mmm," Vivi said, her voice going all soft.

Lane hit the lights. God, he was a lucky son of a bitch.

"When I first saw you on the beach, S.B., I nearly had a heart attack. It was like you'd been all laid out on a towel at my feet, waiting for me to trip over. Literally a gift from the gods."

"When I first opened my eyes, I saw your ankle. It was trim and sexy and athletic."

"And that bow sitting so sweet on top of your round, silky smooth, perfect ass. God, Viv, I got so hard staring at you. And when

I thought you were topless, well, I really needed to go for a run. But all I could think about was you and your ass."

"Is that why you had your hands on my ass within five minutes that night in the parking lot?"

"Guilty as charged. And at the time, I was sort of horrified by that. My body went on autopilot. But if I remember correctly, you didn't seem to mind. I believe the words you used were *life affirming*."

"Mmmmm."

"Sleeping Beauty…are you…touching yourself?"

"Am I under oath?" she sighed. "It's been a long time since I felt your…*life-affirming* apparatus."

"Well, it's feeling pretty life affirming right now. And under oath, I'd have to admit, I am touching said apparatus."

"Does it feel good?"

"When you're whispering in my ear like that, it feels damn good."

"I love you, Lane."

"I love you, too, Miss DuVal."

"You're gonna have to call me Dr. DuVal after five years at Notre Dame together."

"If we last five years at Notre Dame together, I'll be calling you Dr. Kettering."

He could hear her faint giggle. "That has a nice ring to it."

"Just another one of my big dreams," he said.

CHAPTER TWENTY-THREE

January was cold and miserable, except for the Skype sessions Vivi and Lane held every night. Those video chats had a way of keeping things warm, if not downright hot. Careful not to cross any statute lines, they tried to convince themselves they were in the home stretch. Vivi enjoyed hearing the antics of her cousin Tinley. Apparently, she was hell-bent on getting Lane to meet her father and attend a Henderson party so she could prove to everyone they were, indeed, dating.

Lane enjoyed reminding Tinley that they were not, indeed, dating, so she needed to get over herself.

As much as Vivi worried that this could damage Lane's relationship with her cousin forever—even after all of the various charades finally came to an end—she could tell Lane was starting to enjoy bantering with Tinley, thinking of her a little less as a flighty blonde and a little more like a friend.

And Tinley was keeping their secret, as it was serving her own self interest too. She was a high school student after all.

On Valentine's Day, Vivi baked heart-shaped cookies for her Statistics class—because it was the last class of the day, of course. And Lam got all kinds of ribbing for presenting her with a heart-shaped box of chocolates. "What?" he said. "Miss DuVal is hot," he defended. "And I need to pass this class."

March came in like a lion with a rare North Carolina snowstorm, but by the fifth, the Wilson Warriors' brand new lacrosse team was on the field and scrimmaging any school who would line up against them. Lacrosse was new in this part of North Carolina, but it didn't take long for all of the football and soccer players Lane had rounded up to look like they knew what they were doing.

Stopping by to watch their games was a little bit more challenging for *Miss DuVal* since the stands were not full. In fact, they were empty. She stood on the side of the bleachers, half hidden, watching as Lam was forced to play goalie simply because he was big enough to cover most of the goal. His hand-eye coordination was terrible at the beginning of the month, but by the end of the month, he was making more saves than the goals that snuck by.

Mr. L. came out to watch the team. At least that was his cover. He and Vivi chatted about the rules briefly, commented on the speed of the game, and together agreed that Notre Dame's lacrosse coach might be tempted to steal their redshirt running back next year. Lane was a natural and seemed to love the game.

"I'd like an opportunity to sit down with you and discuss your contract for next year, Vivi."

"Oh. Mr. Levendusky. I'm certainly not expecting you to renew my contract."

"I'd like to. I really would. You've been an exemplary first-year teacher. Other than that previous relationship we've had hanging over our heads, I couldn't ask for a more efficient, easy-going, helpful, and well-liked staff member."

"Mr. L.," Vivi sighed. "Your words mean a lot to me. They really do. But you and I both know that once Lane graduates, the wonderful parents here at Wilson High won't want me coming back."

"So you two are still planning to be an item. I would have thought the infatuation might die out, under the circumstances."

"I understand. We're both young," she said, glancing back at the game.

"Have you heard from Notre Dame?"

Vivi eyed her principal. "You know about my application?"

"I know everything that goes on around here."

"Oh," she smiled. "Of course." Then she began to laugh. "That seems like a rather heavy burden, though. Knowing *everything*."

"Don't I know it."

They went back to watching the game.

Finally, Vivi voiced what she had yet to say out loud. "I've been waitlisted."

"Oh? Well, that's too bad. I'm sure Mr. Kettering is disappointed."

"He doesn't know yet."

There was a moment of silence between them with just the sounds of the game going on in the background. Then Mr. Levendusky turned to her and wondered, "Why didn't you ask me to write a recommendation?"

"I didn't want to put you in an awkward situation."

"I could have written an honest and glowing review. You've performed brilliantly and under a good bit of emotional distress. This couldn't have been easy on you. But you've done everything I've asked of you and then some. I'd be happy to send a letter on your behalf now. In fact, let me do a little research to see if I have a connection there."

Vivi gave her mentor a smile. "I'd be grateful, sir."

"And I'd like to hold your contract open for a while longer. Just to give us both some options."

Vivi probably should have told him right then that she wasn't going to change her mind about Lane. And keeping their relationship under wraps after he graduated was not an option. She really had grown to love her job and the kids she taught. But at this point, her nerves were strung out and brittle. Keeping her hands off Lane had started to feel cruel and unnatural. And although she understood the position she was in legally, the real crime was how much it was starting to tear them apart. The two of them had given up a lot, and their months of celibacy were wearing thin. She saw it in Lane's eyes and felt it in every fiber of her body the night they sat in his parents' media room watching a movie, celebrating St. Patrick's Day, and being *Irish*.

There were plenty of places in the world where she could teach. But only one place where she'd be judged.

Still, options were options. And being put on the waiting list for Notre Dame had narrowed hers.

"Thank you, sir," she said. "For everything."

Once the warmth of spring arrived, everyone wanted to be outside. Besides the growing chatter about prom dates and dresses, and the finagling of graduation party dates because—God forbid—best friends wouldn't be able to attend each other's parties, the interest in Wilson's lacrosse team soared. And why not? It was action packed and full of laughs as the lacrosse newbies tried to work out the kinks. There were no expectations for the team, and the atmosphere was more like a party, both on the field and in the stands.

The third Friday in April, Tinley arrived at a Warriors lacrosse game wearing a very high hemline and a very low neckline. She had five friends in tow, all variations of blond, each one prettier than the next. And all of them showing off a whole lot of skin. While Vivi sat at the top of the stands in her "buttoned-up teacher clothes" as Lane called them, she felt her age for the first time ever. Seventeen was fresh and carefree, while twenty-one was tired, stressed out, and feeling a little hopeless.

The seniors had voted for the teachers they most wanted to chaperone the prom, and Vivi was voted in as first alternate. The other staff members told her that was high praise since it was only her first year and most students didn't even know her. Whoopee, she thought begrudgingly. First alternate. Unless somebody got sick, she would not be chaperoning the prom.

Probably all for the best, Vivi thought as she watched Tinley make a spectacle of herself in the middle of the stands, waving frantically to get Lane's attention.

Was I that annoying back in high school? Vivi wondered. Probably. There wasn't much she'd heard come out of her cheerleaders' mouths that she didn't remember thinking or voicing at one time or another. And so often, that thought had made her cringe. Girls were girls were girls, she supposed. She just hoped she'd be able to handle herself with a little more decorum in the stands at Notre Dame. If she ever made it into the stands at Notre Dame.

Yeah, that conversation hadn't been pleasant. Lane had been so patient with all of this, but that patience was wearing very thin right now. Even though their nightly Skype sessions were fun and sweet and seemed to go well, the limited times they managed to be alone together were becoming stilted and strained. Finally, Lane had admitted he was afraid to touch her. That every time he tried, she'd pull away. And that realization broke her heart. Because she was sending mixed signals. Of course she was. And he understood it intellectually. But, emotionally, Vivi worried it was tearing them apart.

Because they couldn't cuddle, or kiss, or even hold hands like normal couples. And the physical tension between them was like static electricity. When Lane said he felt like if he got too close he'd explode, Vivi knew exactly what he meant.

So telling him she'd not been admitted to Notre Dame, something Lane had refused to consider, didn't go well. They'd spent a lot of time imagining how different life would be for them "next year." And now, well...

And since their May sixteenth birthday celebration in Myrtle Beach had to be postponed when they realized graduation wasn't until May 30th, it just seemed like their situation was never going to end.

Six weeks to go, and Vivi felt defeated.

When the game ended, she watched Lane and his teammates line up to shake hands with the opposing team. Vivi stood, eager for his helmet to come off, eager for him to find her in the stands and gift her with his smile. But this time, the moment his helmet came off, Tinley was there, throwing herself into his arms and pulling his head down for a kiss. It wasn't necessarily a loooong kiss, although time really seemed to stand still as Vivi watched it. Tinley was making a show of her and Lane for her friends, Vivi was sure. Still, the emotional punch Vivi felt watching her cousin kiss Lane vibrated throughout her system.

She had to sit down.

And watch.

Maybe Lane tried to find her in the stands. Maybe it looked like he was scolding Tinley right before he began playing the part of her boyfriend, letting Tinley take his arm and lead him over to her friends. He definitely looked adorable, even sweat-covered with his hair askew, smiling and chatting with the blondes from Henderson.

They would love Lane. How could they not? And they would all envy Tinley. Just as Vivi did at that moment.

As the crowd dispersed around them, Vivi heard Lane introduce Lam and a couple of his other teammates to Tinley and her friends. There was a discussion about a party that night. A bonfire back in an old tobacco field, way off the radar. Lam had a truck that could get them out there. They'd bring lawn chairs and coolers. The girls talked about snacks.

Vivi watched and listened as plans were made, as the flirting began, and as Tinley kept touching Lane. She couldn't decide if she wanted to weep over the fact that she couldn't be included in their plans or that she'd thrown away her last year of being a student, or that the chasm that separated her and Lane at this moment made her look at the one thing she'd refused to see.

Vivi DuVal was an adult, an educator, and a professional.

Lane Kettering was still in high school.

CHAPTER TWENTY-FOUR

"Miss DuVal," Lane called out, because he'd had enough of Tinley's crap. Every head turned in Vivi's direction. They hadn't noticed her sitting alone at the top of the stands. "Care to join us tonight? I hear Henderson girls can be a handful. Might be a good idea if they had a little adult supervision," Lane joked.

"Who's that?" one of Tinley's friends asked.

"That's Tinley's cousin," Lane said. "Hottest teacher in the school. Tinley, ask her to come."

"Yeah," Lam agreed. "Ask her to come."

"She's not going to want to come," Tinley said. "She's a teacher. She *can't* come."

"Says who? Besides, I thought all you DuVal cousins partied together."

"We do, but…that's family stuff."

"How 'bout it, Miss DuVal?" Lane said as Vivi approached, coming down the stands slowly, smiling at him. God, he loved her smile. Especially this one. It was the one that conveyed loud and clear that he was still her hero. Good to know after that kiss her cousin planted on him. Freaking little ingrate.

"I'd love to come," she said. Lane had to laugh at the horrified looks around him. "But I've got a late date tonight, so…no thank you."

"A date?" Lane asked.

"A late date," she said.

"Sounds interesting."

"I'm hoping so."

"It's not Mr. Liskey, is it?" Lam asked. "I've seen the way he looks at you."

"Lambert Weber, how does Mr. Liskey look at me?"

"Like you're a rib-eye steak, coming off the grill all hot and juicy."

Lane smacked Lam as Vivi burst with laughter. "He does not," she denied.

"Does too," both Lane and Lam claimed together.

"Hmm, maybe he'll ask me to prom," Vivi teased, all wide-eyed and excited. "Nice game, gentlemen. Have a good weekend everybody." Then she lowered her best bossy-teacher stare at her cousin. "Be good, Tinley."

Lane watched her go, admiring her backside in those stretchy black pants. When he turned his attention back to Tinley, he found her seething. "What?" he asked.

"You asked a teacher? To come to a bonfire?"

"She's your cousin. It would have been rude not to."

"And she's hot," Lam added.

"There is that," Lane said.

Tinley was not appreciating them mooning over their statistics teacher in front of her friends. She deserved it and more, ambushing him like this. But she was Vivi's cousin, and the two of them were striving to become friends…and she could out them, maybe, if he didn't play nice, so Lane decided to cut her a break.

"Come here," he said, pulling Tinley in for a wet, sweaty hug. She and her lack of clothing deserved that too. "Tonight will be fun. We keeping this small or are we telling the world?"

"Small's good. Gives us Henderson girls a chance to meet your Wilson friends."

"All right. My friends are looking forward to meeting you, too," he said, feeling generous. He'd text her his personal list of rules and regulations later. "Am I picking you up?"

"That'd be nice."

"Is your father going to be there?"

"Maybe."

Lane sighed inwardly. Little Miss Tinley was going to get her way come hell or high water. Hollywood had his work cut out for him with this one.

"Eight o'clock?"

"I'll be ready. Do you need my address?"

"Nope," Lane said. When she got all smug and pleased about that, he added, "I'll just ask your cousin."

"You need to stop it with all this cousin crap," Tinley scolded Lane as they walked through the field toward the makings of a bonfire.

"And *you* need to keep your lips as far from mine as humanly possible."

"Hah!"

"I'm not kidding. I did not appreciate you trying to suck face with me in front of Vivi."

"You need to get over her. She's older than you for God's sake. She's a teacher!"

"And Hollywood is an asshole."

"Hollywood?"

"Harv-ard Mich-aels," Lane enunciated.

"You're jealous," Tinley smirked. "You're jealous of me and Harv."

"If I'm jealous, it's of whatever happened between Harv and Vivi."

Tinley put a hand out, stopping their progression.

"What?" Lane asked, exasperated.

"Look, I'm sorry," Tinley said. "I'm sorry about kissing you in front of Vivi. I didn't know she was there."

"How does that matter?"

"I was playing it up for my friends. They've been dying to meet you since New Year's Eve and since you wouldn't come to me, I had to bring them to you."

"Our agreement was for prom. My prom. It did not include Facebook posts or meeting your friends."

"Yes, but then *I* needed a cover and figured what could it hurt? So please, don't embarrass me with any more public acclamations about how hot my cousin is."

"Fine," he snapped.

"Fine," she snapped back.

They continued walking.

"I thought dating Lane Kettering was going to be so much more exciting," Tinley sighed.

"Well, if we were actually dating, I'd care about what you thought."

"Okay, seriously. We need a truce. I mean, if we're stuck in this together, we may as well make the most of it, right?"

"Fine," he grumbled.

Tinley huffed, twirled, and stomped away.

"What'd I say?" Lane asked, walking off after her.

"Yeah, so it started off pretty rocky," Lane told Vivi on the phone later that night. "Bossy has met its match with your cousin. She was setting up chairs, dictating where people should sit, even told Jamie how to arrange the wood for the bonfire. I thought I was going to have to gag her to prevent Lam and Jamie from tying her up and burning her at the stake."

Vivi laughed.

"But once the fire was blazing, and she got half a beer in her, she dialed herself back. She's actually quite funny when she's not telling people what to do."

"She really is funny."

"Oh! I wish you'd seen this. I don't know how it started—I think some music came on—but all of a sudden Lam and Tinley started doing that old cheerleading skit from Saturday Night Live. One of them started doing some cheer dance and the other joined in, and the next thing you know they were feeding off of each other until they had the rest of us in tears we were laughing so hard."

"Wait. I cannot imagine Lam doing a cheer routine," Vivi said.

"I know. That's why it was so funny. *I* had no idea he could do that. He and Tinley definitely bonded over that."

"Well that's good, I guess."

"And her friends were nice too. Sort of reminded me of your friends at the beach. Everybody got along, and because the group was relatively small, everybody got to know each other pretty good. I wouldn't be surprised if there are a few more Henderson girls invited to Wilson's prom."

"That'd be nice for Tinley," Vivi said.

"And make the evening easier on me," Lane claimed. "I wouldn't say I'm dreading prom, but your cousin is a handful and a flirt."

"She was flirting with you?"

"Not me. Everybody but me. Which I have to say was a little bit awkward, since I'm the one she's supposed to be dating. All the guys are looking at me like…is this okay?"

"Is what okay?"

"She sat on everybody's *lap*, Viv. And with the music blaring, in more cases than not, it turned into a lap dance."

"What? Please tell me you're joking."

"I wish I were. But, don't get too freaked out. It wasn't really as bad as it sounds. Everyone was having a good time. And she wasn't the only girl sitting on laps. Or dancing."

"Oh, Lane, I'm sorry."

"Sorry for what? If this is my penance for getting Tinley to intervene with you and Hollywood, I'm happy to suffer a few fake dates. After all, I did get to kiss you at midnight."

"That feels like a long time ago."

"It was. Too long ago. So, look. I've got to go over to Henderson and invite Tinley to the prom next week. In my desperation to keep Hollywood's lips off yours, I promised a big, showy invite. And she's holding me to that. So I want you to be there."

"I'm not going over to my alma mater to watch you invite my cousin to the prom."

"Why not? It's all about you, you know. I might be asking her, but the big, showy invite is really…for you," he said, meaning it.

"I've never had a big, showy invite. What are you planning?"

"Well, you know how Henderson is all about their totally obnoxious state championship winning baseball team?"

"Yes," she laughed.

"With the help of my new best friend, Josh McCourt, I am commandeering their fancy electronic score board."

"Josh the geeky teacher/football coach? The one that's dating my cousin, Molly?"

"The very same. I met him at the New Year's Eve party. Thanked him for putting that recruiting tape together for me. He's a big Lane Kettering fan."

"Isn't everybody?"

"Not everybody in Henderson. I called him, and he's helping me out during the varsity game this week. Unlike our lacrosse games, they draw a big crowd. Tinley will be there."

"So is the score board going to be flashing her name?"

"I'm leaving the details up to Josh. He said he'd make it good, seeing as Tinley is Molly's cousin. I'm a little worried that I'm getting in deep with your extended family because of this Tinley thing. What is going to happen when we finally tell them the truth?"

"I don't know," Vivi said, laughing. "I just hope we get that far."

"What do you mean, hope? I'm not jumping through all these hoops for nothing, S. B. You are going to have to claim me publicly the moment I have that damn diploma in my hand."

"We are not claiming anything while you're holding your diploma. We are going to meet in Myrtle Beach for our long, very much anticipated weekend. And after that, we are going to live our lives normally. But you're right. We may have to make an announcement at a DuVal family event. Explain a few things so my uncles don't think you've dumped one cousin for another. But other than that, we aren't making any grand announcements or proclamations. I'm certain that the news about us will spread all on its own, and rapidly."

"Yeah, I've got a different plan."

"Lane, I'm not going to be able to come back to work at Wilson next year when this gets out. But I'd like to be able to work somewhere."

"Yeah, like in Indiana. South Bend, Indiana."

"You think I'm going to follow you out to godforsaken South Bend?" Vivi laughed.

"If you don't, I'll just have to transfer to some lousy football program in North Carolina and give up my big dream."

"Don't be ridiculous."

"Start sending applications to South Bend. Or at least, consider it. I'm still not giving up hope that you're coming off that waiting list."

"That makes one of us."

"If all goes well, I'm going to be living in South Bend for five years. You've got plenty of time to get into that program."

"I know. It will all work out."

"That sounded kind of forced."

"Did it?" He heard her sigh. "It's starting to feel forced. A little bit. Maybe I'm just tired."

"It's three in the morning. If you drag that sweet ass of yours out of bed and look out the window, I'll let you get some sleep."

"What? Have you been outside this whole time?"

Lane saw her window open. He shut down his phone and got out of his dad's hot rod, watching Vivi's pretty hair fall around her shoulders as she leaned out of the window.

"Lane," she whispered.

"Sleeping Beauty," he whispered back, coming to stand underneath her window.

"You're like my Romeo. Can you climb up here?"

"I'd have to be more like Spiderman to scale the side of your house."

"I'll come down. Wait."

Lane smiled as her head ducked back in the house. *She was coming down.* Then she popped back out. "I can't believe we've been talking on the phone while you've been here the whole time." She left then, and he went to meet her at the side door.

"I wasn't dropping Tinley off two streets over and not doing a drive-by," he said when she opened the door.

"I'd sneak you into my room but then there'd be cops knocking on the front door at daybreak."

"Your dad might not appreciate that. How 'bout we just sit out on the porch a minute."

"Isn't this past curfew?"

"My parents pretend not to notice these days."

"Why?"

"Good grades. Record-breaking season. Admission into Notre Dame. And, ah, what's the other one? Oh, yeah. They know I'm in love with a girl I can't get pregnant."

Vivi burst out laughing.

Lane pulled her into his arms, and man, oh, man, she went with it, folding him up in her own. "That feels good," he whispered into her hair. "I've missed you touching me. Even like this."

"I'm sorry. I don't trust myself."

"Aren't I supposed to be the horny teenager?"

"From the moment I saw you, I went weak in the knees."

"Because you hadn't slept or eaten, and there was that heat stroke thing."

"I just blamed it on that. I'm pretty sure it was you. *You* were the shock to my system."

"It's been just about eleven months since I found Sleeping Beauty and her bare ass on the beach. Mmm, I do miss you without clothes."

"So I can pack that swimsuit when we go? The one with the bow?"

He growled against her head, rocking her gently in his arms. "For my personal enjoyment, yes. Though I'm not sure I can handle all the attention it's going to attract on the beach."

"Ha. As if. And like you'd have anything to worry about anyway. You know how I feel."

"That didn't stop me from wanting to rip Hollywood's head off on New Year's Eve."

"Yeah. I got a little taste of that this afternoon when Tinley kissed you."

"That's why I came by. Hoping to coax you out here in the dark. So I could apologize. Maybe erase that from your memory."

She pulled away and smiled her shy little Sleeping Beauty smile. "How're you gonna do that?" she teased.

"Well, I'm gonna kiss you like I kiss my grandmother, of course. But while I'm doing that, I want you to think about that last night we spent together at the beach."

"Hmm," she sighed as he kissed her forehead.

"That was some kind of night," he said as he kissed her nose.

"Refresh my memory," she said against his lips.

Challenge accepted.

His arms slid up under her nightshirt and stroked over her bare back as they kissed. Lane tried to focus on the feel of her skin under his fingertips and the smell of her soft, sleepy body in his nostrils, distracting himself from how sinfully decadent her mouth felt under his. His tongue, however, started marching to its own beat. A very sensual beat pounding down on him from afar. Lane answered that call by coaxing Vivi to open her mouth and slipping his tongue inside. The fallout from how good that felt shot straight to his groin. And then he wasn't thinking at all. He was taking.

He took Vivi's hand from around his neck and slid it over his shorts, up against his hard-on, holding it there. When she didn't pull away, he slid her hand up and down the length of him, slowly, firmly, just like he'd shown her how he liked it their last night together.

"I remember," she whispered against his lips.

He just moaned into her mouth, thinking about how hot it had been. How hot it was going to be with them again. How hot kissing her was right now.

It took everything he had to drop her hand and end the kiss.

CHAPTER TWENTY-FIVE

"Mr. Liskey invited Miss DuVal to our prom!" Stacey Collins shouted, giddy and out of breath. She'd practically skidded into the pack of cheerleaders leaving the cafeteria.

Lane's head, along with Lam's, snapped to attention at the news. They looked over at each other and then immediately forced their way into the mass of short skirts and saddle shoes as the story was spilling from Stacey's mouth.

"In the middle of calculus class, there was this knock on the door and Mr. Liskey walks in dressed as Prince Charming. He had this big gold crown on his head, wore some kind of fancy white jacket with a red sash running across it from shoulder to hip. He had on white gloves and was carrying a boatload of red roses—way more than a dozen—all wrapped up with a big red and black striped bow. He got down on one knee in front of the whole class and makes like it's a proposal. I mean, for a minute, we all thought he was asking her to marry him! We were all squealing and dying, and then it turns out he asked her to be his date for the prom."

"And what the hell did she say?" Lane barked.

"What could she say? I mean, at first she just stood there, shocked, not saying anything. And the class was oohing and aahing and shouting for her to accept. And then Mr. Liskey sort of motioned the class to egg her on, so finally everybody is shouting "Say, yes. Say, yes," over and over until she finally nodded her head and said she'd go."

"And then what happened?" Lam asked.

"Then he sort of bowed as he gave her all those roses, and once she took them, he stood up with his hands in the air and danced around like he had just won a prize fight. The whole class cheered. It was fantastic."

Lane looked over at Lam. He did not think this was fantastic. He thought this was bullshit. Lam pulled him out of the group and pushed him into a wall.

"You cannot be upset over this."

"Too late for that."

"I mean, you can't be upset with Miss DuVal."

"Really? Because right now I'm very upset with Miss DuVal."

"Says the guy who is taking a girl with enormous tits to the prom."

"It's my prom. And that's a fake date," Lane scowled.

"And you think Miss DuVal going with Liskey is real? Why do you think the asshole went to all the trouble of the big, public invite? So she couldn't say no."

"She could have said no."

"With the whole class cheering like that? Face it, man, she didn't have a choice."

"She had a choice."

"Dude. Do not let this be your Kryptonite. And definitely do not bust her chops about this during school hours."

"Oh my God," a shrill voice came from down the hall. "Did you hear Mr. Liskey invited Miss DuVal to the prom?"

"Perfect," Lane said. "It's going to be all over the school and in my face all day."

"Suck it up, Irish. This is not her fault. Besides, it's not like old Liskey can compete with Notre Dame's new running back."

"How old is Liskey, anyway?" Lane asked, his eyes squinty like he couldn't imagine Vivi going out with such a lech.

"Old. Probably can't even get it up. You have nothing to worry about."

"I'm not worried, I'm pissed. I'm pissed he gets to go with Vivi and I can't. And I'm tired of this shit. I'm tired of acting like I'm okay with the way things are, when I'm not. And I tell you. I'm scared to death she's on the verge of asking me to continue this charade so she can come back and teach here next year. With Liskey."

"Liskey isn't your problem."

"You're wrong," Lane said as he shoved himself off the wall. "He's the newest addition to a long list of problems. Problems I'm starting to drown in."

"But she's worth it, right?" Lam asked as he dogged after Lane. "You've always said that. You've always told me she was worth it."

"I don't know," Lane said. "She's a teacher. I'm a student. She's already finished college. I haven't even started. I can't *change* that. I *tried* to change that."

It was the argument Lane had suffered with the day Vivi became his statistics teacher. But he'd pushed it out of his mind, not wanting to give it too much attention. They'd worked hard to find their way around it, but facts were facts. And right now, circumstances were not helping them modify those facts.

"Look, I'm getting out of here. I've got to be over in Henderson for the ball game this afternoon anyway. Lock in my prom date with the big tits. Tell Vivi if she wants to talk, she can meet me over there. Otherwise…"

"Otherwise what?"

"Otherwise, tell her we can take a break."

"I'm not telling her that," Lam said.

"Fine." Lane pulled out his notebook and scribbled a note. He ripped it out, folded it up and gave it to Lam. "Give her this."

"What's it say?"

"None of your business," Lane said as he turned and headed for the door.

CHAPTER TWENTY-SIX

"So I assume he heard," Vivi said to Lam as he approached her at the end of class.

"There is nobody from here to Henderson who has not heard about Prince Charming, the seven dozen roses, and you going with Liskey to the prom."

"And Lane thought cutting class would help the situation?"

"He thought if he didn't, things might get ugly."

"So he's upset."

"That's an understatement. He said he had to be over at the Henderson ball game this afternoon, and if you wanted to talk you should meet him there."

"I guess I deserve having to watch him ask Tinley to the prom after this Prince Charming incident."

"I don't think either one of you deserves what you're putting yourselves through. It seems like things have gotten a little complicated."

"Ya think?" She smiled.

"He wrote you a note. But it was while he was severely pissed off. So I'm going to do the two of you a favor and not let you read it."

Vivi's heart fell. "What's it say?"

"I don't read them. Ever. Not even today. What's between the two of you is between the two of you. Still, I'm guessing once he cools off about this Liskey prom date business, he might regret what he's written. So I'm gonna look out for my boy and not give it to you."

She held out her hand.

Lam looked from her hand to her face. "Did you not hear what I just said?"

"I heard it, Lam," she said in her bossy-teacher voice. "You're a good friend. And I appreciate that. I also understand that note was written in the moment. I want to know how he felt, in the moment."

"He felt defeated."

"I can definitely relate."

"He was pissed off you agreed to go to the prom with Liskey."

"I'm not too happy about him taking Tinley."

"See, so this is not heading in a good direction right now."

"Lam. I'm the adult. The buck stops with me. Hand the note over. Please."

Lam hesitated. "This is a really bad idea," he said, capitulating. He reached into his pocket and pulled out the note.

"Thank you," she said.

"Aren't you going to read it? Write a response?"

"Not while you're standing here."

"I think I ought to stand here."

"Lam. Trust me. All is well."

"Miss DuVal," he said, laughing. "I'd like to believe that. So, okay. I'm going. I'm going and I'm trusting that you—as the adult—will take care of this situation for my boy. Who was pissed. Really pissed. And at the end of his rope. Hanging by a thread."

"Lam."

"I'm going."

"See you Monday."

Vivi watched him leave. Took a deep breath. Then unfolded the note.

CHAPTER TWENTY-SEVEN

Lane wished he'd been in the right frame of mind for the big invite he laid on Tinley. Because Josh McCourt had done a job messing with the scoreboard. He had it flashing during the game, little things lighting up here and there like there was a problem. It definitely caught the crowd's attention with some sparks and colors and the screen going blank a few times, flashing on and off. So when it finally did go blank, during the seventh-inning stretch, and then flashed Tinley's name over and over and over again, no one who was attending the game could possibly miss it. Then came the big PROM??? flashing over and over and over again, changing colors each time. Then, and Lane really could have done without this part, it flashed a video of him in his football uniform running in for several touchdowns. Yep, no doubt about who was asking whom to the prom. The crowd all started to look around, so he made his move, took his bouquet of roses—thank you, Mr. Liskey—and moved down in front of the center of the stands waiting for Tinley to come out of the crowd and give him her answer.

And right on cue, there she was. Pretty as he'd ever seen her. All dolled up in a pink sundress, coming out of the stands to a round of applause. He plastered a smile on his face, gave her the roses—which she held high in the air to the cheers of the crowd—and then pulled her by the hand off the field and over to the side of the stands where he gave her a quick kiss to make it all look legit.

"That was nice," she said quietly, as the crowd shouted funny things at them. Lane smiled at all the well-wishers, wishing he were with a different DuVal cousin. Then he smiled at his prom date, resigned.

"I'm glad it met your approval."

"It was perfect. Best prom invite ever. I had my friends videotape it. I'm going to put it on Facebook."

"Of course you are. Don't you think that might piss off Hollywood?"

"He's not on Facebook. He says he's too old for Facebook. He's on LinkedIn or something boring."

"That means he's probably a little old for you."

"People who live in glass houses," she said.

"Shouldn't throw stones," he finished. "Come on. Let's watch the rest of the game."

They scooted into the first row, her all snuggled up on him just like Vivi used to do.

Vivi.

He was probably being an ass about this Liskey thing. If Tinley had hung him out to dry while he stood there in front of this entire crowd holding out roses, he would have been mortified. And Vivi was too sweet, too kind to do that to anybody. Especially a coworker, in front of a bunch of unforgiving teenagers. It would have embarrassed everybody in that classroom and word would have spread just as quickly about that nightmare as it did about what actually happened.

So okay. Like Lam said. She had no choice. Just like he didn't have a choice with Tinley.

"Would you mind if I texted Vivi? Something happened at school today."

"What?"

"Another math teacher asked her to go to the prom."

Tinley thought that was the funniest thing she'd ever heard. Her laughter busted right through Lane's dismal mood and got him laughing about it too. He told her the whole story and didn't leave out how pissed off he was.

"Is the teacher cute?"

Lane stared at her like she had lost her mind.

"Text her. Tell her I'll be happy to do a big switch at just the right moment. Like we did on New Year's."

"Maybe we can just double date, being as you're her cousin and all," Lane joked.

"It will certainly make the night interesting," Tinley said.

Lane texted Vivi. *"Sorry I skipped class. Are you here at Henderson?"*
The text came in, *"No."*

No? Just, no? He texted, *"Are you coming to Henderson?"*

"No."

"Why not?"

"WHY NOT??"

Uh-oh.

"Did Lam give you my note?"

When there was no response, Lane was pretty sure Lam had given her his note.

"Ah, Tinley? Can we do a big smoochy goodbye so I can get the hell out of here and go put out a big freaking fire with your cousin?"

"Sure," she said. "I'll walk you to your car."

"I really appreciate this," he said as they left the stands. "Your cousin is being a whole lot less cooperative."

"Lane, when you and Vivi are all done mooning over each other, call me up and ask me out for real," Tinley said as Lane got into his car.

"Tinley," Lane said chuckling. "If I can't handle the soft, sweet, shy one, there is no hope for me ever being able to handle you."

"Oh, don't sell yourself short, Lane Kettering. Love can't be any harder than football. Throw a pass. Catch a pass. Dodge any obstacles." Then she leaned in and whispered. "And don't forget how good it feels when you finally do score."

CHAPTER TWENTY-EIGHT

"Oh, thank God you're still here."

Lane could hardly breathe. He'd sprinted in from the parking lot and raced down the hall, worried he wouldn't find Vivi in her classroom. He panted as he strode forward, collapsing into the chair where he regularly sat.

"I'm sorry," he gasped. "I didn't get it. This Liskey thing. Until I was standing there with roses, asking Tinley to prom in front of hundreds of people, I didn't get it," he panted. "You couldn't say no."

"Well, Mr. Kettering," came a voice from behind him, "that is the point, isn't it? Making sure you don't get turned down."

Shit.

Lane turned to watch Liskey in all his prepped-out preppiness stride forward and pass him, eyes locked on Vivi.

His Vivi.

"Yeah," Lane sneered. "But then I realized, it's kind of an asshole move, don't you think?"

Vivi gasped.

Liskey chuckled. "And here you've just pulled the very same *asshole* move."

"My date had prior warning."

"Well, I'm sure this didn't come out of the blue for Miss DuVal. I've been trying to take her out since September."

"She has a boyfriend."

"So she says. Although there is zero evidence. I've asked around. So I've come to the conclusion she's playing hard to get."

"Are you?" Lane asked Vivi pointedly.

"Am I what?" Vivi asked, startled.

Yep, she definitely had that deer in the headlights look. *Crap.* Lane sighed. He needed to stand down. They had made it all the way to prom. Just a few more weeks to graduation. He was not going to let this blow up on her now.

"I'm sorry," he said. "My bad." He stood and held out his hand to Mr. Liskey. "I apologize," he said as Liskey shook it. "I'm dating Miss DuVal's cousin, Tinley. Have been since New Year's. So I've gotten to know Miss DuVal outside of class. She's only twenty-one, you know. I'm turning twenty soon, so most of the time it seems Miss DuVal is more of a friend than a teacher. Anyway, it's all good. I'll head out and let you two talk prom." As Lane walked away he said, "And if you want to double date, Mr. Liskey, Tinley and I are available."

"Thanks, Lane. I realize we are going to the prom, but double dating is just a little *too* high school for me."

Ouch.

Lane stopped short in the doorway.

His rational mind argued it would be counterproductive to turn around and engage—to let Liskey know exactly who Miss DuVal's phantom boyfriend was. His rational mind insisted no good could come from that. But the asshole high schooler who had been pushed around enough wasn't listening to any rational arguments. The prideful running back and his chained-up libido wanted nothing more than to piss all over his territory.

He turned. "She's not playing hard to get," he told Liskey. "Vivi has a boyfriend. So, you can take her to the prom to increase your popularity among the students because I'm sure the two of you will look good together and I know for a fact Vivi is a hell of a dancer. But in the end, you'll make a move, she'll shut you down, and you'll be lying in bed that night thinking about all the kids getting some while you're not. And that's when you'll start to wish that you were the one still in high school."

He turned, left the classroom, and headed down the hall texting Tinley.

"Just threw a Hail Mary pass."

CHAPTER TWENTY-NINE

Vivi held her breath.

She watched Phil Liskey stare after Lane, a puzzled look on his face. Was he figuring it out? Why Lane was so defensive? Was this going to turn into the nightmare she'd killed herself trying to avoid?

Finally, Phil turned to her, dumbfounded. He raised his arms in quandary and then let them fall against his sides. "The damn kid aced my geometry class his freshman year. What could he possibly have against me?" he said, completely clueless.

Vivi gifted him with her biggest, brightest, the-weight-of-the-world-is-off-my-shoulders smile. "Probably just teenage hormones." She shrugged.

"Vivi, I'm sorry if I put you on the spot today."

"You did put me on the spot, but it was fun. And the kids loved it."

"You and I have a lot of laughs in the faculty lounge," he said. "I thought it'd be cute. Get in the prom spirit."

"It was perfect, Phil. It truly was. My goodness, those roses are beautiful. And who wouldn't want to go to prom with Prince Charming? But, Phil, I do have a boyfriend. Which I've mentioned. Several times. So, as much as I truly appreciate your prom invitation, under the circumstances, if you'd like to find another date, I will certainly understand."

"No," Phil said, a little bit defeated. "I'd like to take you, Vivi, if you're still willing to go. Besides, now that I know you're a helluva dancer, I'd relish the opportunity to sweep you off your feet."

"All right," she said. "You're on."

Lane was waiting for her in her driveway.

"What are you doing out here?" she said.

"Waiting for you. Look, I've got Piper Beaumont ready to swoop in with whatever we need. I thought about calling Principal Levendusky but figured I didn't want to jump the gun. What happened with Liskey?"

Vivi started laughing. "He hasn't a clue. About us. After you left, he sort of stood there in shock, wondering why you were attacking him after he gave you an A in his geometry class."

"Oh," Lane sighed, relief cascading throughout his body. "I thought I had blown it. Oh, thank God. Viv, I'm sorry. I just…"

"I know what you just," she said. "He stepped on your toes—hard—and you reacted like you do. How I love that you do," she said. She stepped forward and wrapped her arms around his neck. "You stood up for yourself, you claimed me as yours, and you didn't let him walk all over you—or us."

"Is that what I did?" He grinned.

"That's how I saw it," she said, grinning back.

And that was the picture—Vivi's arms looped around Lane's neck—that showed up all over social media that night, compliments of Bitchin' Bros.

CHAPTER THIRTY

"Vivi. Wear your hair up, burn the clothes you had on yesterday, and get rid of those shoes."

"Why?" she asked, her voice groggy with sleep. "Lane? What time is it?"

"I don't know. Just turn on your laptop. Or put me on speaker and look at your phone. There's a picture of us everywhere. Only…I don't think anyone knows it's us. Yet."

"What do you mean? Oh shit!"

"That's what I mean."

Vivi studied the photo that had been forwarded over a dozen times on Instagram. "Who took this?"

"I don't know. But they didn't put our names on the photo. I can't figure out if they are toying with us or just don't know who we are. I almost feel like we're going to get a blackmail letter asking for money."

"You aren't kidding. It's clearly us."

"Well, it's clearly us to us. It's blurry. You can't see our faces. No one is suggesting it's us. Some people think that it's me, so I'm going to be getting a haircut first thing this morning. But no one has suggested it's you, yet. They just know it's not the blonde I asked to prom. So it's becoming a big fucking mystery that everyone is trying to solve."

"Okay, well…today is Saturday. Let's hope by Monday there's some new juicy piece of gossip to distract everybody from this. In the meantime, I'll send it on to Piper and you text it to Tinley so she has a head's up."

"All right, okay, I just, you know, needed to inform you."

"Yeah. Thanks." She stared at the photo. "Lane, whoever took the picture had to know who we were. They had to be watching us."

"I think so, too. How well do you know your neighbors?"

"Pretty well. Most of them are old. I can't imagine them posting pictures to the Internet. Or claiming to be Bitchin' Bros. That's a Wilson thing, right? Not a Henderson thing."

"I thought it was a Wilson High thing.

"Me too."

"Okay. Well, so far it's a non-issue."

"Except you're cutting your hair. I love your hair."

"It'll grow back. Go back to sleep, S.B. I've got this." Lane hung up.

Vivi stared at the ceiling for a long time, alternating thoughts between what she'd want to do if she could no longer be a teacher and what her gorgeous boyfriend with that fabulous shaggy hair would look like with a buzz cut. Finally, she felt stupid for feeling sadder about the buzz cut, so she turned over and went back to sleep.

Her phone pinged. A text came in.

"I'm not cutting my hair. Don't get rid of your clothes. Tinley will be over to get them this morning. She and Lam have an idea. You won't see me this weekend, so spend your time figuring out how to get yourself employed in Indiana. ASAP."

"You are sooooo bossy," she texted back. *"Really glad you aren't cutting your hair."*

He sent a smiley face.

Vivi handed over her clothes to Tinley, who told her nothing except to watch Instagram. She was doing that already, reading every comment that came across her cheerleaders' feeds. It seemed that the picture wasn't gaining momentum. Of course, it was early on a Saturday morning. Who knew what would happen when all the high schoolers rolled out of bed.

Vivi spent time finalizing the exams for her algebra and calculus class. Her Advanced Placement Calculus class had to take the specialized AP exam, so she didn't have to worry about that. Her statistics exam was in limbo. It felt unwieldy. It seemed to her the exam should be smarter if it wanted to test the abilities of her students. Smarter, not harder. Just arranged better, or differently, or—

Her phone pinged.

Instagram showed a replica photo of the one of her and Lane. Only in this picture, the girl had long blond hair. It was as close to the original as one could make it, and Vivi guessed that Tinley had dressed in her clothes and posed with Lane. Which was an interesting comeback, she supposed.

It wasn't long before another replica picture showed up. Same pose, same clothes, totally different girl and boy. Unless there were some fancy Photoshop antics going on, because the girl had long brunette hair and looked a whole lot like Vivi from the back, especially in the same dress, but the guy had curly hair. If Vivi were to guess, she would guess it was her cousin, Lolly, and Lolly's boyfriend, Brooks, standing in for her and Lane this time.

Great move.

Pictures streamed in the rest of the day. Most of the girls were blond—Tinley's friends—and with Lane, from what she could tell. All were wearing her clothes and her shoes. By Sunday, all sorts of couples were getting in on the act. Vivi could tell Lane and Tinley weren't posing them because Vivi's clothes were no longer being used.

Late Sunday, a photo with a new twist showed up on social media. Lam, in his very visible football jersey, was posing in place of Vivi, hands around Lane's neck, almost completely obscuring him from view. You could see a little of Lane's hair and a little of Lane's jersey as well. Even without much else, it was very obviously Lam and Lane—BFFs—in a hilarious parody of all the pictures that had come before. Lam had even lifted one foot off the ground, as if the two of them were kissing. Most of the comments made about the photo were clever and funny. A few, Vivi worried, would offend Lam.

When she addressed that with Lane Sunday night during a Skype session, Lane told her it had all been Lam's idea. That he was prepared to come out if he had to, just to get things spinning in a different direction—away from Vivi and Lane.

Now that was pure loyalty. Vivi had a lot of great friends, but she didn't think any of them would come out of the closet in order to save her reputation. She sure didn't want Lam to do it.

Vivi stopped by the principal's office first thing Monday morning. He'd seen the photo. He knew who it was. He showed her a comment she'd missed suggesting it was Miss DuVal hugging Lane Kettering, but the comments that followed—started by a "LamtheMan"—suggested that Miss DuVal was too smoking hot to go slumming it with the likes of Lane Kettering. That served to prompt a long line of vividly disparaging comments about Lane and how he wouldn't know what the hell to do with a woman if one landed in his lap.

"I'm sorry about this," Vivi told her principal, trying to stifle her laughter. No wonder Lane hadn't told her about this thread. "How did you find out? Your own personal Instagram account? Or were you on Facebook?"

"Miss, DuVal," he scolded. "I'm not as out of touch as you think I am."

"Mr. L., I didn't mean…"

"I know you didn't. I'm kidding you. Unfortunately another teacher brought it to my attention. Your prom date."

"Phil Liskey?" Hmm, Vivi thought. Maybe that clueless thing was an act.

"I heard about the big prom proposal."

"What did my *prom date* have to say?"

"He said he thought it looked suspiciously like you and Lane. He said he was concerned for your reputation as an educator. He suggested I speak with you."

Vivi sank down into a chair.

"He knows," she breathed. "Of course he knows. I'm wearing the same thing in the photo I had on when he did his Prince Charming proposal earlier that day. So what does this mean?"

"Nothing," Principal L., said. "I told him I'd look into it. I told him I'd speak to you. I've done both. As far as I'm concerned, this matter is complete."

"Complete?"

"Yes."

"Okay, but I feel like I'm getting off easy."

"Really? You're going to the prom with Phil Liskey."

Vivi burst out laughing.

"We've got a week until prom, three weeks until graduation. Vivi, you and Lane have handled yourself beautifully up to this point. Just do me a favor and keep your guard up through the rest of the year. And, frankly, I'd like you to rethink your contract and come back to Wilson next year. I'll take the heat for whatever happens after graduation. I know the truth. And I know what an outstanding teacher you are."

"Thanks, Mr. L. I'll think about it."

At the end of Statistics class, Lane and Lam were filling Vivi in on what the seniors were saying about all the couple photos over the weekend. Turns out one of the couples was in a lot of hot water, totally derailing any interest in the photo of Vivi and Lane. Seems everybody thought the photo of Sandy Watkins and Greg Sengstack, the couple voted "most likely to marry," turned out to be Sandy's twin sister, Cindy and Greg, as Sandy had gone away for the weekend to attend to college registration. The boys were suggesting just how stupid Greg was when Phil Liskey entered the classroom.

Instead of stopping the merriment, Vivi motioned Phil to join them. "Phil, come in. We're talking about all those pictures that came out over the weekend. Did you see my *picture* with Lane?" she asked as if it was the biggest scandal to ever hit Wilson.

"Your picture with Lane?" he asked, as if this was news to him.

"Well, nobody believes it's us. But it is," she claimed.

"Bullshit," said Lam.

"See, I told you," Lane said to Vivi. "Nobody believes that a smoking hot teacher like you would ever be caught with a lowly senior like me."

"What do you think, Phil?" Vivi asked with a smile.

"What do I think of what?" Phil asked cautiously.

"Oh, he totally thinks you're a smoking hot teacher, Miss DuVal," Lam said. "It's a good thing you asked her to prom when you did, Mr. Liskey. I was working up the courage to do it myself, but you got there first."

"Who have you not asked to the prom?" Lane teased Lam. "He's been turned down by so many girls it's just embarrassing."

"One. One girl has turned me down," Lam argued. "Because I didn't ride in on a horse or blow up a fireworks factory. I'm telling you, it's not easy getting a date these days in the *you've-gotta-top-that* age of prom invitations. I don't know if it's worth it. I might just show up stag so that all the ladies can enjoy time with Lam the Man."

"As if," Lane huffed. "All I know is I'm taking the smoking hot teacher's cousin, and she's a handful. Mr. Liskey, that invitation for a double date still stands."

"Thanks, Lane, I'll think about it."

"Come on, Lam. Let's let the old people practice their waltz."

"Right behind you. See you, Miss DuVal. Mr. Liskey."

"See you, Lam. Bye Lane. Say hi to Tinley for me," Vivi called.

"Will do," Lane said as he exited her classroom.

"Well," Vivi said brightly, smiling at Phil. "Shall we practice our waltz?"

CHAPTER THIRTY-ONE

"You look beautiful," Lane said, caught off guard and floored by the vision in front of him.

He'd been fixing his boutonniere in the mirror outside of the ladies room at the Oxford Inn waiting for Tinley when he looked up to find Vivi standing in the hallway alone. She wore a pale blue strapless dress that fell to the floor over layers of tulle. Her Sleeping Beauty hair was partially up, partially down, curled and enticing. Her lips were pink, her eyes deep brown, and when she batted those long eyelashes at him, all he could think about was how much he wanted to kiss her.

It must have shown on his face, because she stepped close to him and brushed at his lapel. "I wore this for you."

"Viv," he breathed.

"I've encouraged all my sweet, docile cheerleaders to give Mr. Liskey a thrill and ask him to dance. Maybe while he's otherwise engaged…"

"Lam and I can ask you to dance."

Vivi laughed. "There are going to be rumors about Lam and you if you're not careful."

"There are going to be rumors about Lam and me *and you* if we're not careful." He laughed.

"Bring 'em. How are things going with Tinley?"

"She's the biggest flirt ever. But I think that's going to work out okay for me. No one is going to question me dumping her at the end of the night."

"Ha," Vivi laughed. "Is she aware of your plan?"

"Hell, no. I want it to look real. How are things going with Liskey?"

"Perfect gentleman."

"It's early yet."

"I can handle myself."

"Yeah, but here's the thing. You don't have to. Lam and I are going to be all over following the two of you out of here, making sure our favorite statistics teacher gets home safely."

"Don't you have after parties to attend?"

"Not after my ugly breakup. Pretty sure Tinley will hook up with some other guy and show up at those parties. I'm going to be too busted up to want to see all that."

Vivi couldn't help but laugh. "Lane, this doesn't sound like much of a prom night for you."

"You'd be surprised. Trust me. I'm gonna have a helluva time."

"You two look good together," Lane's friend, Jamie said innocently as he came up on them.

Lane tilted his head as if studying Vivi. "You know, Jamie. We do look good together."

"Have fun, boys," Vivi said as she headed into the restroom.

"You should ask Miss DuVal out," Jamie suggested. "I mean, after the school year and all. She's a smoke show."

"You think she'd go out with me?" Lane asked, curious.

"Why not? You're going to fucking Notre Dame," he said, patting him on the back and moving down the hall.

The evening was rather extravagant for Wilson teens. The ballroom, the dinner, the band—who was killing it—all sent the message that this was their time for fun. And the Wilson seniors took full advantage. Tinley was tipsy after sneaking in a flask stashed in a secret compartment in her purse. Half the guys on the football team had flasks strapped to their calves. Lane thought he had enough to worry about without getting caught with alcohol, although he did appreciate the quick guzzle of tequila he'd had before entering the prom. It helped him not worry so much about Vivi and focus on enjoying his friends.

Tinley dragged him onto the dance floor once things really got rocking, and Lane tried not to notice her enormous rack moving to the music. Unlike her cousin's gently alluring gown, Tinley's dress was nothing but white, glittery, body-hugging sequins with a low-low neckline and a low-low-*low* back. It wasn't necessarily out of place in the room, but it did attract a lot of attention for what it showed off.

Apparently, Tinley liked to show off.

Lane had left his jacket at their table, but right now Tinley's hands were working on loosening his bow tie. Then they were on his shoulders and drifting down his chest, his stomach, and…what the hell did she just touch?

"Tinley. Jesus."

"Just wanted to see what you were packing."

"You did not just cup my junk on the dance floor."

She smirked.

"What is wrong with you?"

"What is wrong with you? Stop being such a pussy and let's have a little fun."

"A pussy? You're wasted."

"I'm not wasted. I'm dancing. I'm young. I'm not stuck on some old teacher who's never gonna give me what I want."

"No, you're stuck on some old guy on LinkedIn who lives on the other side of the country."

"Yes, and until he moves back, I told him I am playing the field. And right now, you're the field I want to play on."

"Well, that's a big problem for you because the equipment on this field is all locked up. And only your cousin knows the combination."

"Pfft. Pretty sure, given half a chance, I could figure out the combination to your…equipment."

"That's a half a chance you're never gonna see."

"I can be persistent."

Lane grabbed Tinley in his arms and hugged her to him, whispering in her ear and making it appear as if she was his dream date for the prom. "If you want some action, you need to look elsewhere. In fact, I'd appreciate it if you'd look elsewhere aggressively so you and I can have a big public break up at the end of the night and there'd be somebody willing to give you a ride home."

"So this is the thanks I get?" she feigned. "For saving your sorry affair with my cousin? I swear Lane Kettering, you are so booooring. You're probably a lousy kisser."

"Don't try to bait me. It isn't going to work."

Tinley laughed, stepping back out of his embrace. "I bet I could get you to kiss me if Vivi weren't here."

"There's pretty much an entire room full of guys willing to kiss you. You can have your pick."

"But none of them are you," she pouted. "And if no one has seen you kiss me, our big break up is never gonna fly. You need to kiss me. For your own good."

"Really? Are you listening to yourself?"

"Kiss me."

"Nope."

"Chicken!"

Lane burst out laughing.

"You are," Tinley claimed. "You're afraid to kiss your seventeen-year-old prom date because it might upset your statistics teacher."

"I'm not afraid of anything."

"Prove it."

"Stop goading me."

"Prove it. Here, I'll help." Tinley launched herself into Lane's arms, pressing her lips against his as he staggered back into other dancers.

"Hey, man! What the hell?" he heard as Tinley opened her mouth and tried to swallow him whole. Her feet were off the floor and his balance was precarious trying to keep them from falling. His hands were all over her, searching for something to grab on to in order to pull her off, and his anger was escalating.

Tinley wrapped him up harder, pressed his mouth to hers and kept right on kissing him until he felt like every last breath had been sucked from his lungs. When she finally let him pull them apart, he was gasping and furious.

Tinley stood in the center of the dance floor, laughing. At him.

"You think that's funny?" he said, wiping at his mouth.

"I do," Tinley said.

"I'm in love with somebody else," he yelled. "You know that!"

"Vivi's a boring math teacher. I really don't get why you're so hung up on her," Tinley shouted back.

"Vivi?" Olivia Thompson asked.

"My cousin," Tinley answered, rolling her eyes.

Lane snapped out of his tirade then. He took a look around and saw that they were the center of attention, at least on this part of the dance floor. Big ears and wide eyes all taking in the argument between him and Tinley.

"Who's her cousin?" somebody asked.

"I don't know. Her last name is DuVal," some helpful bystander answered.

"Vivi DuVal?" somebody asked. "Sounds familiar."

Lane grabbed Tinley by her arm and spun her around to head off the dance floor. "Please, not another word," he begged her. "We may have just outed your cousin."

"Shit! Lane, I really didn't mean to do that."

"Yeah. Neither did I."

Vivi was having a surprisingly good time with Phil Liskey. He was an attentive date. He had great insight into most of the kids at the prom, having known them for all four years they'd been at Wilson. It was obvious to Vivi why he was well liked and why the senior class had voted for him to be a chaperone at the prom. Phil was fun. He loved teaching. Loved his students. And he was a very good dancer. In fact, many girls other than her cheerleaders approached Mr. Liskey and drew him out on the dance floor.

Vivi happened to be dancing with Lam when the scuttlebutt on the other side of the dance floor broke out. They didn't see what happened and really weren't aware of anything going on at all. Until a number of giggling girls raced up to them and asked Miss DuVal her first name.

"Vivian," she told them proudly. "My parents named me Vivian Leigh after the famous actress."

"What actress?" The three of them stood there confused.

"Scarlett O'Hara in *Gone With the Wind*?"

They shrugged.

"Girls. Please tell me you've heard of the book *Gone With the Wind*," Vivi insisted.

Blank stares. "No, but we did just hear Lane Kettering profess his love for a Vivi DuVal. And now we're pretty certain he meant you."

"What?" Vivi scoffed. "Why, that's…ridiculous."

"What's ridiculous?" Phil asked, coming to join her and Lam as the song ended.

"Lane Kettering has a thing for your date, Mr. Liskey. Better watch out," the girls said before giggling and walking away.

Phil turned toward Vivi, folding his arms over his chest. "So my suspicions weren't unfounded," he said. "I knew that kid was pissed off about me asking you to the prom. I just figured—" Phil stopped talking as his eyes lit up. As if the fog had suddenly cleared and he could see everything that had been in front of him all along. He scowled and pulled her abruptly off the dance floor.

"Miss DuVal?" Lam called.

"It's okay, Lam," she said over her shoulder.

Once they were on the sidelines, up against a wall, Phil laid into her. "A football player?" he growled. "A fucking *high school* football player? That is your mysterious boyfriend?"

"Phil, please. Hear me out."

"Oh my God. All this time you've been turning me down because you're screwing Lane Kettering."

"I'm not screwing anybody," Vivi said, exasperated. "Trust me."

"He's always in your classroom after Statistics. He and his diversionary sidekick. It was right under my nose this entire time. No wonder none of the other teachers ever heard you mention a boyfriend. Because you couldn't. Because *fucking a student is against the law.*"

"I am well aware. In fact, Lane and I can both recite the Intercourse and Sexual Offense with Certain Victims statute. We've got the Indecent Liberties with a Student statute down pat too. Would you like to hear them?"

When Liskey just rolled his eyes, Vivi went on. "Look, Phil, I have too much respect for the teaching profession to knowingly violate the law. I love this job. I've worked too hard to put it in jeopardy."

"But you admit there's something going on between you and Kettering. I'm sorry Vivi, but I'm informing Principal Levendusky about it first thing Monday."

"I'll join the two of you for coffee, because Principal Levendusky already knows."

"What?"

"I told him myself the first day of school, right after Lane walked into my Statistics class."

"The principal knows you're screwing Lane Kettering?"

"I'm not screwing Lane," Vivi said softly. "Phil, the truth is that I'm in love with Lane. I've worked really, really hard to keep my hands off him for the entire year. We met at the beach last May. I didn't know he was a student at Wilson when I took this job."

"What do you mean you didn't know? How could you not know?"

Vivi blushed. "I knew he was a senior. I just assumed he was a senior in college."

"What?" Phil said, starting to laugh.

"It's not funny," she said, smacking his arm.

"I don't know. It's starting to sound a little funny."

A slow song started. "Come dance with me," he said. "Start from the beginning. Tell me everything. And, you know, do your best to make me believe it."

"I don't care if you believe it," she grumbled, letting him take her hand and lead her onto the dance floor. "I'm tired of hiding it. It's hard work denying who I love, and frankly, it feels just as wrong. So I'm done with that. You can go ahead and get up on stage with the band and tell everybody about Lane and me. I'm tired of denying it."

"Oh, no," Phil said.

"What?"

"Looks like somebody else might be tired of denying it."

CHAPTER THIRTY-TWO

Lane was willing to take the heat. What the hell did he care? He wasn't going to see half of these people again for a long time after graduation. He was heading to the Midwest. And the only thing he wanted to take with him his heart. So if he had to pour it out in front of the entire school to protect Vivi DuVal, he'd do it.

He tapped the microphone a couple times like he was a rock star. Thought it was kinda funny when he said, "One, two, one, two, testing," into the thing. Shit, that last swig from Tinley's flask must be getting to him.

"Okay," he started. "The band has agreed to give me thirty seconds to address a rumor going around. The rumor, in case you are one of the three people who have yet to hear it, is that I've got a thing for Miss DuVal." The woo-hoos and whistles that went up were deafening. Lane started to laugh. He had to wave them all down before he could go on. "You're right. You're right," he said. "She definitely is smokin' hot." A lot of cheers went up. "But there's a rule about teachers dating students," Lane said, prompting a lot of boos. "Yeah, I know. But rules are rules. And you know I'm a rule follower." He grinned. "I mean, there isn't anybody here who's breaking a rule right now is there?" Laughter and catcalls resounded through the ballroom. "Okay, okay. I've got about ten seconds left, so let me say this. With all due respect to my beautiful prom date, who happens to be Miss DuVal's cousin—I'll let y'all figure that out—the moment...*the moment* I have that diploma in my hand, I am asking Miss DuVal out." Cheers erupted. "I'm not letting Principal

Levendusky stop me," he said as if he were leading a cheer. "I'm not letting my mother stop me," he yelled and everybody laughed. "And Mr. Liskey, you've got a big fan club here, and that Prince Charming stuff worked like a charm. But even you are not going to stop me. Your days are numbered, man, because I am gunning for your prom date."

Lane handed over the microphone to the lead singer and jumped off the stage. Tinley was there, throwing her arms around him, and his teammates were there pounding him on his back. And then the crowd parted and up waltzed—literally waltzed—Mr. Liskey and the love of his young life, the smoking hot statistics teacher in a sorority girl's dress. Vivi. His Vivi. And they were both smiling.

For the first time in about nine months, Lane Kettering breathed a sigh of relief.

It was going to work out, he told himself. It was all going to work out.

The storybooks must have gotten it all wrong. Sleeping Beauty was never meant to end up with Prince Charming. Not when she had the power to make him feel like Superman.

CHAPTER THIRTY-THREE

Bump.

Hmm?

Bump, bump.

What the hell?

Bump—bump, rock, rock, rock.

Vivi opened her eyes and groaned. "I do not believe you're toeing my ass…again."

"Ah, come on, Sleeping Beauty," Lane said, lying down wet and drippy on the beach blanket beside her. "It worked out so well for me last time."

She turned her head toward him and pouted. "You left me this morning. Alone."

"I let you sleep in while I went for my run. I'm a student athlete, S.B.," he said while rolling over onto his back. "Gotta keep in shape."

"This Notre Dame stuff is totally going to your head."

"Fighting Irish. Long, proud history."

"You mean long, cold winter. I'm not sure I'm gonna look good in Ugg boots and a parka from November until April."

"When you come out to see me, you can wear whatever you want. I'll happily keep you warm."

"Yeah, but what if your classes are on the other side of campus from my classes?" She rolled over on her back as well and closed her eyes against the sun. "I think I better get a pair of Ugg boots. And a parka."

Vivi felt the shade created as Lane loomed over her. She opened her eyes.

"Is there something you forgot to tell me?" he asked.

She shrugged. "Nope. I didn't forget. I had it all planned out to tell you in bed—this morning—right after I used my mouth to commit a lewd and indecent act. Because I can do that, you know. Touch you. Wherever the hell I want. Because I am no longer employed as your statistics teacher. In fact, I am currently enrolled as a graduate student at The University of Notre Dame."

Ruggedly handsome, completely tantalizing Lane Kettering grinned down at her. Big. Like she'd just delivered the best news ever. And then his grin shifted, sort of making him look more like the Big Bad Wolf. He was definitely making her feel like Red Riding Hood. Or...lunch.

"Come on," Lane whispered before rolling off the blanket. He held out his hand to Vivi.

"Where are we going?"

"To get naked in the water."

"We're not getting naked in the water."

"We are sooo getting naked in the water," he said, swooping in and pulling at her hands to tug her up into a sitting position. "And I probably ought to warn you. Your bossy-teacher shit? It just jacks me up." He leaned over, put her hands around his neck, and then wrapped his arms around her back, pulling her up against his body. He leaned down, flipped her legs into his arms and then looked right at her as if to say, "I'm Lane Kettering and this is my world." They started toward the water.

"I really liked when you did this last year. Of course, I was feeling woozy at the time."

"How are you feeling now?" he asked as his feet splashed into the surf.

"Humbled."

He cocked his head, his green eyes curious, as he studied her.

"All you did for me. For us. A year of sacrifice."

"Pfft. I was highly motivated. When times got tough, I just pictured last night. You, flat on your back, on a king-size bed in my uncle's condo."

"My horny teenager is back."

"Yeah, but as you know, this is no longer my rookie season."

"You made the all-star team your rookie season."

"Yeah? Good. This season I plan to break a whole lot of records. Especially in the lewd and indecent department. Starting with public sex in the ocean." He turned his back on the breaking surf as he moved them out deeper into the water.

"I'm certain there are rules and regulations about this sort of thing."

"Nobody's looking at us."

Vivi looked toward the beach. The late morning hour was bringing a lot of activity. People staking out spots on the beach, setting up umbrellas, and laying out towels. "We're the only ones in the water. *Everybody* will be looking at us."

The water lapped around her shoulders. Lane turned her in his arms and guided her legs around his waist. "Let 'em," he said. "We've been dodging being seen together for a year. It feels good to have free access to your lips," he said leaning in for a kiss, "and your hips," he laughed, kissing her again, running his hands around her hips and cupping her ass. "Jesus, you are hot. Make sure you buy a big puffy parka. That's the only way I'm going to get any studying done. "

"Oh, you'll be studying. I'm not about to let my favorite statistics student squander his college education."

"Sounds like I've already got my own personal tutor all lined up."

"We're going to college," she said, smiling. "Together."

"The world is full of big dreams, S.B. Somebody's got to live 'em."

Thank you for reading *Tempting Vivi*.

If you'd like to read more about Annabelle, the Keeper of the Debutantes, who helped Vivi shape up her Cheerleaders, pick up ***Playin' Cop, Heroes of Henderson ~ Prequel.***

Vivi's dress-designing cousin *Lolly* gets caught up in a hilarious and sexy love triangle in ***Good Cop, Heroes of Henderson ~ Book 1.***

Piper Beaumont, the adorable love struck lawyer gets her man in ***Bad Cop, Heroes of Henderson ~ Book 2.***

And *Josh McCourt,* the geeky football coach who sent Lane's touchdown video off to Notre Dame has his own little romance in ***Taming Molly, Heroes of Henderson ~ Book 2.5.***

For more information and excerpts from all my novels, please visit my website: www.LizKellyBooks.com and sign up for my newsletter to learn about future releases.

Thanks so much! *Liz*

Liz Kelly Books

All of my Heroes of Henderson novels and novellas are complete
romances in and of themselves and do not need to be read in any
particular order. However, it's a little more fun that way.
Taming Molly and *Tempting Vivi* are part of The
DuVal Cousins series showcasing Lolly's Henderson
cousins as heroines of their own stories.

Heroes of Henderson full-length Novels

Good Cop
Bad Cop
Top Dog
Tempting Vivi
Under Dog
Mr. Wrong

Heroes of Henderson Novellas

Playin' Cop
Taming Molly
Kissing Cooper

About the Author

Growing up every summer in a place where dancing and romancing are literally part of its theme song, Liz Kelly can't help but be a romantic at heart. And since her favorite author, Kathleen E. Woodiwiss wrote some of the world's greatest romances, she's just trying to give the world a little more of that. (Okay, maybe a little sexier that, but we are now in a new millennium after all.)

A graduate of Wake Forest University, where she met her handsome golf-addicted husband, (who is now sporting dark glasses everywhere he goes) Liz is a mother of two grown sons (also sporting dark glasses) and a miniature Labradoodle named Isabelle. They split their time between The Windy City of Chicago and the Fountain of Youth, a.k.a. Naples, FL where dancing and romancing continues on ad infinitum.